To my husband, thank you for always believing in me, supporting my passions, and helping me make all my dreams come true.

CRUEL DECEPTION BOOK IV

DEGREES of POWER

INTERNATIONAL BESTSELLING AUTHOR

VIA MARI

ONE

The look in his eyes is mesmerizing, and as we lay naked, tangled in the sheets, the reality of what I've said registers.

"Katarina, you need to know what you are agreeing to," Chase says, sitting up on one elbow, looking at me with an odd intensity.

I shake my head, holding his deep green eyes captured with my own. "Not this time. As I recall you said you needed my unbridled trust."

"Baby, I do need that and the ability to control situations around us, but I don't want it at the cost of you giving up something personally," he says.

"How much control do you need?" I ask softly, watching the color of his eyes grow deeper.

"I want to control everything, right down to your orgasms. This is what transcends ordinary relationships. Total commitment, total trust, total power," he says, pushing the strands of auburn hair behind my shoulders and kissing the sensitive skin of my neck right below my earlobe.

I shiver and push into the warmth of his touch. "Chase, you have my total trust and I'm working on letting go," I say hesitantly.

"Control is hard for you to relinquish, Baby?" he asks.

"A little … possessive, always there when I need you, I love that. The bedroom, well it's like every woman's fantasy. I may even have learned to appreciate patience and anticipation," I say, trying not to focus on the fingers tracing the curve of my neck.

He raises his eyebrows at that. "Indeed?" he asks, his mouth turning up in a quirk.

"Well, I'm working on it," I concede, trying to contain the blush that I feel warming my cheeks.

"Tell me what it is that you find difficult to give up in the way of control?" he asks, continuing to trace patterns along my neck.

"Okay."

"You're blushing," he says, his penetrating eyes holding mine.

"The conversations we have still embarrass me a little."

"Baby, it's not my intent to make you uncomfortable, but to ensure I can take care of all of your needs, emotionally and sexually," he says, kissing my lips gingerly.

I nod. "I love that you want to understand my feelings," I say, trying to decide how best to explain my thoughts. "We may have discussed a few of these things before, but I admittedly may not have been as forthright as I should have been," I say.

"It's important for me to understand whatever it is, Katarina. You can tell me anything,"

he says, encouraging me with the stroke of his finger against my cheek.

"It bothers me when you tell me to stop working, especially when I feel like I'm making a difference in patient's lives. I'm proud of the work I do and at times it can be professionally stifling," I say.

His eyebrows rise in genuine surprise. "Katarina, I have absolutely no intention of curbing your work, but I do want to control the time you have to spend on it personally. As a continuous improvement professional I'm surprised you're not more open to alternative ways of getting the same work done, perhaps even more efficiently."

"Really?" I say, rising to the challenge shining in his eyes.

"Perhaps we can agree on some ground rules related to this particular issue," he says, rubbing my lower lip with his forefinger.

Just thinking about it makes my core clench and I feel myself begin to moisten. "Rules that I would need to follow?"

"Indeed," he says.

"And what happens if I don't follow them?" I ask breathlessly.

"Agreeing to a ground rule and then disobeying would most definitely call for firm punishment," he says, stroking my bare thigh and lower belly under the cover.

"This may not be a great deterrent," I say, recalling my pleasure when he's punished me in the past.

"Oh, Baby. The punishment for play and that for infraction of ground rules have completely distinct intensity levels," he says as his fingers find and heat the sensitive skin of my mound.

"You're intriguing me," I say huskily, feeling the warmth of a blush rise onto my cheeks.

"The entire intent. We'll start slowly, two ground rules to begin with," he says, as his fingers find the moistened folds below.

"The time I spend working and what else?" I ask, looking into the intensity of his deep green eyes.

"Taking your security precautions seriously," he says without pause.

"Hmm... So, when you found me in my office working late and not in the car with Jay as planned, you were tempering yourself?" I ask, recalling with a smile the night when he was irritated with me for not letting security know about the change in plans.

"Baby, you have no idea how much I wanted to paddle your lovely little ass! All I could think about on the way home was seeing your skin warm beneath me," he says as his smoldering eyes hold my own.

"I have no clue why that makes me so hot, but it absolutely does," I say, moistening at the thought.

He gently presses his thumb and rubs circles over the top of my sensitive nub. "Katarina, can you agree to the rules?" he asks, his eyes wide with challenge.

"Oh, Honey, right there, please don't stop."

"I like it when you tell me what you want, Baby," he says, teasing me, applying brief pressure and then allowing me to cool before starting over.

"I can't take it when you do this," I moan, my hips raising of their own accord, meeting his fingers, pushing into them over and over. I grasp the sheets unable to suppress a moan as he continues stroking me, my body poised right on the edge.

He finally lengthens his stroke and applies pressure to my clit. "I want to feel you shake in my arms. Cum for me now, Katarina," he says, and the sound of his voice sends me plummeting over the edge, trembling against his fingers while he holds me close against him and my breathing returns to normal.

"What were we talking about now?" I ask playfully, stroking his chest with my fingers.

"I think it was about rules until you completely distracted me," he says, kissing the top of my head, gently pushing the hair from my face.

"I can agree to trial a couple ground rules," I say.

"Kararina, tell me where you want to start," he says, lifting my chin so that I meet his eyes, still alight with desire as he gazes at me.

I feel my cheeks heat at the memory of him first spanking me with the long paddle. The angst I originally felt that quickly turned to lust, wanting to feel it even harder as my body pulsed and my core clenched with desire. I had never been so turned on before. Will I like it even more when he's doing it for punishment?

"Katarina?" he says, pulling me from my reverie.

"Work time and security, I can live with both," I say, "but let's go slow on the work hours at first. We are in the process of bringing up the entire division," I say, as his hand splays across my breast.

"We could hire others to assist you in that work."

I don't respond at first, too caught up in the delight of his hands on my body. "Hmm, I could probably agree to anything right now as long as you keep doing that," I say, as he strokes my nipples.

"Katarina, I do understand what this project means to you and I can agree to compromise for a little while longer. I know what a big step this is for you, Baby," he says.

"Tell me what you wanted to do to me when I went to Brazil," I say, changing topics and immediately delighting in the sea of emotions that play over his handsome features.

"All I could think about was getting you safely home and punishing you. You have no idea how worried I was," he says, continuing his leisurely pattern over my nipples.

"What would you have done to me if we had the ground rules in place then?" I ask, looking into his heated eyes.

"When I learned that you took the security team and confiscated my jet in order to fly to the other side of the world and meet Vicenti? All I could think about was restraining you, punishing you unmercifully until you assured me that you would never put yourself in that much danger again," he says.

"You wanted to spank me?"

"Baby, I wanted to do more than that. I ached to see your beautiful ass warm beneath my touch, to torture you, keep you on the edge, so close but so far, unable to do a damn thing about it, the same way I felt the entire time you were gone. I wanted to watch you moan with agony while I was in total control," he says, mesmerizing me with his intensity.

"Would you have eventually let me cum?" I ask, looking into his passionate green depths.

"Not that night. You would have gone to bed with a sore ass and an unquenchable ache between your legs," he says.

"Chase, that's horrible!"

He shrugs, smiling down at me. "Perhaps, but you have to admit it would have been well deserved," he says.

"I have no issue with the spanking, but you know how I feel about denial," I say, pouting.

"Punishment is intended to correct behavior," he says, running his finger across my protruded lips.

"So control is satisfying to you?" I say.

"Control in ensuring your safety and well being? You have absolutely no idea how much I need that Baby," he says, kissing my lips before he captures my arms, placing them above me, rolling on top of me and pushing my thighs apart with his own.

I gasp at the feel of his hardness pressing into me, rubbing against the most sensitive part of my body. "Honey," I moan as he continues.

"Baby, I want to feel you wrapped around my cock," he says, pushing into my wetness with one move.

"Aahh!"

"Wrap your legs around my back. Your hips will tilt and it will be that much more pleasurable," he instructs.

I do and feel the penetration deep in my core, making me moan softly beneath him. "It

feels so good," I say, my breath shallow as he slowly moves in and out, leisurely teasing me with his hardened length.

"We fit together perfectly," he says, pushing deep inside of me.

"Oh, God, it's so slow, so amazingly good this way," I say, raising my hips to take him in as far as I can.

"Chase, Honey," I pant as he lifts my legs over his shoulders. I connect my ankles around his neck, holding him in place as he leisurely dips in and out, deep and then slowly withdrawing, time and time again for what seems like forever.

"Ready Baby?" he asks, eyes glazed over, mirroring the passion and intensity of my own.

I nod and he begins to gain momentum, driving deeper and deeper until finally both of us are left trembling around each other in the aftermath of our passion. I can barely catch my breath, holding him close until he slowly lets my legs down from around his neck. I stretch my limbs before wrapping them around the back of his thighs, keeping his body resting atop my own.

"Do you have any idea how much I love you," he says, kissing my lips gently.

"As much as I love you?" I say, opening as he deepens our kiss and my legs tighten around the back of his thighs, clenching tightly around him.

TWO

I roll over to an empty bed and groan at the time registered on the clock before pulling on my robe and heading downstairs to find Chase. He is at the breakfast bar reading stocks and eating a bowl of oatmeal with blueberries and nuts. His cell is on the table and Sid is on speakerphone. "The teams are in place and we've got increased levels of effort on the communication front," he says.

"Good. Let me know when you and Jay settle on the plans for Christmas Eve," he says before disconnecting.

"Morning Baby," he says.

"Well, I wouldn't exactly call four a.m. morning, but you weren't in bed and I couldn't sleep," I say, pouring myself a cup of coffee.

"Sid and I had a lot to talk about," he says.

"Are you concerned about security for our wedding?"

"It's been in every social column in and out of the country. I want to mitigate any risk of it becoming a problem," he says.

"I was surprised to see it in just about every tabloid, too," I say, taking the seat next to him.

"Good news travels fast. Is it a problem?" he says, grinning.

"No, you warned me, I just didn't realize it would be this widespread," I say.

"Unfortunately we're going to be in the spotlight for a little while with the wedding and the Prestian Corp and Torzial expansions. Did you see the email from Brian about the customer requests he's been getting and passing along to Jenny? She may want to set up offices in our L.A. and Vegas towers, too," he says.

"Yes, and actually I was thinking the same thing. The medical facilities on the West Coast are expansive. It's going to take local boots on the ground to get all the preliminary work done," I say, chewing my lip.

"Tell me what you're worried about, Katarina?" he urges.

"I just want Jenny to be able to spend quality time with her mom and not have all of this on her mind. I'm excited to talk to her about it, but I hope she's offline enjoying time with her family before Christmas. She was struggling with how to tell her mom about the rape."

"I didn't realize she hadn't told her mom," Chase says.

"She wanted to do it in person. Thought it would be easier if her mom saw firsthand that she was physically okay."

"Probably a good idea to spend time with her mom after she tells her," Chase says.

"Do you travel there often?" I ask, wondering how much of our time will now need to be spent on the West Coast. While I know the importance to the business, I was hoping to spend more time in the New York office getting to know my father.

"Quarterly board meetings, forums, but otherwise much of the work is done remotely now. The technological age has really transformed the way we interact in the last several years, but I would envision us traveling there a little more as we build relationships, at least initially," he says, putting my mind at ease.

"Good. I was worried it may pull us away from the New York office, but it doesn't sound as physically demanding as I first thought. With everything going on it sounds like we'll both be busy after the New Year," I say.

"Put good systems and structures in place and the work will take care of itself," he says, his eyebrows raised.

"I'm pretty sure I'll have to push a boundary or two with the ground rules for a while," I say, smiling sweetly at him over my coffee.

"Oh, by all means, Katarina, please do. It will be the highlight of my day," he says, his eyes alight with mischief.

"Well if you had stayed in bed, having your wife give you an incredibly slow, leisurely blow job would have been today's highlight," I say, smirking.

"Baby, the day is just beginning and there's absolutely no time like the present," he says, scooping me into his arms.

"Chase!"

"Shh, Baby," he says, carrying me to the elevator and pushing the button to take us upstairs.

IT IS late morning before we are showered and head downstairs. "I'm absolutely famished," I say, walking into the kitchen.

Gaby looks up from behind the counter. "Well it's about time you two lazy birds got up for breakfast. In fact, it's so late I think we'll have to call breakfast brunch, although I see someone dipped into the blueberry and nut oatmeal already," she clucks.

"Brunch looks fabulous," Chase says grinning, lifting the lid to the top of the 9 x 13 pan sitting on the stove.

"Sit, sit, sit," she says, shooing him from the cooking area as I look on and take a seat at the small table in the corner of the kitchen.

"It would appear you've been kicked out of the kitchen," I say, laughing at the pair.

"Indeed," he says, scowling at his cell and then looking up at me with hooded eyes.

"Since I haven't been very productive this morning, I'm planning to spend the rest of the day and tomorrow catching up and reviewing the West Coast healthcare organizations and dynamics," I say.

"Oh, I think you've been highly productive Miss Meilers, but on a serious note, you're not even the slightest bit interested in what's going on with Alfreita?" he says.

"Maybe curious, but I don't have to know. There's a difference," I say, as Gaby places an egg bake and fresh fruit in front of us.

"You said you didn't want me to worry about what's swirling on around us and how you're handling things. I'm trying to do just that and I trust the best interests of our family is your utmost concern."

"Baby, you're so brave, but I still think we should discuss what is being recommended," he says, taking a sip of his coffee.

"You asked me to trust you about these things and I sincerely do not have a need to know what your conversation with Sid was about. I have faith that you will do what has to be done."

"Trust aside, Katarina. This time it's a little different, there are things you really should be aware of, Baby," he says.

I shake my head. "No, that man is evil. I still have an incredibly hard time thinking about what would have happened if that shipment had reached it's destination. How many kids would have died after ingesting that stuff?"

"Your father and Vicenti are working to shut other production sites down so that doesn't happen," Chase says.

"Okay, now you have my interest. I didn't know Vicenti was involved in helping with that, but Dad did mention the men from Miami were assisting. I thought you were closing them down to spite Alfreita?"

"Clearly you know quite a bit for someone that's not supposed to be aware of anything," Chase says, eyebrows raised.

"Blame my father. He spilled his guts," I say, grinning.

"And yet you aren't interested in what I would share with you?" he says, gazing intently at me.

"I have to admit, it surprises me too, but honestly, I don't have any desire to know," I say.

"You need only ask if you change your mind," he says before taking a bite of his breakfast.

"The dish is made from egg whites. I'm pretty sure it's only the yolks you find too rich, so I altered the recipe. Chase, I think you'll like it, too," Gaby says.

"That's awesome, Gaby. Thank you so much. I'm sure Chase will love it!" I say, trying not to laugh at his upturned eyebrows and look of appall as he chews and she sashays out of the room.

"I'm pretty sure participation in the altering of my breakfast routine should be considered along with security and work. So it would appear now is a good time to talk about ground rules," he says, smirking.

"Seriously, we're going to discuss this now?"

"You threw down the gauntlet, Baby," he says, toying with his egg white bake. "Why don't we agree to four hours of work this afternoon and four tomorrow? It seems you've been quite productive already this morning," he says, eyes dancing with amusement.

"What about four hours today and eight tomorrow?"

"I would counter that. A paddling of my choosing with any implement I see fit for every hour past four tomorrow."

"For every hour? So you would bank them up?" I ask.

"Indeed, and would let you pay them off with various other acts of indiscretion," he says, his eyes sparkling.

"How about a paddling for each hour over four with the implement of my choosing? That sounds like a fair compromise, considering it's my first time."

"I concur, spending time selecting instruments together would be most pleasing indeed," he says.

"And just how would you suggest doing this?" I ask right before Gaby walks in.

He raises his eyebrows and tries to hide his smirk as she begins clearing dishes and discussing dinner. "Did Katarina tell you we set the wedding date?" he says to Gaby.

"Oh, good Lord. She most certainly did not," she says, grinning widely. "That most definitely calls for a celebration dinner. Will you be home tonight?" she asks.

"Yes, until next Wednesday. Then the three of us will be flying with Jay and the crew to New York. We'll all be staying with Katarina's parents for the wedding on Christmas Eve," he says.

"This year! And you're taking me with you?" she says, wide eyed.

"Gaby, you know you're much more than the person that takes care of this home to me. You've been like a second mom," he says.

"Young man, do you have any idea how much I love you!" she says, hugging his neck.

"The feeling is mutual Gaby," he says, laughing. "I've asked my assistant to contact you tomorrow. She and Katarina's mom will help coordinate your dress for the occasion. If I recall it will be a theme of sapphire and black," he says.

"Good memory, Chase. Gaby, you're going to look absolutely amazing and we would be delighted to have you at our wedding."

"My goodness. I am so excited I don't know where to start. I better get a plan together for the staff if we're going to be gallivanting all over the countryside," she says, sashaying out of the kitchen.

"I love that she'll be part of the wedding, Honey," I say.

"Wouldn't dream of having it any other way, Baby."

I walk around the table and put my arms around his neck. "Call whoever texted you. I know you're dying to get this resolved. In the meantime, I need to get a little work done and will be in the library."

"Don't be too long," he says, trying to hide his grin before giving me a kiss on the cheek.

"You seem to like this agreement quite a bit."

"Katarina, you have no idea how much it excites me," he says.

"Well, I hate to disappoint you, but my ass will be safe tonight as I only plan on spending a few hours working today. I understand a celebratory meal is on the menu for supper," I say, giving him a smile and quick kiss on the lips.

"Pity, perhaps another time, Baby," he says, smiling as I head towards the library. The room has two floor-to-ceiling windows and a stone fireplace in between. The view overlooks the property, which is surrounded by a wall of towering blue spruce pines adorned with a fresh winter's coating of snow. The only thing missing is a warm fire and I text Chase.

Message: Where can I get wood for the fireplace in the library?

Reply: Will send someone.

Message: I can start a fire. You know I was a Girl Scout.

Reply: I have no doubt your skills are impeccable. I will send you some hard wood.

Message: You talk so dirty!

Reply: Remember who started this.

I look up and expect to see Chase, but instead a tall man with greying hair pushing a

cart of oak wood enters the room. "Ma'am, Mr. Prestian asked me to start a fire and leave you with plenty of logs," he says, setting about his task.

"Thank you. I apologize, but I don't recall meeting you before. I'm Kate," I say.

"Pleasure to meet you miss. My name is Glen," he says, extending a tanned arm to shake my hand.

"How long have you worked for Chase? I haven't seen you around, been somewhere warm lately?" I say, referencing his tan as he loads the wood from the cart into the fireplace.

He gives me a broad smile. "Oh, yeah, I was down in the Keys with my boy, doing some fishing."

"Well it's very nice to meet you. I really appreciate you starting the fire, it's been some time since I've built one myself," I admit.

"Don't worry, it'll be roaring in no time. If you like the library, I'll be sure to keep the fireplace going," he says.

"That would be lovely. It's my favorite room in the entire house," I say, before leaving him to his task and texting Chase.

Message: And here I thought you would deliver the hard wood personally!

Reply: Careful, Baby. I do know where to find you.

I smile, opening my keyboard and curling into the large cushy chair to enjoy the warmth of the logs as they begin to smolder. It is late afternoon when my cell alerts me to a message. I glance at the clock and realize I've been working for a few hours already. I look down expecting a text from Chase, but it's from Jenny.

Message: See the expansion news?

Reply: It's happening so fast! Southwest & Cali? OMG!

Message: Incredible! Have time to work on this with me the next couple of days?

Reply: Absolutely! I'll send through a couple meeting invites.

Message: Great. If we can get a proposal packaged up for Chase by end of day Friday that will give him and his attorneys time to review the following week, so we don't have to worry about anything the week of your wedding.

Reply: Sounds good. When do you leave for your parents'?

Message: Tonight, I'll be there until next Weds. I can help with last minute wedding details on Thursday.

Reply: Perfect, now I need to go before I end up in hot water for working too long!

I smile, secretly wondering what it is that Mr. Intense has in store for me as I close my notebook and go in search of him.

THREE

It is **Wednesday evening,** two days before our Christmas Eve wedding and barely dusk when we touch down in New York. Jay has the limo waiting on the tarmac and our driver greets us as we get into the back seat. Jay and his team follow closely in the car behind us as we head into the heavily congested pre-holiday traffic. The snow is softly falling, glistening in the lights of the city as we make the forty-minute drive upstate. The snowfall becomes heavier, denser, already weighing the boughs of the spruce and pines that are lined along the country road leading to my father's estate. The driver slows at the stone and wrought iron gate, speaking with the guard before being allowed entry onto the property. Another mile and my father's home comes into view, an impressive three story white Victorian looking mansion with tall pillars that frame the doorway. We pass the ten-car parking garage as the driver pulls along the circular drive in front of the home. Chase gets out and opens my door for me, guiding me to the entrance just as my father opens the door.

"Katarina, Chase, welcome," my father says, shaking Chase's hand as my mother and I hug and we are led into the impressive marble floored foyer.

"We'll have someone put your luggage in the same suite you were in the last time you and Chase stayed here together." I smile at the recollection of Chase showing up unexpectedly after a day of shopping for a wedding dress with Jenny and my mom and what he did to me in that room. "Most of the family have arrived or will be coming in tomorrow," Mom is saying as we walk through the foyer.

"Jenny texted me to let me know that she had a few things come up unexpectedly and that she plans to arrive sometime tomorrow, and we dropped Gaby off at her family's home," I say, as our coats are taken by the staff.

"Jenny can stay in the main house, same room she was in when you visited. Most of your father's family have settled into the guest houses on the property," Mom says.

"I'm sure that will be fine," I say, gasping as we walk into the great room. The vast space has been completely transformed into a world of white twinkling lights hanging from the ceiling and wrapped around the curved marble staircase. A bluish-green Christmas tree is decorated with white angels, silver ribbons and a brilliant five-pointed star that does not quite, but almost touches the high vaulted ceiling.

"It's beautiful, Mom," I say, gazing up at the banister that has silver ribbon and twinkling lights adorning the staircase that I will soon be walking down and my mother walked down before me.

"I'm glad that you like it, Sweetie," she says, guiding Chase and I through the room to the formal dining area. She is animated as she announces us to family members already seated and I realize how excited I am to spend the holiday and share our special moment with family.

The night is filled with laughter, a wonderful meal and lots of wine. It is well past mid-night before Chase and I make it up the curved marble staircase.

I wake earlier than normal after such a late night and glance at the empty spot beside me. How he runs on such little amounts of sleep is beyond me. The weather icon on my phone displays ten degrees, one of the colder days New York has had in quite some time. I stretch and decide to get up, scouring through my belongings for yoga pants, sports bra and a t-shirt, donning them before lacing up my shoes and going in search of the indoor gym.

I make my way to the first floor where the staircase ends, recalling my mom's mention of it being on the lower level the last time I was here. I finally find an elevator right off the hallway adjacent to the dining room. I enter it and push the lower level button, amazed at the magnitude and luxury of the wealthy. The gym is every bit as impressive as Chase's with a treadmill, elliptical and lots of circuit training equipment arranged to one side. The Olympic size pool takes up the remainder of the space and off to the end is a set of doors, which I presume to be the shower and bathroom area. I peel off my shirt, select my playlist and begin my run, thinking back to the night before. It was wonderful getting to know more of our family and a much better way to spend the evening than at a bachelorette party. Chase and I had both been approached by well-meaning friends who wanted to throw us pre-wedding parties. We both declined, wanting to spend the time together with family.

I go over the list of my to-dos for the day which is minimal, but includes a haircut, nails, and eyebrow and body wax mid-morning. I finish my run, slowing the last four minutes to the sound of my cooldown song, grab my t-shirt and decide to use the bathroom before heading upstairs. I open one of the doors and to my surprise enter a sauna that is already heated and smells heavenly. Deciding to partake I close the door to keep the heat in, exploring the dials and options on the panel. There are buttons that denote infusion therapy with choices of eucalyptus, lemon grass, and chamomile, and when I make a selection I'm awestruck as the entire room is infused with a steamy eucalyptus-scented spray. I take a seat on the horizontal bench and lay face down on its length luxuriating in the feel of the warmth and scent wafting around me. I close my eyes, relaxed after a late night and early morning, thinking about my wedding day when the door opens and a shot of unexpected cool air hits my skin.

"We've got her," Sheldon says into a crackling walky-talky looking device.

"What the hell is going on Sheldon?" I ask, embarrassed at my state of undress, hurriedly pulling my t-shirt on over my sports bra.

"Chase couldn't find you and you weren't answering your cell," he says, looking flustered at my annoyance. "I can't cover for you if you don't tell me where you're going," he says, clearly as frustrated with the situation as I am.

"So, even at my parents' house I am to give you a play by play of my movements? Are you kidding me?" I ask.

"Kate, we're trying to keep you safe. There's a lot of shit going down right now. I need to know where you are at all times," he says, running his hands through his hair.

"Okay, that's it. Take me to Chase," I say, now exasperated with my ignorance of whatever situation we are dealing with.

"Sure, he's upstairs. The guy called in every security team in the state. They asked me if I knew where you were and I didn't. I'm sorry Kate. I checked all the rooms down here except the sauna and shower," he says.

"This is not your fault, Sheldon. I've been listening to my cell for the last hour and a half. I didn't get any phone calls or texts," I say.

"Secure room," he says, gesturing to the space around us. "There's a safe room, well, more like another little house down here with bedrooms and kitchens through this door. It's designed in the event a longer stay is needed," he says as we get into the elevator. We arrive on the main floor and my phone explodes with ring tones alerting me to numerous missed calls and texts. My anger immediately dissolves as I see the look of sheer relief in Chase and my father's eyes as we walk into my dad's study.

Chase crosses the space in a few easy steps, pulling me into his arms and squeezing me tight. "What happened? Where were you?" he asks, looking down at me, not yet comprehending what has transpired.

"I was working out, saw the sauna and decided to indulge. I didn't know anyone would be looking for me and had absolutely no idea that you couldn't reach me down there. I'm sorry. My music was still playing," I say, gesturing to my cell phone.

"Thank God. Chase, I'm going to make a few calls," my dad says, leaving us to our conversation as he begins punching numbers on his office line telephone. "Sid, this is Carlos Larussio. You can call off the teams, we've got her," he says over the speakerphone.

"Thanks, Carlos. Glad to hear it, but I'm gonna need confirmation of that from the big guy," he says.

"Sid, this is Chase. She was downstairs working out and didn't realize she had gone off the grid. Sorry for the worry. If you would contact everyone, let them know she's safe and call everyone off I would appreciate it," he says, keeping his arms firmly around my waist.

"Chase, I'm sorry about this. It's my job to make sure I know where she is at all times. I checked the gym, but everything was dark. I realized I missed the sauna the first time around and went back down," Sheldon says.

"I didn't tell Katarina the severity of the situation with Alfreita because I wanted to keep her sheltered. I should have told her how determined he has become in trying to gain any leverage that he can. She clearly didn't realize the danger in not keeping you informed and that's my fault. I'll fill her in and we'll meet with you and Jay after that to establish guidelines going forward," Chase says.

"Sounds good," Sheldon says.

I look at the clock and cringe as I realize that most of the morning is gone. "Chase, I'm supposed to be in the city by eleven. I thought Jenny was coming in last night so I made appointments for both of us, but it looks like she won't arrive until later in the day," I say, embarrassed that I neglected to let anyone know my plans.

His eyebrows raise in question. "Appointments for what?" he says.

I whisper in his ear. "Haircut, wax, you know..."

"I thought your mom arranged that for tomorrow," he says.

I widen my eyes at him. "Not that," I say quietly, letting my meaning register.

"Sheldon, Katarina needs to go into the city. Can you arrange security rather quickly?" he asks.

"Chase, use some of our men. Jay has already brought a few of my men up to speed and has synced technology with your own. They've been briefed on the situation," Carlos says.

"Very good. Sheldon, make sure no one takes their eyes off of her. I want heavy guards around the perimeter and at least three female details inside the salon. Katarina will give you the address so you can make arrangements. Unfortunately, the appointment is soon. We'll use Carlos's team and have your men meet us there," he says.

"You're going to the salon with me?" I ask.

"We can't be sure that someone wasn't listening when you set up the appointment and unfortunately we don't have time to run intel. I'm not about to let you out of my sight right now. I plan on marrying you tomorrow," he says, kissing me soundly on the lips right in front of Sheldon and my dad.

I have barely gotten out of the shower and changed when Chase enters the room. "Baby, we have to hurry if we're going to make it on time. The helicopter's waiting," he says, as I pull my towel-dried hair into a pony and we dash downstairs and outside toward the helipad that is already heavily surrounded by security.

Chase helps me into the shiny new blue helicopter. "I have to admit, the amenities, especially the custom soundproofing, are much nicer than the older model," I say, curling into the soft leather sofa and buckling my seat belt.

"Glad you like it, Baby," Chase says, sliding in beside me as the pilot prepares for liftoff.

"It's definitely nice to hear each other talk on the way to the airport and not have to wear the headset," I say as we begin our ascent.

"Would agree. It was never an issue before as I didn't travel with anyone other than security and they all have three-ways," he says, rubbing the tops of my shoulders with his hand.

"I'm sorry for all the fuss today. I seriously feel awful that we are using so many security people just so I can go get, you know..." I say, blushing.

"Oh, Baby, I would move mountains and then some to make sure that how you display your body to me on our wedding night is exactly what you want," he says, pulling me close and kissing me lightly on the lips.

"I love you, Chase," I say against the warmth of his lips.

"I love you, too, Katarina, and while I would like nothing more than to show you how much and break this helicopter in right, we are going to be landing in less than six minutes," he says, rubbing his finger against my lips.

"I'd like to break it in, too," I murmur, curling my face into the crook of his neck and breathing in the crisp clean smell of soap on his skin.

"Tell me what you'd like to do," he murmurs against my lips.

"As soon as the pilot lifts off next time, I'd like to get out of my buckle and climb into your lap, straddling my legs around you," I say.

"And then what?" he asks huskily.

"I'll be wearing a short skirt, so you can reach underneath and put your hands on my ass and guide me onto your hard cock. Once I'm positioned, you'll bring me down hard," I say.

He kisses my lips passionately, lifting my hair and encircling my neck with his hand, pulling me closer. "Baby, if we weren't going to be landing in the next few moments I would have my cock so deep inside of you," he says.

The pilot's announcement of the impending landing comes over the digital speakers. "Next time, Honey," I say, bending to kiss his lips.

The pilot puts us down on the Prestian Towers helipad. "We're about twenty minutes from the salon in midday traffic," Jay says to Chase.

"Sounds good. Let's hope it isn't too bad," Chase says, holding my hand as we are guided from the helicopter to the safety of a stretch limousine. The driver navigates the congested traffic with a sense of ease and obvious knowledge of the city, pulling up street-side to Briena's boutique, a chic little salon with a red brick exterior. Jay opens my door and Chase walks around the back, placing his hand on the small of my back to escort me inside.

"I'm Kate Meilers and I have an appointment this morning," I say to the receptionist who greets me from behind the contemporary cherry wood credenza. She has short spiky brunette hair with tinges of purple throughout and a warm smile. I glance around as she looks up my reservation. The security detail is completely unobtrusive, blending in so well that I am unable to distinguish who from the women in the waiting area may be working on the payroll.

"I'll be waiting here, catching up on a little light reading," Chase says grinning, holding up the latest copy of People magazine. I shake my head at his antics as I am led to the back of the salon, knowing full-well that he'll be working within minutes using his phone's secure-net software.

The rest of the late morning is relaxing, spent having my nails french tipped and square cut, my hair slightly trimmed and thinned, and getting my eyebrows, legs, and lady bits waxed. By the time we get back into the car it is three in the afternoon. The beep on my phone alerts me to an incoming text from Jenny.

Message: Just arrived. I'm visiting with your mom.

Reply: Glad you made it. We are just leaving the city. See you at home shortly.

Message: They frikken doubled all of my security.

Reply: For everyone!!

"Jenny said you doubled all of her security, too," I say, glancing up from my cell at Chase.

"Just precautionary, but things are escalating. I'll bring you up to speed when we are alone," he says.

It takes another fifteen minutes to get back to Prestian Corp by car and from there we are escorted through the opulent tunnel system that leads us to the helipad that overlooks the water. I see what Jenny means about the escalation of security. It does feel like the entire team has almost doubled. The pilot takes off quickly after we are seated and the aircraft is soon skirting around the island, over the bay, and heading north toward Chappaqua. The flight is uneventful and I snuggle into the crook of Chase's arm, determined not to let my concern with whatever is going on put a damper on our evening.

"Tired, Baby?"

"I had hoped to take a nap before the dinner rehearsal, but didn't realize the appointment would take quite as long as it did."

We land and Chase shakes everyone's hand as we get out of the helicopter, letting them know how much he appreciated their assistance on such short notice. I feel completely embarrassed that it took so many people to make the trip into the city possible, but it does not seem to faze him or anyone else at all.

Chase and I head upstairs to get ready for the evening. He showers before me and is gone when I finish. I unpin my hair and let the long loose curls the stylist put in fall to my chest before applying fresh makeup. My legs are waxed and glistening with the freshly applied Aloe spritz I brought back with us from Aruba. Chase walks into the bedroom dressed in a black suit with a sapphire colored tie just as I finish dressing.

"You look absolutely stunning, Katarina," he says, spinning me around, taking in the formfitting, off the shoulder, long sleeved, sapphire blue dress. The dress is thigh length and the four-inch Louboutin heels that crisscross and circle around my ankles are a perfect match to its length. He kisses me gently on the lips and his hand glides down the expanse of bare skin from the bottom of my jaw, along the length of my neck and around the top of my bare shoulder. "This dress is very hot, but I think it may be missing something," he says.

"What's that?" I ask, twirling before him.

"Close your eyes for a moment," he says.

I let them shut, listening to the sounds around me. I can hear him walking around the bedroom, a drawer opening, and things being shuffled. His hands lift my hair before the chilly feel of metal brushes my neck and something cool rests against the start of my cleavage. He moves me across the room, guiding me so I do not trip.

"Open your eyes, Baby," he says.

I am facing the mirror and audibly gasp when I do. It is a sparkling necklace; three strands of diamonds, twisted and braided to hold a single heart-shaped sapphire that now lies against my chest.

"Chase, it's gorgeous," I exclaim, tracing the diamond ropes with my finger down to the brilliantly blue heart which has to be the largest stone I've ever seen, let alone worn.

"My father gave it to my mother as a wedding gift. She wanted me to keep it in the family and give it to my wife someday. You've had my heart since the day I met you, and I'd be honored for you to have it," he says, turning me around to face him.

"I absolutely love it," I say, reaching up to kiss his lips.

"Now we better go downstairs before we miss our own celebration dinner," he says, rubbing his hands over my hips and ass. "Thong?" he asks mischievously.

"Chase, you're not supposed to know that, yet," I say, feigning exasperation with his antics.

The rest of the family members have been arriving throughout the day and are mingling in the great room, my father's study and the dining room. Chase catches the attention of a waiter who brings both of us a glass of white wine. "To us," he says, lifting his glass.

"To us," I say as he puts his arm around my shoulders escorting me further into the great room, passing several waiters who are walking around with shrimp and a multitude of other fancy looking hors d'oeuvres.

"I see that Mom has taken my request for a small informal gathering to heart," I say.

"She's excited," Chase says, pulling me close.

"I know, it's pretty hard to be upset with her. There's Jenny," I say, spying her across the room visiting with a few members of my family. Chase and I spot his dad and Emily at the same time and he guides me to where they are sitting on a love seat talking with one of my aunts.

Don stands and shakes Chase's hand, but his eyes immediately fall to the sapphire shimmering around my neck, gazing at it. Finally, he takes my hand in his own, turning it before bringing it to his lips. "You look absolutely stunning this evening, Katarina. You can't know how happy it makes me that Chase has found someone as lovely as you for a wife and that he has given you his mother's necklace."

"Thank you, Don. I know how special it is and you have my word that it will always be cherished," I say.

"I have no doubt that it will, Katarina. Emily and I are looking forward to seeing you both a little more often now that the medical centers are expanding," he says, putting his arm around her shoulders and drawing her into the conversation.

"We should mingle a bit Dad, but we'll round back a little later," Chase says after we've visited for a short while. We find Jenny and chat with her and a few other guests until dinner is announced and then make our way to the place reserved for us at the conference-size dining room table. Chase pulls out the seats for both Jenny and I before taking his place to my right.

"I thought Brian was going to be here," I say to Chase.

"He got caught in negotiations, but he'll be here tomorrow. At least he better be, otherwise, I'm going to have to pull in one of your uncles to stand in for best man," he says, grinning.

"Brian won't be here tonight but Chase expects him to be here for the wedding," I explain to Jenny who is sitting beside me but did not hear our conversation.

"We've emailed each other tons since Torzial started working on the Prestian accounts. I was hoping to get to meet him in person when we toured Prestian Corp last week, but he wasn't around," she says.

"He was out of the country working on something," I say as dinner is served.

The meal is a true Italian feast as is tradition in the Larussio family. The seafood scialatelli smells wonderfully of basil, garlic and butter. The prawns have been perfectly sautéed and are displayed on a bed of pasta, laden with roasted cherry tomatoes, sprinkled with parsley and a unique cheese that is delicious in taste, but unique and unfamiliar.

"Do you know what the cheese is called? It's so good," I ask Chase.

"It's Pecorino, a little stronger than Romano and imported straight from Italy," he says.

"It's very flavorful," I say, murmuring my appreciation for the dish. The meal has been nicely planned, allowing time to socialize between courses. I take another sip of the crisp but delicately sweet wine and look around in wonder at the family who I never knew existed only a few short months ago.

I am pulled from my reverie as the waiters place a dish of Sea Bass alla Fiorentina in front of us. The smell of the fish, roasted tomatoes, garlic, basil and parsley lend off a wonderful aroma. I marvel at how pretty they have presented this course of the meal. The fish sits upon a ladled pool of freshly diced roasted tomatoes and the sauce surrounding it is sprinkled with parsley and served with a mixed green salad. Jenny is sitting next to my single aunt and they seem to have hit it off fabulously, deeply engrossed in conversation.

The wait staff has cleared the tables and is setting before each of the diners a small dish of sorbet. "I'm glad the dessert looks light. I am so full," I whisper to Chase.

He gives me a boyish grin. "Baby this is just to cleanse your palette. It will prepare you for the next delicious taste you are about to experience. The real dessert will be sinfully decadent," he says, his lips turned up in a smirk at my dismay.

I dutifully spoon the cold, pale yellow sorbet to my lips and scowl playfully at his look of amusement.

"Your mom told me they are serving Tiramisu," he says with a wide smile. I inwardly groan as I see the progression of waiters pour coffee for the guests, while others begin carrying large porcelain platters that hold small plates into the dining room. It is a beautiful dessert, layered with creamy mascarpone cheese, Italian chocolate shavings, crème and espresso.

"It's absolutely delicious, sinful even," I say, taking a bite and murmuring my appreciation for the dessert.

"See what you would have missed if you had stopped at the sorbet?" he asks.

I narrow my eyes at him. "I know what you're getting at," I say, taking in the raised eyebrows.

"Whatever do you mean, Katarina?" he asks mischievously.

"You know, I'll tell you later," I say, feeling the warmth of a blush rise to my cheeks.

"I'll be looking forward to it," he says before the staff clears our dishes and people begin meandering into the great room where wine and other alcoholic beverages are being served. It feels good to stand after such a large meal. I have a brief opportunity to chat with Jenny before she is pulled into a discussion about Torzial with Don and a few others.

I notice my parents mingling amongst the family and every time I catch site of them they seem to be laughing or smiling. Chase and I continue to circulate but by the end of the evening the long day has taken its toll. "You look exhausted, Baby," Chase says.

"I think someone kept me up a little late last night, that and I was up a little earlier than normal," I say, narrowing my eyes at him.

"Yes, up early causing my security team grief as I recall," he says.

"Who was causing them grief? Also, I distinctly recall you mentioning filling me in on all this added security," I say, raising my eyebrows at him.

"I'm teasing you, Baby, but you did say that you didn't want to know. I'll bring you up to speed a little later but for now why don't you head upstairs? I'll make the rounds one more time and let everyone know we are retiring for the evening," he says, kissing me on the lips before I tiredly climb the stairs to our room. I close the door and look at my reflection in the wall-sized mirror. The sapphire necklace glitters at me and I rub my finger over its shimmering surface. Tomorrow I will no longer be Kate Meilers, but instead will be Katarina Prestian. I wonder how Chase's mom felt when she married his dad. The door opens and I realize I am still staring in the mirror.

"You look a million miles away, Baby," Chase says, putting his arms around my waist and kissing my neck from behind.

"I was just wondering how our moms felt the night before their weddings," I say, rubbing the stone between my fingers. "Chase, are you sure you want to marry me?"

"Katarina, of course I do, why would you ask that?"

"I'm not the type of girl that people like you marry," I say, hating the catch in my voice.

"People like me?"

I turn to face him. "Chase, look at this stone. I've seen pictures of you and other women. They were duchesses, princesses, and daughters of diplomats. Do you really think your mom wanted you to give such a magnificent stone to someone like me?"

"Listen to me. My mother wanted it to go to the woman I love, want to marry and will carry on our family. Why would you even compare yourself to the other women I've been with? It concerns me that you're such an intelligent, kind person, but so self-deprecating when it comes to feeling like you belong with me. Katarina, the money's a package deal, but it shouldn't define us," he says, unzipping my gown and letting it fall to the floor.

"Now, since you went against all traditional wedding plans, I think we'll just skip the part about not seeing the bride-to-be the night before the wedding and all of those other little rules," he says, spinning me so he can capture my lips with his own.

FOUR

It has been a full day, with a family breakfast followed by an all-day affair of facials, massages, hair styling and makeup. "We have to hurry up. Otherwise, you're seriously going to be late for your own wedding," Jenny chastises, scooting me into her room as we get to the top of the stairs.

My mother has seen to it that all of the ladies in our family have been thoroughly pampered while the gentlemen have been exiled to the nature trails that Carlos recently had created and donated to the state for public enjoyment. Mom has had all of my clothes for the evening placed in Jenny's suite to allow us privacy while we get ready and afford Chase a space to do the same, insisting we follow some traditions.

"I'll change in the bathroom while you put your little unmention-ables on," Jenny jokes as she heads into the bathroom to get dressed. I smile at her reference to the brief little thong I bought to go under my wedding dress. I quickly undress and slip it on, the only undergarment I will wear. The custom design of my dress and plunging, deep V-neck trails past my cleavage to the top of my navel and does not allow for anything under it.

I spin around just as Jenny comes back in the room. She looks amazing in a stunning long strapless gown that dips low in the front, cinches around her perfect waist and falls gracefully around her in soft gentle folds. The sapphire wedding color accentuates her long dark chestnut colored hair. She is wearing silver and diamond drop earrings and a matching necklace that sits right at the start of her cleavage.

"Kate, you look absolutely beautiful," she says, spinning me around in front of the mirror. The seamstress has done an excellent job. Thin spaghetti straps cross over my shoulder and trail to the top of my hips, leaving my back completely exposed and the satiny material flowing to the floor and beyond. Jenny holds out the graceful train so I can see it in the mirror.

"Here, I'm supposed to make sure you wear this," she says, clasping the sapphire necklace into place. It really is much more gorgeous than all the pictures," she says, spinning me around.

"What pictures?"

"Kate, seriously, haven't you seen all the tabloids and social columns? It's all anyone has been gossiping about since last night," she says.

"Jenny, I don't have the slightest idea what you're talking about," I say.

"Apparently, Chase's dad gave this to his wife as a wedding gift."

"Chase told me that," I say, turning to look at the long train in the mirror.

"Did he tell you that it's rumored to be the largest heart-shaped sapphire in the world?" Jenny asks.

"No, we were up late, I slept in. We didn't really talk about it," I say, letting what she said register.

"The tabloids are in a frenzy. Apparently Don outbid a Saudi prince who collects rare stones like this and believed at one time it belonged to his family. Don refused the guy's attempts to buy it for millions more than it was worth even after Chase's mom passed away. The newspapers are recounting all the stories that were published about it even years ago."

"I hope Don isn't uncomfortable with all the press," I say, touching the stone.

"I'm not sure. All the articles say that he's made no comment, but apparently the stone sitting around your neck is worth more than forty million dollars, Kate. Seriously, when Chase gave it to me to put on you tonight, I was actually scared to take it," she says.

I look at the stone in the mirror. The cool blue glistening gem lays against my chest, the point of the heart perfectly settled between the gentle sloping of my breasts. I touch its surface, recalling only a few short months ago I didn't trust any man and now I'm about to commit to a man whose controlling tendencies know no bounds and nothing feels more right.

"It's time, Kate. We have to go," she says, pulling me from my reverie, helping me from her room to the top of the stairs. The wedding planner has orchestrated things down to the minute and Jenny gives me a hug as she leaves me with my father at the top of the stairs.

He is dressed in a black tuxedo with a sharp sapphire-colored tie. He takes my hands and his eyes meet mine. "Katarina, there's something that I need to say to you."

"Okay," I say, squeezing his hands.

"There's not a day that goes by that I don't wish I could turn back time and do things all over again, but unfortunately that's not possible. I can only hope that you give me a chance to be a good father and grandfather in the future. There's nothing I regret more than the decisions I made early in life that caused me to miss the first twenty-six years of your life," he says.

"Dad, there's nothing I would like better than to spend many years getting to know each other even better. I'm so glad that you agreed to walk me down the stairs," I say, hugging him close to me and trying desperately to keep my tears at bay.

"It's an honor. Let's go to a wedding baby girl," he says, taking my hand as the music to "Here Comes the Bride" begins to play on the grand piano. We walk slowly, down the long winding circular staircase. The officiant is at the bottom of the steps and the wedding planner has arranged the guests so they can witness the ceremony.

My mother is in a sapphire gown that falls softly off her shoulders, hugging her slim waist before draping into soft folds around her and her eyes are misty as she watches my father and me. The color of the dress accentuates her strawberry blonde hair and sparkling blue eyes perfectly. Don is dressed in black dress pants, a sapphire blue shirt with black tie, while Emily is in a lovely floor-length gown of flowing sapphire. I catch a glimpse of Gaby standing next to Don and Emily. She is dressed in a beautiful soft sapphire colored dress that folds gently around her rotund curves and she smiles warmly at me as our eyes connect. Jenny's long flowing brown hair is a perfect contrast to the dress that hugs her hips and slim waist. She is standing next to Brian who has finally arrived and is wearing a black tux, sapphire-colored shirt and black tie.

At the bottom of the steps my father hugs me tightly before placing my hand in Chase's and taking a seat next to my mother. I look up and my eyes are captured and held in place by the green swirling depths of raw emotion I see there. It is impossible to focus on anything else until the officiant begins to speak.

"Friends and family, we are gathered here tonight to celebrate the love of Katarina Meilers and Chase Prestian, joining them in a life of marriage. In front of friends and family you are committing to promises you make to each other today, blending two unique families. This day is not about traditions or grand ceremonies, but instead a simple acknowledgement in front of the most treasured family and friends the love and commitment of two people. Please join hands."

"Chase, do you take Katarina in marriage; to love, honor and keep her in sickness and in health, through hardship or prosperity as long as you both shall live?"

"I do."

"Katarina, do you take Chase in marriage; to love, honor and keep him in sickness and in health, through hardship or prosperity as long as you both shall live?

"I do."

"Chase and Katarina, you have chosen to exchange rings as a symbol of your never ending journey together. Chase, as you place this ring on Katarina's finger, repeat after me."

"This ring represents my promise to you for an unending life of commitment and love," he says, placing a silver band inlaid with diamonds onto my ring finger.

"Katarina, as you place this ring on Chase's finger, repeat after me."

"This ring represents my promise to you for an unending life of commitment and love," I say, placing a wide silver band inlaid with diamonds onto his ring finger.

Chase has my eyes captured in his, holding them in his gaze as the officiant says, "Chase and Katarina you have professed your love and commitment to each other today, before God, family, and your closest friends. In accordance with New York State laws and by the power invested in me, I now pronounce you man and wife. You may kiss your bride."

Chase takes me in his arms kissing me, pulling me closer, enveloping my lips with his, sealing our commitment to each other as the room erupts around us with cheers, well wishes, and camera flashes.

My parents are the first to congratulate and hug us, followed by Don and Emily. "Chase, I couldn't ask for a better son-in-law," my father says, shaking Chase's hand.

"That means a great deal coming from you Carlos," Chase says, placing his arm around my shoulders. You can be assured I'll take good care of her," he says, grinning widely.

"Katarina, I was hoping to have you for my daughter-in-law from the moment I met you. I can't tell you how pleased I am," Don says, pulling me to him, kissing one cheek and then the other.

Brian shakes hands with Chase. "Congratulations," he says.

"Thanks, Brian, I'm glad you were able to make it," he says, smiling widely.

"I wouldn't have missed it for the world, Chase. I'm just sorry I got here so late. Negotiations were a little more difficult than I thought they would be."

"I'm glad you made it and we didn't have to sub you with one of my uncles. Pretty sure Chase would have picked Uncle Vito to stand in for you if you didn't make it. Same height, look, well, you know," I say.

He laughs at my joke but his shocking blue eyes are riveted on

Jenny as she comes to stand next to me. "Brian, let me officially introduce you to Jenny Torzial, Katarina's best friend, and the maid of honor," Chase says to Brian.

"Oh, that Jenny," he says.

She laughs. "Yeah, that Jenny.

"I didn't make the connection. Very nice to meet you officially," Brian says, extending his hand.

"Likewise, Brian," she says as Chase leads me to the great room which has been turned into a vast marble dance floor with an array of small and large Christmas pines and a thousand little twinkling lights that have been strung along the banner of the staircase.

The band commences and Chase leads me onto the dance floor. "Now you're officially mine, Baby," he whispers into my ear, holding me closely until the song comes to an end and he has to relinquish me to my dad for the father of the bride dance.

My father is a strong competent dancer, guiding me slowly across the floor as Chase dances with my mother. He is commanding, head of the mafia, controlling vast portions of industry in New York City, but the look in his eyes tonight is full of love for me, his daughter.

"Your mother and I are very happy for you both. We wish you a long and meaningful life together," he says before Chase takes me back into his arms, allowing Carlos to dance with my mom again and Don and Emily, and Brian and Jenny to join us on the dance floor.

The night is filled with fun and laughter and it is approaching midnight by the time Chase leads me back on the dance floor for the closing number. "Baby, you look absolutely amazing. I will always remember the way you looked tonight and I can't wait to take you upstairs and peel you out of this dress," he says.

He holds me close, guiding me to the music with his powerful thighs, allowing me to feel his desire as he does. "Your breathing is changing, Baby. Are you getting wet for me?" he whispers so only I can hear.

"Yes," I say, breathlessly feeling myself moisten at the feel of his body pressing against mine and the sound of his voice in my ear. "Just a short while longer before I can have you all to myself," he says, as the song ends and we walk to where we begin cutting the cake. I can't help but smile at my mom, who is standing by my father's side across from us. A small, simple little get together has turned into quite a wedding with a custom designed, four-tier cake created by New York's top chef.

We spend the rest of the evening mingling and being pulled into one dance or another by the band and well-meaning friends and family.

As the last song of the evening ends Chase kisses me gently before we say good night to our parents and a few of our relatives who are still visiting. "Now, if you don't mind, I think I'd like to have my bride to myself for the rest of the evening," Chase says, scooping me up into arms.

"Wait," Jenny says laughing, lifting my train and placing it over my arms, so we don't trip as Chase carries me up the curved marble staircase to our suite. He closes the door behind him with his foot before he lets me glide down the length of his body allowing my feet to slowly find the floor.

"Baby, I've been dying to see what you have on underneath this gown all evening," he says, slowly turning me to unzip the small amount of material holding my dress together in the back.

He turns me to face him, pushing my long curled auburn locks away from my face and kisses my lips gently. I open for him, relishing in the feel of his growing desire and urgency of our kiss. "You are such a beautiful bride and now you're all mine," he says, caressing the curve of my breasts before rubbing my nipples through the satiny material. They tighten immediately and strain against the material. "So lovely," he says, sliding the delicate straps from my shoulder. My core clenches as I see the passion in his eyes as he watches my dress fall to the floor, leaving me completely nude except for a miniscule white lacy thong and jewelry.

"Katarina, you are absolutely gorgeous," he says, removing my necklace as he kisses my neck and collar bone, sending a shiver of anticipation down my spine before slowly taking a nipple into his mouth. I feel myself moisten and moan as he grasps my hips, running his hands over the curves of my ass while nibbling the tender flesh of my nipple causing my desire to flare.

"Baby, this thong is perfect, but it's not going to be on you very long," he says, tracing his fingers along the delicate and miniscule piece of designer lace that adorns my ass cheeks. He kisses his way down my abdomen and pauses as he pulls the panties down slowly over my hips and mound. "Sweet Jesus," he says, tracing his fingers over my completely bare, silky, and hypersensitive sex. He kisses me and my insides clench as he runs his tongue across my mound and then slowly dips inside my folds.

"Oh, Honey," I moan, my hands grasping his hair as he finds my clit, caressing it gently with the warmth of his tongue.

"All mine," he murmurs, licking and caressing, escalating my desire and need.

"I want to hear you say it, Katarina," he says, his eyes smoldering, watching me intently from below.

"All yours, Honey," I moan, finding it difficult to even think or talk.

"Mine always," he says, before capturing my sensitive nub with his mouth, sucking hard, leaving me panting and crying out as I shatter around him, trembling uncontrollably until the waves begin to subside.

"Yours always," I say, panting as he scoops me up and carries me to bed.

"Tonight, no restraints," he says, laying me against the luxurious silk bedding and kissing my lips. "I want to make love to you slowly. I'm going to explore every inch of your magnificent body and make you cum, over and over, all night long. I want you so sore and satisfied tomorrow that you'll always remember our wedding night," he says, carrying me to the bed and laying me down before he begins to remove his clothes.

I WAKE SLOWLY and glance at my phone to check the time, knowing that Chase has already worked out and will be reading downstairs. I smile at the folded piece of paper laying on the pillow next to me with only my name scrawled on its surface.

· · ·

KATARINA,

You can not begin to imagine how happy you've made me. You are the best Christmas gift I could have ever imagined and I will treasure you forever. I love you with all my heart, now come downstairs so we can enjoy the holiday with your parents before I whisk you away to the place we first met.

Yours always, Chase.

I SIGH, feeling absolutely giddy and scramble to get showered and ready for the day before heading downstairs. I smile as his eyes meet mine when I enter the kitchen where he is sitting with my parents. "Merry Christmas, Mrs. Prestian," he says, pulling me into his lap for a kiss.

"Chase," I say, laughing and trying without success to ward off the blush flooding my cheeks.

"Are you two at it again?" Jenny says, walking into the kitchen.

"Coffee, ladies?" my dad asks, holding up the carafe to pour us each a cup.

"Jenny," I think you've embarrassed my father," I say teasingly, slipping into the chair beside Chase and adding some creamer to my coffee.

"Oh, nonsense. You forget, I was in the suite between both of yours," she says, causing my mom to swallow her coffee wrong and her face to pinken.

"Jenny!" she says, laughing.

Chase grins widely. "So it would appear we're off to a wonderful Christmas Eve tradition," he says, grasping my hand.

"Indeed it does," my father says, beaming.

"Jenny, Katarina and I will be staying until after lunch and then leaving for our honeymoon. Gaby is visiting family in the area for a few days and then will fly back to Chicago. Matt can have the jet take you back whenever you want, just connect with him directly," he says.

"Thanks, Chase. That's very generous of you. I'll let him know that I'd like to head back to New York shortly after you leave. These two love birds should have a little more time to themselves on their first Christmas together," she says.

"You are welcome here as long as you'd like to stay, Jenny," my mom says, blushing.

"I greatly appreciate the offer Karissa, but I'd like to get back home, too," she says.

The morning is special, the first Christmas that I have ever spent with my father, my parents together, my best friend, and married to the man that I love. Lunch consists of an herb crusted prime rib that smells heavily of garlic, butter, wine, and rosemary. The potatoes are slow roasted with a side of almond flavored green beans.

My mother and I are talking in the kitchen before dessert is served when Chase walks in eyeing the variety of fruit and cream pies that adorn the countertops.

"Mom, you know the pies are not safe with Chase around," I say, grinning at him as he eyes them with obvious delight.

"Here," I say, taking a knife from the kitchen counter. "We can split a few different types," I say, cutting several in half.

"I knew there was a reason I married you," he says, grinning.

"Save room for the real dessert," I say quietly, as my mom walks out of the room to return to the dining room.

"Oh, Baby, you need ask only once," he says, standing behind me, pushing his growing hardness into my behind while slipping his hands under my skirt to cup my ass cheeks.

"Chase," I say barely above a whisper, hoping no one walks back into the kitchen.

"I believe you started this. Always so ready for me, Baby. You have no idea how much I like that," he says, rubbing the wetness along my sex and slipping a finger inside of me while kissing and suckling the sensitive skin of my earlobe and neck. His strokes are slow and long, curling into that special spot that makes my desire flame.

"Hmm, that feels so good," I say, softly pushing back into the fingers that are making me needy with want before he slows their movement and then abruptly removes them.

I sigh, trying to regulate my breathing and to gain control of my want, knowing that I am in for a long day spent on the edge of neediness.

He turns me to face him and places his fingers between his lips, licking my desire from them. "You're right, the real dessert is amazing, just a small taste to tide me over for a bit," he says, parting my lips so that I can taste my own desire on his tongue. "Now quit provoking your husband and go spend some time with your family. We'll be leaving shortly," he says, kissing the tip of my nose.

FIVE

The helicopter ride to the airport from Chappaqua is uneventful and the Gulfstream is on the private tarmac waiting for us to board. Chase guides me toward the plane and I squeal as he unexpectedly scoops me into his arms and carries me up the ramp while security hoots and hollers in the background.

"Chase!"

"It's tradition, Baby. Behave," he says, laughing.

"I hear congratulations are in order," the pilot says, greeting us at the entrance and grinning from ear to ear as Chase sets me down.

"Thanks, Paul. I appreciate you making the trip with us today. I hope you were able to spend time with your family this morning," Chase says, shaking his hand.

"Oh, yes. We had a great morning watching the kids open gifts, attended church service and even had time for lunch with the family. And, thank you for the generous bonus. I'm going to use it take the wife and kids on vacation over spring break and remodel the house a bit," he says.

"Excellent, I'll have my assistant connect with you when we return. Let's talk about dates so we can ensure one of the Gulfstreams and a pilot is available. I appreciate you giving up part of your family's holiday for us this year," Chase says, guiding me past the security suite behind the cockpit and into the living space.

The main cabin boasts a beige leather sofa with extended chaise in front of a floor-to- ceiling stone fireplace, which is already glowing, and emitting warmth throughout the cozy room. There is a small dining table and two chairs on one side of the plane positioned in front of an oblong window, with various leather reclining chairs scattered throughout the cabin.

Chase pulls me onto the sofa with him as the captain announces an impeding take off. "You know how much I enjoy restraining you?" he asks, buckling me in for takeoff.

"As much as I like it?" I ask, kissing his lip.

"Even when you want to cum and I won't allow it?" he asks, sucking my lip and then dipping into the sensitive skin of my neck.

I groan. "Honey, it's still hard for me to wait, but I have to admit it makes me exceptionally wet," I say, capturing his lower lip in my own as we lift off.

"I'll need to confirm this," he says, waiting until after we've taken off to unbuckle me and lead me to the master bedroom. The room is impressive with a large cherry wood bed, armoire, fireplace and wall mounted big screen monitor in the corner.

"Have a Christmas drink," he says, pouring me a glass of wine from a little bar by the fireplace.

I raise my eyes, knowing he is purposefully drawing this out, building my anticipation, and I take my drink wanting to please him and be pleasured in return.

"Taste it, Baby, I want to hear you tell me how the wine feels on your tongue. What are you experiencing?" he urges, guiding me toward the bed.

I slowly take a sip, letting it resonate on my tongue before swallowing. "Hmm. So good, it's a little crisp, but deliciously sweet. Unfortunately, I'm in the mood for something a little on the savory side, salty even, and I can feel myself moistening just thinking about it," I say, taking another sip.

"Patience Baby, we will get there," he says, watching me intently as he slowly begins to undress himself. My breathing hitches as he removes his shirt revealing his lean cut physique and I run my tongue across my lower lip as he removes his pants, allowing me to take in the trail of hair that extends from the bottom of his navel to the area encompassing his rigid cock.

My core clenches and my nipples harden, growing more erect as he caresses them through the satiny material of my blouse before beginning to unbutton it. He leaves trails of kisses along my sensitive skin as he exposes it, pushing the material from my shoulders and undoing the clasp of my bra to free my breasts to his view. He lingers to explore, caressing each one, using his tongue to create and build the now familiar slow ache and desire I have come to know so well. He reaches behind me and unzips my skirt, sliding it along with my panties, down the length of my body, easing them over my hips and past my thighs before slipping them off and laying me gently on the bed.

"I believe someone offered me dessert and I want to taste my Christmas present," he says, gently rubbing my clit with his thumb until my hips raise of their own accord and I feel myself moistening even more under his touch.

"Tell me what you want," he instructs, continuing to stroke me while continuing to kiss and suckle my inner thighs.

"Hmm. Honey, I want you to taste me."

"Tell me where, Baby. You need to guide me."

"Honey, here," I say, pushing his face closer to my sex.

"Words, Katarina. What do you want?"

"I want you to touch me, there, with your tongue," I pant, trying to maintain my composure as he nips at the sensitive skin of my mound.

"Tell me where there is," he says, his eyes watching me intently.

I moan as he nips my mound with his teeth and squeezes my nipples simultaneously, flaming my desire even further. "I want to be your dessert. Kiss my pussy," I say, running my hands through his hair and pulling him close.

"That's what I wanted to hear, Baby," he says, finally letting his tongue wash over my clit, gently caressing it.

"Chase," I say, pushing into him.

"What Baby, tell me what you're feeling, what you like," he says, slowly stroking my clit and folds.

"I'm so turned on, I want to cum, but I know you want me to wait," I say, trying not to push into his mouth.

"Very good, Baby. I do want you to wait, at least until I do this," he says, nipping the sensitive skin between his teeth.

"Chase!" I moan, pushing into him, struggling to control my body's response, wanting to cum, but desperately holding on.

"Cum for me now," he says and I am unable to control the orgasm that overtakes me as he continues to suck and lick the most intimate part of my body through my pleasure.

"Baby, the next time you come, I want to feel you around the end of my cock," he says, pushing his hardened length into me.

My body responds to his urgency, our rhythm in perfect sync as we meet each other's need, stroke for stroke, our desires soaring. "I want you to cum again with me, Baby. Push back and feel me deep inside of you," he instructs.

As I do, he takes me by the hips, grinding his body deeper into mine, pushing repeatedly against that special spot deep inside until I can feel myself building again. He drives into the most sensitive spot of my body, thrusting against it, over and over. I can barely breathe as he continues to take me and all of a sudden the release is so near again. My hands find his neck, pulling him closer, tightening my legs around his body, trying desperately to hold on.

"Cum with me, Baby," he says and the deep timber of his voice pushes me over the edge as we find our release together, trembling around each other in wave after wave until we are completely spent.

He holds me tight, kissing me deeply before releasing me. "I'm looking forward to having you to myself this week," he says, stroking the side of my face to push my dampened hair back from my eyes.

"That sounds heavenly. Maybe you should tie me up for the week. You know, an intense week of kinky sex," I say.

"Baby, don't tempt me," he says, looking down at me bemused.

"Sounds pretty amazing though, doesn't it?" I ask through sated and sleepy eyes.

"Indeed, it does, Katarina. Now, I think you should close your beautiful eyes and get a little sleep while you can. We've got a few hours before we land," he says, pulling the luxurious satin sheets over my body and kissing me on the lips just before I drift to sleep.

JAY AND SHELDON have the limo waiting on the tarmac when we land and we are soon on our way to the resort. The driver navigates the island traffic easily and I sigh as I take in the turquoise seascape shimmering in the distance. The palm trees are gently swaying in the island breeze as we drive toward the sprawling resort that sits atop the white pristine sand beach around it. The car doors are opened for us as we pull up to the entrance. Chase greets the doorman by name as he guides me to the Mayan Tower elevators and enters the code for the penthouse.

"I remember the first time we rode this upstairs together," I say, looking out over the resort and ocean below from the glass encased elevator.

He pulls me close and kisses my hair. "I was completely enchanted with you. I contemplated taking you somewhere else for our honeymoon, but you originally wanted to get married on the island, so I thought this might be nice."

"It's perfect, Chase. I wouldn't have wanted to go anywhere else. This island will always hold a very special place in my heart."

"I'm glad. We'll go out on the yacht tomorrow. Mickael was excited to hear that we were going to be back on the island."

"Are you having him come with us?" I ask.

"Yes, it would be almost impossible to man the yacht and do what I have in mind," he says, grinning mischievously.

"Hmm... I seem to recall a pair of soft suede wrist restraints being involved the last time," I say.

"Indeed. I might just have to find them," he says, guiding me out of the elevator and towards the door of his suite. Sheldon has taken the elevator before us and is already awaiting our arrival.

"Everything's clear Chase," Sheldon says, opening the penthouse for us.

"Excellent, now I believe I need to carry Mrs. Prestian across the threshold," Chase says, scooping me into his arms.

"Chase, how many doors are you going to carry me across?" I say, placing my arms around his neck, looking into his eyes alight with amusement.

"I'm pretty sure we have a few more to go," he says, eyes twinkling as I hear the door close behind us. Chase slowly lets me slide down his body and my feet find the floor. "Welcome home, Mrs. Prestian," he says, kissing my lips.

"It's absolutely perfect," I say, looking around. A window that stretches the expanse of the room allows us the perfect view of the white sand beaches, blue-green water, swaying palm trees and yachts that dot the ocean beyond.

On the dining room table sits a vase overflowing with white calla lilies encircled with greenery. "Chase they are absolutely beautiful," I say, inhaling deeply.

"I'm glad that you like them," he says, kissing my neck.

"I love them. They're even more magnificent than what you sent me the first time. I don't think I'll ever be able to look at an arrangement of calla lilies and not think of you and Aruba," I say, reaching up to kiss his lips.

"The night is still early. You'll find clothes in the closet and dressers. Go change and then we'll go out dancing. I need to spend a few moments with Jay to discuss security for tomorrow, but it shouldn't take long," he says, kissing my lips before I head into the master bedroom.

I open the closet and shake my head at the array of clothes—sundresses, floral skirts and camis, formal dresses, little sweaters and sandals. I open the top dresser drawer and smile at the selection of lingerie, pulling out one of the thongs, smirking at how little covering there really is.

I slip into the shower, rinsing off the day's travel before sliding into a flowy floral skirt, white cami, and thong-style sandals. I scrunch my long curly hair and decide to let the unruly curls do as they wish tonight, letting it hang down naturally before slipping the silver and diamond bangles onto my wrist and clasping the necklace that doubles as nipple clamps Chase gave me into place. I can't help but smirk as I place the thong I originally laid out back into the drawer, recalling how turned on Chase was when we went dancing and I wore no panties the last time.

I find him in the dining room. He has removed his suit jacket, loosened his tie and is sitting at the table sipping a Balashi while he talks on the phone.

I walk to the refrigerator, feeling the heat of his eyes on my body as I remove a beer for myself from the refrigerator and pour it into an hourglass-shaped glass. I take a sip, enjoying the taste of the island brewed drink before setting it down so I can rub the top of Chase's shoulders. His muscles feel tense and I massage them while he talks. He places Jay on mute and groans. "Baby, that feels amazing," he says, as Jay continues to talk.

"I think you have on way too many clothes," I say, sliding his tie from around his neckline, gently kissing the skin above it.

"Jay, it sounds like you've got everything under control. Call me back if you need anything," he says as I begin to unbutton his dress shirt from behind him.

"Your breasts feel good pushed into my back, Katarina. I can feel how hard your nipples are. I'm going to enjoy spending the evening dancing with you," he says.

"That's good. You need to relax a little bit. Your muscles are so tight," I say, pushing his shirt down to expose his bare shoulders.

"You're right. There's been so much going on that it's been hard to decompress, but I'm all yours now. Let me go change. It won't take long since I've been helped out of some of my clothes already," he says, smirking at me.

"Sorry, surely worthy of some sort of kinky punishment," I say, winking at him as I take a seat across from him and sip my beer.

"I'm sure I can think of something, Baby. Now let me go and get dressed, I want to show the world my beautiful wife," he says, taking a pull from his beer before heading into the bedroom.

I use the time to text Jenny and my mom letting them know we have arrived on the island and are settled in. Then I send Jay a text to tell him that I'd like to go for a run in the morning.

I scowl at the message I receive back.

Message: Talk to Chase, see if it works.

"What's that look about?" Chase says, walking back into the room in a pair of khakis, and a button down short sleeve shirt and boat shoes.

"I sent Jay a note that I plan on going for a run tomorrow and he says to ask you if it works. What's that all about? It's beautiful and warm and I wanted to go for a run outside instead of on a treadmill," I say.

"Hmm. I have a surprise for you that involves early morning plans," he says, grasping my waist.

"Oh, well in that case, I can definitely skip my run," I say, as he pulls me into his body.

"I plan to give you plenty of cardiovascular activity this week, Katarina," he says, kissing my lips gently.

"Hmm, I like that," I say.

"Starting with dancing. I'll let Jay know we are heading downstairs," he says.

The pathway is lit up with little white lights and lined with greenery as we make our way down the beach to where the band is set up. He guides me to a table in the front that has a reserved sign on it and pulls out my chair for me.

The server arrives almost immediately, removing the sign as I take in the surroundings, relishing in the warm breeze dancing over my skin while Chase gives him our order for drinks and appetizers.

"I love this little bar area. It's completely open to the ocean and beach, but can be enclosed at a moment's notice. The design is amazing," I say, looking out at the whitecaps gently rolling across the sea in the distance.

"Señor Ridalgo had an amazing vision. The intent was to maximize nature views from wherever a patron stands, whether it be in their room, the elevator, a restaurant, or a bar," Chase says.

"I think he succeeded. It's absolutely perfect," I say.

"I couldn't agree more. Now, Mrs. Prestian, may I have this dance?" he asks as the band begins playing a slow sultry beat.

"Of course, Mr. Prestian," I say, allowing him to lead me onto the dance floor and pull me into his arms.

The band continues to play requests throughout the night as we enjoy cocktails and dance to the songs we like best. The evening is finally starting to wind down and the group begins to play a few of their closing numbers as Chase leads me back onto the dance floor.

"I don't think I'll ever forget the first time I held your body in my arms on this very floor. I could feel your heart beating and your shallow breathing. All I could think about was making you mine," he says, kissing the top of my hair.

"I had never felt desire like that before," I say quietly.

"I know, Baby. I could feel your body's response to my touch. It was the same for me," he says, guiding me to the music.

"Tonight was magical. I'm wondering what will happen when we get back to our room?" I say.

"We're not going back to our room tonight," Chase says, pulling me closer as the band begins to play a slower song.

"Where are we going?" I ask.

"To the yacht," he says, pushing the hair over my shoulder to keep it from blowing in my face.

"I didn't pack anything from the room," I say, shaking my head slightly as I realize he has the entire evening planned. "Silly me, my clothes and swimsuits were probably in place on the yacht long before now, huh?" I ask.

"Does that kind of control bother you?" he asks, searching my eyes.

"Honey, that's the kind of control that makes me so wet," I whisper.

"You know, control freak that I am will need to confirm that for myself. Luckily you have not worn any panties so access won't be an issue tonight," he says, grinning mischievously.

"You already know! I was going to surprise you," I say, pretending to pout.

"Oh Baby, did you think I wouldn't be able to tell that you weren't wearing them? I know every inch of your body and what it looks like in and out of panties. Now put those pretty little lips away, but only for a short while. I have something else in mind for them later," he says.

I blush and he runs a hand over my cheek. "Talking like this in public excites you and embarrasses you at the same time. I can't wait to feel how wet you are,'" he says.

I press my face into his chest, listening to the steady beat of his heart as he guides me around the dance floor until the song ends.

"Time for the evening to begin Baby," he says, kissing the top of my hair, nodding to Jay and Sheldon who I see standing by the door as he guides me towards the exit with his hand on the small of my back.

A long black limo is waiting for us as we reach the front entrance of the Ridalgo and Jay and Sheldon open our doors and close them before getting into the middle seats, presumably where they can talk to the driver.

The privacy glass is in place and we have not even started driving before Chase kisses me. "Now, if you had opted to wear panties this is where I would have told you to remove them for me, but since you decided not to wear any I want to see how wet you are, Katarina," he says, pulling my skirt up around my waist.

"The windows, Chase," I say, glancing around.

"No one can see us," he says, making his way up my thigh and gently caressing my bare mound. "I like the smoothness of this very much," he says before running his fingers along my folds.

I moan as my desire builds and push into his fingers, rubbing his rigid cock through the material of his pants.

"So wet Baby. Now, I would like nothing better than to have my wife's pouty little lips wrapped around my cock," he says, unzipping himself as I eagerly shift around to take his swollen member into my mouth.

"Hmm," I say, tasting the precum and moaning softly as he inserts two fingers into me, sliding them deep and curling them up to find that special spot that has been aching for hours.

"Baby, you're so needy," he says, as my hips move into him and I suck him deeper into my mouth, covering my teeth to allow them to glide over his hardened girth. He shifts his hips slightly and I feel the pulsing of his cock and take him in deeper, allowing my hand to massage his balls while my other hand rubs the root of his shaft. He moans, shifting again and I can feel him pulse. I take my time, teasing him, sliding my lips and tongue along his length, slow and then fast until I know he's getting as close as I am before I begin picking up the pace.

"Katarina, I want to cum in your mouth while you cum all over my hand," he says, running his thumb along my clit. "You're almost there, Baby," he says, rubbing my clit and pumping his two fingers in long firm strokes as he pushes deeper into my mouth. "Cum for me now, Katarina," he says, and at his command we both topple over the edge and he continues stroking me through my pleasure as he trembles and convulses, shooting warm strands of his desire into my mouth. I look up at him, and his eyes reflect the passion of my own as I swallow everything that he has to offer, pleasuring him until he is completely finished.

"Jesus Katarina," he says, zipping his pants before pulling me into his lap and licking his fingers one at a time, watching me intently before kissing me hungrily as the car pulls off the highway and towards the loading zone.

Mickael greets us as we walk up the ramp to the large, three-story white yacht. The Prestian Corporation logo is proudly displayed on the side and visible by the lights on the side of the craft. "Congratulations, I'm so happy for you both," he says, shaking Chase's hand and kissing my own.

"Thank you, Mickael. You know Jay and Sheldon, they'll be getting the team aboard and will assist you with anything that you need," Chase says, guiding me up to the main floor.

"Would you like a drink?" he asks, as we enter the spacious living area.

"Yes please," I say, slipping my sandals off and settling onto one of the soft leather couches as he brings me a glass of wine. He takes the remote from the side table and presses a button and the long drapes begin to close on both sides of the room.

"Is this where you got the idea for the blinds in my office?" I ask, recalling how at a touch of a button they close, allowing us complete privacy.

"You have to admit they came in quite handy, especially when you were texting me about how wet your panties were," he says.

"Yes, absolutely shameful. I can't wait to see how we use the room in the future," I say.

"I couldn't agree more. It was designed with fucking you in mind," he says.

"That makes me so hot," I say.

"You know I'm going to need to confirm that for myself," he says, slipping his hand under my skirt to rub his finger along my slit.

"Jesus Katarina. You're everything a man could want. Always so wet and ready for me," he says, kissing my lips.

"I love being on the yacht. How long are we staying?" I ask, wishing he hadn't removed his finger.

"As long as you want, Baby," he says.

"We're not even moving and it already feels so relaxing," I say.

"I think you may have had something to do with how relaxed I'm feeling right now, Katarina. Your mouth is like silk sliding over me," he says, sitting next to me, clasping his hand at the back of my neck and pulling me to him. His lips capture my own and I open for him, his tongue swirling gently, but growing as our passion ignites.

"I want to make love to you all night long, take my time, torture you all night so when you wake up you'll feel where I was, recall what we did and know that you're mine," he says, picking me up and carrying me into the master bedroom.

———

I AM ROUSED from sleep and look up to find Chase leaning over me, his intense deep green eyes watching. "You're such a morning person," I groan, reaching up to pull his face down so that I can kiss his lips.

"As much as I'd like to keep you deliciously naked in bed, I want to show you something. We're going outside for a bit so you'll need clothes," he says, pulling me reluctantly into a sitting position.

I stretch finding my muscles tight and sore. "Your devious plan worked Mr. Prestian. My body and insides are deliciously sore this morning," I say, finally pulling myself out of bed.

"How are your nipples?" he asks.

I feel the warmth of my blush as I recall last night. "Sore too, Mr. Prestian," I say, raising my eyebrows at him.

"Too rough, Baby?" he asks.

"Umm, no, not at all. I love my nipple clamp necklace and what you do to me with it," I say.

"Good, I like that you can feel where I've been," he says.

"What exactly are we going to do?" I ask, rummaging for a pair of shorts, a long sleeve shirt and a pair of sandals.

"It's a surprise, but that will work," he says, gesturing to the outfit I've tossed onto the bed.

"Well I'm certainly glad it meets with your approval so early in the morning," I say, slipping into the minuscule white lace panties and a pair of denim shorts.

"You're just going to stand there and watch me dress?" I ask, feeling the warmth rise to my cheeks as he gazes at me.

"I can't think of anywhere I would rather be at this exact moment and don't tell me you don't like my eyes on you. Your nipples give you away, Baby," he says, watching as I slip into a cami and then pull on a longer sleeve shirt over the top.

"Alright Mr. Prestian. Let me go wash my face and brush my teeth and I'm all yours," I say, heading for the bathroom.

When I come out he is on the phone. "No, it's fine. Just make sure everything is in place and keep me posted," he says before disconnecting.

"Ready?" he says, taking my hand and leading me to the deck. It's still relatively dark, but the yacht lights are on and he takes me to the cabana area by the pool. A small round table has been adorned with overhead lighting, a white linen table cloth and a long fluted glass of orange juice sits at each of the two place settings.

"Take a seat, Baby, the sun will be coming up soon," he says, pulling my chair out for me.

"This is wonderful, Chase," I say, taking a sip of my orange juice and noticing the champagne and glass container of juice that are sitting in a silver ice bucket to his right.

"Mimosa's seemed the perfect drink to watch the sun rise," he says, lifting one of the containers to take an omelet for himself before placing one on my dish.

"It's wonderful. I've never had one before," I say, enjoying the mixture of flavors in the drink as he places a fresh tomato relish atop the omelets.

"The chef made them with egg whites," he says.

"Yours too?" I ask, recalling his reaction the last time Gaby fixed them for him.

"No, real egg for me," he says, smirking.

"Thank you. It is really quite good and for some reason I'm ravenous this morning," I say.

"You're most welcome, Mrs. Prestian. Now watch closely," he says as the light begins to dance over the horizon. "We are so close to the equator that it will take a matter of minutes from the time the sun is first visible until we can see the entire show," he says, glancing into the distance.

"Chase, it's starting," I say, awed at the spray of purples, blues and pinks dancing across the horizon as the sun begins rising and continues its ascent into the sky.

"To my amazing wife and a life full of beautiful sunrises," Chase says, toasting me.

My heart aches with the love that I feel for this man. "Absolutely gorgeous, the only thing I've seen that comes close to that is when we watched the sunset from this very deck," I say, recalling the night we spent on the yacht the week we met.

The rest of the day is spent swimming and laying in the shade of the cabanas. "I think worrying about Alfrieta and the wedding preparations really took their toll. It feels amazingly relaxing and indulgent, just swimming, talking, eating and napping," I say.

"And the sex?" Chase asks, taking my hand in his own.

"Oh, that's the best part, Mr. Prestian."

"Something about hot sex and being on the water," he says, smiling at me.

"We should stay here for the next few days. It's the best honeymoon," I say.

"Anything you want, but we'll go back to the resort the night before we leave," he says.

"We can do whatever you want," I say, feeling myself drifting off under the shade of the cabana as the warmth of the ocean breeze blows over me.

The rest of the week is spent traveling on the yacht and touring the ABC islands; Aruba, Bonaire and Curacao. Chase regales me with the history of the islands and ensures we see the least commercialized attractions, spend time swimming in the sea and dining in the best local and authentic restaurants.

The Bonaire restaurant Chase chooses for dinner on our last night overlooks pristine white sand beaches and our table faces the turquoise sea. The whitecaps dancing and rolling onto shore are mesmerizing, but notice him scowling at his phone again, twice in the last half hour.

"What's wrong, Chase? You've been so relaxed all week and now you look concerned. You're much less tense when we're on the water," I say.

"Sorry, Baby. We can see anything coming on the yacht," he says truthfully.

"It's been pretty quiet this week. Alfreita must not have read the news," I say.

"I'm sure he has but Jay's been feeding the paparazzi pictures of us tromping all over Europe," he says.

"Really? How so?" I ask, genuinely surprised.

"Mostly pictures of us in the sea. It's hard to tell the difference between bodies of water," he says, shrugging.

"I guess I didn't have time to read all the tabloids. You've been keeping me too busy with all of your sexual activities," I say.

"Just the way I like it, Baby."

<h1 style="text-align:center">SIX</h1>

We say goodbye to Mickael before walking to the car with Jay and Sheldon, as their team gets into the car that will follow us back to the Ridalgo resort for our last night on the island. We spend the early evening having a light meal and dancing, Chase guiding me to the sultry music using his thighs to steer me around the dance floor. My face is pressed into his chest and the steady beat of his heart is against my cheek. "I think it's time we leave, Katarina," Chase says huskily a few hours later, guiding me towards the Mayan Tower elevator.

"Go and change into a swim suit while I take a quick call," Chase says, once we enter the room.

I open the drawer and look at my options, selecting a black two piece that leaves little to the imagination. I slip it on and spin in front of the mirror. I shake my head at the lack of material, rummaging in the closet before I find a lacy black thigh length cover-up, pull it over my head and slip into a pair of sandals. He has already changed when I come out of the bathroom and is in a pair of blue trunks and sandals.

"Ready?" he asks.

"I am," I say, running my eyes over his body as he pulls a t-shirt on over his bare chest.

His eyes are alight with mischief. "Patience and anticipation, Baby," he says. I feel myself blush realizing that he knows exactly what my body wants.

We leave our sandals at the resort's edge and he takes my hand as we walk across the white sand beach to the shore beyond. The beach is empty since most of the groups are eating dinner and still dancing. "Leave your cover here," he says, pulling it over my head and tossing it onto an empty lounge chair as we walk into the shallow water. It is still relatively warm due to the sun's intensity, but we take our time, allowing our bodies to acclimate to the cooler night temperatures and blowing breeze as we walk in.

I plunge under the water allowing my body to adapt to the temperature as it drenches my hair, and taste the saltiness of my lips. I stand up in the water which is chest level and feel his gaze lingering upon my erect nipples.

"Come here," Chase says, pulling me closer, kissing me gently, his hand on my neck beneath my hair as I open for him, transferring the saltiness of my lips to his own.

"Take my cock out and stroke it in the ocean," he says.

I watch him as I rub his hardness through his trunks before finding the waistband and pulling it down a little. "Chase, you're so hard," I say, freeing him and rubbing his length underneath the water.

"I've always dreamt of this, now come here and wrap your legs around my waist," he says. I do, the buoyancy of the water making it an easy feat.

He pushes my swimsuit to the side, and rubs his rigid tip against my moistness. "Open for me, Baby," he says, pushing in slowly until he is firmly rooted inside of me.

He does not move me, just holds me, kissing me while my body screams for him to create the friction I so desperately need.

"Chase this is torture," I say, moaning into him.

"I can feel your pussy tightening against my cock, holding me so firmly, you're so needy, Baby. Tell me what you want to do right now," he urges.

I moan softly. "I want to ride on your cock, Honey. I want to feel you slide in and out of me while you hit that special spot until I cum," I say.

He laughs softly. "Katarina, you're so hot Baby. While I would love to feel you riding my cock right now, I don't think your parents would appreciate me allowing you to make the front page of all the gossip rags."

"I don't care who sees us, we're on our honeymoon," I huff.

"Patience, Baby. I care who sees my wife in the throes of passion and there is a cameraman just outside the Ridalgo area. I'm pretty sure he's been able to get a few shots, but right now all he can see is us kissing. He has no clue that I have my cock balls deep inside of you and that your cunt is dripping all over me. Now be a good girl and slowly unwrap your legs and we'll walk back to the resort and I will fuck you so hard you will still feel me tomorrow," he says.

I moan as I slowly unravel myself from around his waist and he rubs his cock purposely against my clit as he pulls out before adjusting his clothing under the water.

We slowly walk out of the sea and he stands in front of me, slipping my cover-up over my head before we walk back to the resort and head upstairs to our room.

"As nice as this swimsuit looks on you, Baby, I want to see your bare skin," he says, unfastening the straps of my halter, letting my top fall to the tile floor below. He trails a finger along a drop of water traveling down my neck and across the swell of my breast, lingering and caressing a cold and erect nipple.

"Now these," he says, pulling my wet suit bottoms past my hips and letting them find their way to the floor as he takes turns warming each nipple.

"Let's get you in the hot tub," he says, dropping his own clothes and assisting me into it's bubbling warmth, placing the glass of wine he's poured on its ledge.

I sink into its depths as he gets in across from me, droplets of wetness still visible on his skin from the brisk sea. "It's been such a wonderful time. I'm going to be sad to leave tomorrow," I say.

"Indeed. It's been a great week. It will be hard to let you go back to work after having you all to myself for this long," he says.

"I feel the same way," I say, placing my toes on his manhood. His eyes are watching me intently.

"I'm glad. No concerns about what we've done the past few nights?" he asks.

"Why do you ask?" I ask, trying to escape his penetrating gaze.

"Katarina, you're relatively inexperienced and it's my responsibility to make sure that as we experiment we don't cross over any physical, emotional or ethical limits. I know you enjoyed the things we did like being restrained, spanked for fun, anal pleasure, but I want to make sure you're emotionally okay with what we did last night."

"I can't control the blush on my face and his face softens. "Katarina, am I embarrassing you?" he asks.

I nod my affirmation. "Baby, it's not intentional. I just need to make sure we have good communication. If something gets too intense, I need you to be able to tell me. What we did last night transcends what we've done before and I want to make sure that we didn't do anything that made you uncomfortable."

"I'm still trying to work through it, Chase," I say.

"Baby, tell me what's wrong," he says, lifting me by the waist and pulling me atop his lap so that I am eye level with him.

"I'm not completely sure, myself."

"Was it too intense? We talked about safe words, but I thought we worked through that and you knew you could tell me to stop," he says, rubbing his fingers down the side of my face.

I shake my head. "No, no, Honey, it's not that Chase. I didn't want you to stop anything that you were doing. I loved every minute of it. It's reconciling how I feel to what most people think I should be feeling if I'm being honest."

He kisses my lips gently and pushes my wet tendrils behind my back, kissing the nape of my neck. "Tell me what's bothering you, Baby," he says, breathing close to my ear.

"I love what you did to me last night, but it goes against everything that I've grown up thinking is right. You know, feminist movement and all that," I say.

"What goes against what you think is right? Giving up control, feeling pleasure from a spanking that you think should not be pleasurable, but abhorrent?"

"Maybe both," I say.

"Did the spanking turn you on? It was harder than previous ones and you were restrained, gagged and blindfolded," he says.

"Chase, I loved it, but I think you already know that."

"I do indeed. I was the one on the receiving end of your body's response, I'm just trying to figure out what part made you question how you felt," he says, kissing me gently.

"I thought I was frigid for so long, then you come along and I learn not only am I not miss ice queen, but that I love engaging in sexual activities that most people, especially professional women, would raise their eyebrows at," I say.

"So we're back to what people think being more important than what you feel?" he asks, holding my eyes captured.

"I'm trying not to let it. I loved what we did and how it made me feel— completely yours— but it's submissive in nature. I seem to love you in control, but most women that I know would see that as a total weakness in this day and age."

"Baby, many incredibly successful people engage in this activity and oftentimes many use a safe word if they are acting out scenes with each other. They choose a word that can be used if the act is becoming too intense or encroaching on emotional discomfort. You have all the power, Katarina."

"I know if something is getting too intense I can just tell you to stop. It wasn't last night, so I didn't," I say.

He smiles. "Yes, of course and I would stop immediately. However, now think about this. You are tied up, in an extreme state of arousal... you are so near, but say, honey stop, I can't take it anymore.... Do I stop?" he asks, his eyes lit up with undisguised amusement.

"Aaah... I guess I see the dilemma," I respond.

"Or more importantly, what if you are enjoying the physical plea-sures, but then emotionally become overwhelmed with feelings that you shouldn't be, it's a way to take a pause," he says.

"Okay, I'm intrigued," I say.

"There are some pretty standard practices that people use that we could follow. Some of the norms are green for good, yellow for caution, which lets the other person know they are near to reaching toleration, and red usually means stop now."

"So even if I'm enjoying what it is that you're doing, but I have doubts about whether I should be enjoying it, I would choose yellow?" I ask.

"Exactly Baby. It would give me time to pause, for us to connect. It's important to me that we have a very open communication and trust when we are experimenting in order to learn what you don't like and what feelings we need to transcend."

I nod. "I love that you care so much. I just need time to think about my feelings and how using a safe word might make sense in some certain situations."

"Katarina, I much prefer open conversation, but I want you to be aware of them in case they are easier for you since talking about your feelings seems to embarrass you," he says, pulling me astride his manhood.

"Now, I want to be inside of you, Baby," he says, rubbing his precum against my folds before pushing into me.

I am so wet and he is so hard that I slide easily down the length of him, savoring the way he feels as I rest against his thighs before coming back up, squeezing his length as I do. He takes some of the bubbles and places them on each of my breasts, rolling each of my nipples between firm fingers as he does, pulling softly, watching them become erect again under his touch. I moan softly and increase my rhythm.

"Baby, slow... I want to feel all of you around me," he says, grasping my hips to pull me down deep, holding me there, and then helping to guide me up and down over his hardness, slowly. He captures the delicate skin of my neck with his lips, kissing along the side until he reaches the hypersensitive area between my neck and shoulders, making me squirm with longing. He repeats the pattern, over and over, sending shivers through my body all the while controlling the speed and depth of my penetration.

"Are you ready, Baby?" he asks finally.

I nod and he increases our speed, hands grasping my hips and pulling me down deep and hard, over and over until we're left trembling with a climax that leaves us both breathless and spent. I rest against his chest and can hear the pounding of his heart in my ears as we recover and our breathing eventually starts to return to normal.

I deftly raise up and my legs feel a little wobbly. "I think I am going to stay in this swimming pool that you call a whirlpool, relax and enjoy a glass of wine," I say, pushing the button to refill the whirlpool, emptying some more of the jasmine-scented crystals that he used earlier before sipping my wine, stretching out and resting my neck against one of the plush pillows affixed to the edge of the tub.

"I need to return a couple calls while you relax but will be back shortly," he says, rising from the whirlpool, drying the water droplets from his moist skin and donning a pair of lounge pants from the adjacent closet.

I sink into the warm depths soaking in the majestic descending moon and the view of the coast and crashing waves of the sea below. I am pulled out of my reverie when he abruptly returns.

"Katarina, I'm sorry, but it appears we're going to need to leave a little earlier than anticipated," Chase says.

"In the morning?" I ask, swishing the bubbles around with my toes.

"I'm afraid tonight. Jay's communication system picked up movement of Alfreita's people and he wants us in the air."

"He thinks we're in danger here?"

"Just a precaution, Katarina, but we need to hurry. Get dressed quickly," he says, taking my hand to assist me from the tub and handing me a towel.

"I already started packing so it won't take long," I say, drying off quickly before pulling on a pair of yoga pants and a cami, and slipping into my sandals.

"No time, Baby. Security will come for our stuff," he says, handing me a long sleeve shirt, my purse, and laptop bag before leading me to the back of the closet.

"Chase?"

"I'll explain later," he says, pushing something behind one of the hanging suit jackets which causes the entire panel to open. "Come," he says.

"Oh, my God," I say as the door closes behind us and he leads me down a short hall where we are met by Matt and Sheldon as we reach an open elevator.

"We don't have a lot of time, Chase. Jay is downstairs with the team and wants us in the air before they land," Sheldon says.

"Alfreita's teams?" I ask.

"Yes, Baby. They have men on the island and a few more heading this way," Chase says.

"Did something happen?"

"Your dad and his family have cut off much of the product supply that Alfreita's operation depends on. It's all-out war now, I'm afraid," Chase says as we get out of the elevator and Jay moves us steadily down another hall.

"The limo should arrive in two minutes," Jay says, gauging the time on his phone. "He's going to pull up and I want everyone loaded quickly. I'll feel a lot better once we are in the air. Let's go," he says, pushing open the glass door we are standing behind as the long black limo pulls up. The doors are thrown open for us by the guards inside and we are quickly situated and on our way to the airport.

"We've got good ground support, but I have the Augusta in the air in the event we have issues," Jay says to Chase.

"Did you connect with Carlos?" Chase says to Jay.

"Yes, his family has support in the air. I don't think Alfreita's teams will get through it, but lets not take any chances," he says.

"Agree," Chase says, putting his arm around my shoulder and pulling me close after he notices me peeking out the rear window. Black cars identical to those by our side are behind us as well. The thwap, thwap, thwap sound alerts us to the low flying Augusta that Jay has in position overhead as we make the fifteen minute drive to Oranjestad.

"Sounds like Carlos is running ops on this one himself," Jay says to Chase, glancing up from his phone.

"I'd be doing the same thing if my daughter were involved," Chase says, smiling at me.

"How are we doing for time?" Chase asks.

"Good, they were watching your room. They still have men in place and don't appear to have noticed your departure just yet, but as soon as this plane takes off they're going to know it's you," Jay says as we are escorted by a barrage of guards to the awaiting white Gulfstream.

"Buckle up everyone. The pilot has clearance to get this thing in the air ASAP," Jay says as Matt and Sheldon take their seats next to him at the table by the windows and the pilot begins moving toward the runway. Chase and I are comfortably seated on the taupe- colored sofa adjacent to the floor-to-ceiling fireplace, which is emitting a soft blue glow for ambiance while Jay works on his tablet.

"The Larussio family must have some significant pull in that area. Alfreita's planes just got rerouted and will need to await an in-air confirmation of alternative flight plans," Jays says, smiling widely.

"Good going, Dad," I say aloud.

"We've got a skirmish on the ground," Jay says scowling.

"What's happening?" Chase asks.

Jay glances fervently in my direction. "Katarina can hear anything that you need to share," Chase says.

"They had troops positioned around your tower which is why we got you out before more of their support came in, but they must have gotten word of your departure and tried to storm the penthouse."

"Shit, everyone okay?"

"Physically yes, but two of them got the drop on Johnny. Keith had to take them out. Fortunately he didn't need to take a shot or the police would have been alerted to the gunfire. They're scrubbing the scene now. The last thing we need is publicity around this. Two incidents in less than a month?" Jay says, shaking his head.

"Keep me informed and make sure Keith gets anything he needs in the way of emotional support. Job or not, taking a life leaves its mark," Chase says.

"Will do. On a brighter note it looks like you're clear of paparazzi. They didn't expect you to arrive in Chicago until morning. Any issue with heading to the house tonight? I'd feel a little better knowing you are both tucked into the compound," Jay says.

"No, I assumed you would. I'm pretty sure we had a cameraman on us while we were in the ocean."

"Yeah, I know. We had men surrounding him just to be sure he was actually just a cameraman. He was harmless," Jay says.

"I assumed you did. I let Gaby know we're coming in before we left. If you'll excuse us now, Katarina and I are going to get a little rest before we arrive in the states," he says, taking my hand and leading me towards the back of the plane and into the master bedroom.

"You're very quiet, Katarina," he says, closing the door and settling into the overstuffed armchair to remove his socks and shoes.

"I know, I'm just taking it all in right now. We barely escaped before they got to us," I say.

"Well, I wouldn't say quite that, Katarina. They were on the island for the better part of the day. They just weren't a concern at the time because we had all the crews on the island. Once Jay learned they were sending in support, he had us move. We were never really in danger, Katarina."

"How can you say that? Keith had to take people out and you don't think we were in harms way?"

"Baby, they were under strict surveillance all day. Jay knew the moment they sent in for backup and got us out."

"I'm glad to hear they had it all under control but I guess it was just a surprise. I didn't expect to leave so abruptly on our last night together," I say, walking to the armchair.

"Just what did you have in mind, Baby? It would appear we have about five hours to kill," he says, pulling me into his lap. I shift so my feet are straddled on either side of his, and open to him as his lips descend upon my own.

SEVEN

The plane lands at O'Hare and I am instantly alerted to the multiple missed messages that I've received in flight. I read the texts from Jenny first as we are ushered into the awaiting helicopter.

Message: When are you arriving in the states tomorrow?

Reply: Actually, just touched down. Lots to catch up on!!

Message: Really? I must be a day off? Lunch tomorrow?

Reply: Long story. Can you come to the Prestian estate? On lock down again.

Message: Yes! We have time blocked on our calendars next week, but things are happening fast with the L.A. project.

Reply: Sounds good. Let me know.

"Jenny?" Chase asks.

"Yep, she's stressing over the L.A. expansion. Mentioned things are happening pretty quick. I should probably catch up to the details before we meet tomorrow."

"The Prestian Corporation has just taken over the brand new sky-rise in downtown Los Angeles. While we weren't originally intending to expand our own company footprint, for multiple reasons having a presence on the West Coast makes sense. The property unexpectedly became available and is every bit as prestigious as our other towers, so

I bought it. I sent Jenny a note yesterday to let her know the same deal for Torzial expansion on the West Coast would exist. My guess is she will want your help with that as the grand opening for the property is already next week. See, all caught up. I probably just saved you an hours worth of reading," he says, smiling.

"Yeah? I'm pretty sure there is a punishment in store that we won't mention," I say, mindful that security has the panel wall between our cabin and theirs open.

His smile is wide as he pushes a button on the remote and the privacy panels slide into place effectively ensuring our privacy. "Baby, while my intent is to keep you from working so much it is a challenge indeed not to turn the tables in my favor when such tantalizing pleasures are at stake."

"You know I'm going to need to get caught up and now I have a meeting with Jenny who is probably freaking out. It's going to take a lot of work, especially if you only gave her a weeks notice and expect her or a Torzial representative to be able to discuss an expansion plan with any degree of intelligence," I say.

"Since I've summarized the highlights, you have already developed the expansion plan for New York and it need only be replicated, I don't see why you would need to work more than four hours."

"Chase! Totally unreasonable, besides she is going to come to the house tomorrow so we can work and have lunch," I say, trying to give him my best stern look but failing miserably.

"Perfect. I'll have her picked up in the morning and you can work until noon, have lunch, and then we can spend the rest of the day unwrapping the multitude of wedding gifts that Gaby says are laying all over the dining room table," he says.

"Fine," I say at the amusement in his eyes. "I'll let her know the plan, but I will probably start early," I say.

"Whatever the lady chooses. While you are busy working, I will be developing a plan for such deliberate and disobedient behavior," he says, grinning widely as the pilot begins lowering the craft and we put down on the Prestian helipad. The estate is lit up and the magnificent archways of the chateau are visible from this close away. I shake my head at his antics as the panel slides open and Jay gets out with Dereck and Sheldon. They open our doors so Chase can assist me from the helicopter.

"Alfreita's men turned back. Once they got re-routed they had no chance to catch up. We've got eyes and ears in the air and on the ground. We should know more about locations shortly," Jay says as we make our way into the house.

Gaby greets us with a warm welcome. A delicious aroma of cinnamon permeates the kitchen. "I just took the apple pies out of the oven if anyone is hungry," she says, pulling dessert plates out of the cupboard.

"Katarina, men, take a seat. I'll get the ice cream," Chase says as Gaby begins dishing up generous servings of overfilled apple pie with a cinnamon and brown sugar topping. Chase places large scoops of vanilla on each plate and serves them to the men around the table as Gaby hands out silverware and napkins.

"Coffee anyone, we have decaf and regular?" she says.

"Would love a cup of decaf, Gaby," Jay says. "Same here," Dereck and Sheldon say in unison.

I hold up my hand as Gaby comes around to me. "I'm so tired. I think I'll turn in as soon as I finish this pie," I say, conscious of Chase's watchful gaze without glancing in his direction. He continues his conversation with the team, but his eyes capture mine in question as I tell everyone goodnight for the evening.

Alone in our room I brush my teeth and change into one of the short lacy nighties that Jenny thought was a must have on a recent shopping spree. I settle into bed reaching for my Mac which is one of the only things that Chase grabbed before our hasty departure. I skim emails about the acquisition which only offer the same information that Chase has already provided me. I shake my head in annoyance before placing the computer on the nightstand. It is hard to get the fear of the evening out of my mind, but my eyes become heavy in a matter of moments and I am unable to keep myself from drifting into a deep troubled sleep.

It is seven a.m. when I wake, glancing at my phone to read the message from Jenny.

Message: I'll be at the house around 8.

Reply: Sounds good!

I scurry to the shower, making quick work of shampooing and conditioning the long auburn tresses that are always so unruly in nature. I pat myself dry with the luxurious body towel pulled from the warmer before slipping into leggings, a long warm sweater, socks with a lacy top and a pair of slouchy boots. I grimace at my hair as I let it fall out of the towel it's been wrapped in, slowing running a wet brush through the curls before blow drying them so they frame my face and fall in layers against my chest before heading downstairs to find Chase.

The kitchen still smells like cinnamon and I find Gaby alone sipping a cup of coffee while she reviews one of her recipe cards. "Good morning," she says, looking up.

"Morning, Gaby. Do you know where Chase is?" I ask.

"That young man was to bed late and up early. I believe he's in his study now though. Would you like breakfast? I saved you some french toast."

"Yes, please. In fact, I think I'll take it with me into the study," I say.

"Run along... I'll bring it in with a fresh pot of coffee for the both of you," she says.

"Thanks," I say, already on my way across the dining room and toward the closed door of his study. I knock lightly and let myself in. Chase is sitting behind his desk engrossed on the two monitors, intently listening to the voices on the speakerphone. He waves me in and I take one of the chairs across from him.

Chase reaches over and releases the mute button. "Gentlemen, while cutting off all the product supplies has certainly caught their attention and drawn Alfreita and his men out, it has not, however, impaired their ability to get planes in the air. I want the entire supply curtailed—use every ounce of our access or influence. Cut them off at the knees," he says, placing the call on mute while the team begins discussing options and Gaby walks in with a tray containing french toast, fruit, small plates and a carafe of fresh coffee.

"Thanks, Gaby," I say, pouring each of us a cup and serving myself a healthy portion of french toast, trying hard not to succumb to the magnetism of his gaze in case he sees the fear and anxiety.

I finally look up, motioning an offer of french toast to Chase but he shakes his head slighltly, pushing the button to speak again. "Gentleman, I'd like a fully developed plan put together for my review at twelve thirty this afternoon. Sidney, set up another call for the team. Thanks for your time," he says, disconnecting.

"I was trying to wait up for you last night, but couldn't keep my eyes open," I say, still attempting to avoid the pull of his eyes.

"Yes, I came to bed shortly after you and found you in a sound sleep so went back downstairs to work," he says.

"Thought I would get something to eat before Jenny arrives. She's due here in a few moments," I say, taking a bite of my french toast.

"They should be touching down right now. She'll stay for lunch and then head back to the city. She has an in-person meeting this afternoon," Chase says.

"So are you planning to work in here all morning?" I ask.

"Yes, while I'm not concerned that we were in any true danger yesterday, I am disturbed that Alfreita appears to have readily ascertainable financial support. His product supply has been cut off by both the Larussios and Vicenti, but that has not been as effective as we thought it would be," Chase says.

"I'd be lying if I said I wasn't concerned," I say.

"I know, you were pretty quiet last night," he says, caressing my cheek.

"I trust whatever you and my father are doing will resolve the matter," I say just as Gaby announces Jenny's arrival on the intercom.

"The staff will show her to your office," Chase says.

Everything always planned down to the finest of details. "Looks like it's time to go to work," I say, taking a final sip of my coffee before walking to the door.

"The grand opening is scheduled for next Friday night and all the arrangements have been made. All you and Jenny need to do is show up and represent the Torzial interests," he says as his conference line rings.

"See you later," I mouth, closing the door behind me to find Jenny in what has now become my office.

"Hi there," she says, getting out of her chair and wrapping her arms tightly around me as I enter the door.

"It's so good to see you in person and not just over my phone," I say, laughing at her exuberance.

"So, how was the honeymoon? Everyone is dying to know where you went and all the details," she says.

"Yeah, I think Jay and his team kept the paparazzi pretty busy with leaked sightings in countries that we were supposedly in during our honeymoon. I didn't have a clue it was going on until after we were home," I say.

"Yes, it looked like you were jet-setting around the world," Jenny says.

"Chase wanted to be extra careful with Alfreita still lurking around. It really couldn't have been a more perfect vacation. We flew to Aruba and spent most of our time on the ocean and stayed on the yacht," I say, wishing we were still lazing in the sun and not in the middle of an all-out war between my father and Alfreita.

"I'm glad that he didn't let what is happening with that guy mar your honeymoon. The pictures you sent were absolutely amazing. I'm so happy for you," she says.

"Thanks, I never thought I would find someone that I cared so much about. Oh, and speaking of my controlling husband, he's had all the arrangements for the grand opening taken care of and told me we should just focus on being able to explain the expansion plans," I say.

"Seriously? I thought it would take us hours of preparation this week and just like that it's done?" Jenny says.

"I know," I say shrugging and smiling ruefully at my friend. "He filled me in a little about the expansion on the way home," I say, pulling up a couple documents on the large screen situated on the corner of the desk.

"If we follow the same project plan we used for New York we should be able to expedite things pretty quickly. We have all the structural components in place, but there are a few things we should consider doing differently, but not much," I say pointing to the areas I've highlighted.

"Yes, these look great," she says, reviewing the recommended modifications. "So now all we need are time frames and that should be relatively easy," she says.

"We might even be able to get it done before you're back in the air," I say.

"That would be a huge relief. You saw all the emails about Vegas?"

"I did, it sounds as though Chase is seriously considering a major build in Vegas and is looking for a pretty aggressive timeline. He's intending to use the same footprint as the Chicago and New York office, but we have opportunities to make the interior adjacencies more efficient. He agreed to let us work with the design groups, but we're going to be scrambling to finish before final sign off," I say.

The rest of the morning is spent working through preparations, setting time frames and when we are finished we are as prepared for Friday night as possible. It is just before noon when I hear the sound of an incoming message.

Message: Almost done?

Reply: I thought I would work until approximately 12:05

Message: Aaah. Still struggling with control?

Reply: Or, maybe I like the consequences.

Message: I may have been too gentle.

Reply: Maybe... On our way. Join us if able.

We walk into the dining room and Chase is already sitting at the table. He glances at the clock in the corner and stands as we take our seats, a look of amusement in his hazel eyes. "Ladies, I see you're just slightly late," Chase says, smirking at me.

"We were able to use a lot of the previous expansion plans so there wasn't a lot of what Kate would call rework," Jenny says.

"Very good. I was hoping the initial plans would be similar," he says as one of the servers fills our glasses with water and another one places a colorful kale and grilled chicken salad in front of us.

"I thought we could discuss the L.A. sky-rise today. As you are both aware this is not a standard Prestian tower. While state of the art in design, different than what we typically build. However, we were able to acquire the building at a fraction of what it is worth. Initially the Prestian Corp name will be on the building. The industry is changing in that area and the building is in a prime location. It already occupies some long-term tenants, but I have no doubt it will soon fill to capacity. Jenny, it would be an ideal location for the headquarters of the consulting firm that is taking the nation by storm and has Prestian Corp as their top client."

"I agree, I mean after Friday we'll officially be tenants," she says.

"Actually, what I'm proposing is that we keep the Prestian Corp name on it for a year while we build our standard tower in L.A. In that time, the sky-rise will begin making money as soon as I take ownership, due in large part to the purchase price. Torzial will then purchase the building and I will transfer sole ownership to you and Prestian Corp will move into its new facility. This will give you far greater visibility on the West Coast and allow you to compete on an entirely different level. Now is the time to prepare that path, Jenny," he says.

Jenny audibly gasps and I look from her shocked face to his. "It would be like a dream come true to have the Torzial name on a sky-rise, but you really think I can afford it?" she asks.

"Most definitely. The income from the leases will far exceed any output. You will be making a small fortune the day you sign."

"I don't really know what to say, Chase."

"Yes will work," Chase says.

"Yes!" Jenny says laughing. "I have no idea how to repay you for all your kindness."

"Keep putting out quality designs and consulting services. Your company is starting to get quite a reputation not only for the Prestian Medical facility work, but for the efficiencies of the specialty centers, as well."

"I'm so excited for you, Jenny. I can't wait to take a tour," I say.

"I'm glad you are happy with the plan. Unfortunately, I have a couple calls that require my attention but look forward to seeing you at the grand opening. Ladies, I've taken the liberty of arranging a professional shopper to help you with gowns for the event," he says, kissing me lightly on the lips before returning to his study.

"Did you know about this?" Jenny asks.

"About the sky-rise? No, I didn't have a clue," I say.

"He is certainly the most intense, over the top, and generous man I have ever met," she says.

"That he is," I say, my heart warm knowing how much he takes care of the people that mean the most to me. We finish our lunch, discussing the details for Friday night before we hear Gaby's voice over the intercom announcing that the helicopter is ready to take Jenny back to the city.

"I guess that's your ride," I say, hugging her as she gathers her belongings for the trip.

"I'll see you Friday night," she says, passing Gaby on the way out of the dining room as I head to our bedroom. Chase is nowhere to be seen and I pull down the purplish-grey duvet, slip out of my clothes and lay underneath the plush down softness of the comforter. It feels like only moments instead of hours when I feel a light touch gently caressing my cheek. I look up through half open eyes to see Chase, sitting nude on the bed beside me, his eyes intent upon me.

"Are you feeling ill, Katarina?" he says, pushing the long strands of hair that have fallen over my face in sleep out of my eyes.

"No, just so incredibly tired. Must have been all the excitement of the last few days. I was looking for you and saw the bed," I say.

"I noticed the pile on the floor," he says, pulling the comforter down and trailing a path from underneath my hair, down my spine, and sensually tracing the curve over my ass. His touch leaves a burning trail where it has been and it is hard to stay still as his fingers begin to roam. I audibly moan and push back against him as he explores my folds.

"So wet already, Baby," he says, kissing the small of my back and trailing his tongue where his fingers have just been as he continues to move them slowly in and out of me, grazing my clit with each forward motion.

I audibly moan again, pushing back against the rhythm of his fingers. "Still Baby," he says, pushing my legs apart slightly. "You look so lovely laid out in front of me, wet and ready. Tell me what you want," he instructs.

"Don't stop, Chase. I'm so close," I say.

"Yes, but so far away," he says, slowly removing his fingers, lingering over my wetness and my erect clit, leaving me with a slow burning ache.

"Chase..."

"I know, Baby. You hate being made to wait... on the brink, right there, yet denied the pleasure. Tell me how much you hate being deprived," he says.

"Incredibly frustrating," I moan as he flips me over and rubs his erect cock across the entrance of my wetness.

"We will trade a tardiness punishment in the future, my time and choosing. Deal, Katarina?" he says.

"Yes," I moan as he slowly penetrates me. Gliding into me, little by little, teasing me until I am arched and pushing against him.

"Easy, Baby," we'll trade today's punishment for Friday night," he says, rooting himself deeply inside of me, pulling back, poised and then deeply penetrating me again, rubbing against that special spot that leaves me clawing the sheets and clamoring for release.

"Chase," I moan, rising up to meet him, stroke for stroke, over and over, until we are finally trembling in each others arms and our labored breathing begins to shallow.

"Are you going to tell me what sort of delicious punishment you have in store for Friday?" I ask, circling the light patch of hair on his chest.

"And ruin the surprise? I think not, Katarina," he says, smiling mischieviously at me.

"You don't play fair," I say, pretending to pout.

"On the contrary, I think your punishments are well thought out and always quite appropriate, especially when I know your disobedience is so well planned," he says, smirking.

It is impossible not to delight in our game and I push out my lips to pout at him again. He runs a forefinger over my bottom lip. "You should be careful Katarina, I think now we're going to have to put those pouty little lips of yours to good use," he says.

EIGHT

I wake on Friday morning to an empty bed and groan at the temperature displayed on my phone. Negative five degrees. I slowly come alive, pulling on yoga pants, a sports bra, socks and shoes in anticipation of a good workout on the treadmill before I look for Chase. I make my way to the gym room overlooking the lapping shores of Lake Michigan, turn on the machine, put in my earbuds and slowly acclimate my breathing to the sultry wails of the steamy sound track.

A few messages come through on my phone, but I disregard them as I continue to work out, pushing myself until sweat drips from my body. My cooldown song comes on and I slow to a walk, patting down with a towel before pulling on a hoodie at the end of my run and checking messages. I read the one from Jenny.

Message: I'll meet you tonight. I need to go on a few tours with prospective tenants.

Reply: Sounds good. Will text when we land.

Message: Perfect! Tell Chase thanks for the dress!

Reply: I will thank him multiple times, multiple ways for us!

Message: You seem to have gotten over your shyness about the money!

Reply: I have. He knows I don't give a shit about it!

I go in search of Chase and find him in the kitchen reading the newspaper. "I woke up and you were already gone," I say, pouring myself a tall glass of water.

"You looked so peaceful I didn't want to wake you," he says, glancing up from his computer.

"I missed the way you usually wake me up," I say.

"The lady wanted to play?" he says with a smirk.

"I thought you knew that was a given. In fact, I do believe someone owes me a punishment night," I say, kissing him lightly on the lips.

"Patience and anticipation, Katarina. It will give me great pleasure to watch your body this evening," he says, caressing my already erect nipples.

"You didn't wake me up on purpose and you're not going to tell me what you're planning," I say, pretending to pout.

"Delayed gratification, Baby."

"Hmm... you know I hate that."

"Exactly the point of punishment. Now go and get ready, we have a plane to catch," he says, swatting my behind playfully.

"It shouldn't take me long to shower and I can get ready for tonight on the plane. How long of a flight is it?" I say.

"About four hours in the air. I'll have the items that arrived for tonight taken to the jet," he says as I head to the shower.

THE HELICOPTER IS WAITING and Jay and Sheldon walk with us to the bright blue rig awaiting us on the helipad. "I have to admit this is so much more luxurious than the other helicopter you had," I say, getting into the private compartment that was custom designed with soundproofing, the best in digital music and communication technologies. I take my seat on the soft leather sofa and Chase sits next to me while Jay and the crew open the doorway into the security cabin and close the door behind them, allowing us privacy on the short ride to O'Hare. The flight is uneventful and we are soon boarding the Gulfstream that awaits us on the tarmac. We are no sooner seated than the captain announces an imminent take off and we begin moving slowly towards the runway.

"Jenny just texted me. She's already in L.A. and was able to meet with a few of Torzial's other clients from the West Coast earlier today."

"Good. They could be crucial to her national success," Chase says.

"Yeah, she was pretty excited about the opportunity you gave her," I say as we lift off and Jay comes into the cabin.

"The security detail have swept the entire facility and nothing causes them concern. We still have our communications team staying close to Alfreita's crews, but the radio waves have been quiet up to this point. Our men have mitigation strategies for just about any scenario you could imagine laid out, but I'd feel a lot better with that guy out of the picture," Jay says.

"Briefing in about an hour or so?" Chase asks, glancing at his phone.

"Yes, I want to make sure everyone is comfortable with the drill," he says, stealing a quick look in my direction.

"I promise, I will behave and not cause you one bit of concern tonight," I say.

"I'll be sure of it," Chase says, eyes alight with amusement.

Jay shakes his head and smiles good naturedly at our antics. "We'll see about that," he says, walking towards the cabin door.

"I'm not quite sure how to take Jay's comment. He thinks I am up to trouble all the time," I say, pouting.

"Yes, Jay definitely calls it like he sees it," Chase says, grinning widely.

"Chase!"

"I'll have to think of some way to keep you out of trouble with my security team tonight," he says.

"I am clearly not going to win at this conversation," I say, bemused.

"On a more serious note did you see the email about state approvals for our Vegas tower?" Chase asks.

"Yes, I just saw it. I'm glad that Jenny didn't or she would have really been stressed with the timelines. I can't believe it came back so fast."

"Dad and I had a little help from Carlos getting it pushed through. He owns quite a bit of property in the Vegas area."

"I knew you both had properties all over, but I thought he was more East coast based. At least that's what all the papers always seem to allude to," I say.

"He and your family got their start on the East Coast, but Vegas is a hot bed of activity and your dad has been settled into the legitimate side of the city's business district for years," he says.

"You anticipate Vegas being the Prestian location for all the West Coast activity

around healthcare improvements?

"Yes, with the way we're expanding I'd like to make sure we give the community the advantage of having a strong presence in those areas," he says.

I suppress a yawn and his eyebrows raise in question. "Am I boring you, Katarina?" he asks with a smirk.

"Hmm... not at all. In fact, I think I'm going to go catch up on a few emails and take a little nap so I can stay up late tonight," I say, unbuckling and kissing him gently on the lips before heading towards the master suite.

The thought of skimming through emails is long forgotten as the king size master bed beckons to me. I check the closet to make sure my outfit is onboard and set the alarm on my phone, allowing plenty of time to get ready before slipping under the luxurious quilt and drifting off into a deep sleep. A couple hours later the steady drone of the alarm rouses me and I reach for my phone to turn the offending disruption off. I stretch and slowly begin to wake up deciding to catch up on email before getting ready. I skim through the list responding to a few and delete the informational ones which don't require referencing in the future. The sound of my phone alerts me to an incoming message.

Message: Finally awake?

Reply: Yes, just feeling incredibly lazy lately!

It is an hour later before I finish straightening my hair and have applied a light dusting of makeup. The normally unruly mass of auburn curls has been styled straight, sleek and shiny, and there is a slight rosiness to my cheeks and a gloss to my lips. I step into the midnight blue ball gown, sliding into the delicate straps that hold the material in place, leaving the expanse of my back bare until the silky cloth meets the straps at my hips. I adjust the silver and diamond restraints on my wrists that appear to everyone else as a perfect set of bangles and clasp the diamond necklace that shimmers against my neck when it's not adorned to my nipples in place before slipping into the four inch strappy Louboutin heels. The sparkling diamond and silver theme of my jewelry is a perfect complement to the color and design of the dress. I feel him, the pull that exists between us and turn towards the door, not having heard him enter.

"You are absolutely stunning," he says, shutting the bedroom door behind him, closing the gap between us in quick strides. He pushes my freshly brushed hair behind my shoulders and kisses my neck, letting his lips trail down the side of my sensitive skin and over the curves of my breasts exposed by the material's design.

"The slit on this dress is absolutely perfect for what I have in mind tonight, Katarina. Turn towards the mirror and watch," he says, lifting the material up to reveal the pale skin of my womanhood below.

"So beautiful," he says, caressing my clit gently with the top of his thumb while I watch in the mirror.

I moan softly, unable to control my body's response and the ache it causes deep in my core.

He continues circling, reaches into his pocket and holds up a delicate twirled length of diamonds. "Do you know what this is, Katarina?" he asks, huskily.

I shake my head, too mesmerized by the scene in front of me to speak.

"It is a clit chain that was custom designed for you. It would be a shame not to adorn something so beautiful with something special."

I look at the chain he holds, it's reflection glimmering at me in the mirror in front of us.

"Do you still want to play, Baby?" he asks, holding up the sparkling chain with one hand while he continues caressing, but slightly off the mark, holding me poised at the brink, and simmering with need.

I nod as I watch our reflections. "You will feel a slight suction-like sensation until it is well adhered. This is to ensure it stays in place until I remove it. The length of the jewelry is perfect. It will hang unseen by anyone, but easily within my grasp," he says, placing the jewelry next to my overly stimulated nub, where only moments ago his thumb had been. I audibly gasp at the sensual feel of the suction as it begins, controlled by the little black device between his fingers.

"The pull should feel quite pleasant by now," he says, allowing it to affix itself and the delicate chain of diamonds to hang on their own from my newly captured clit. He tugs on the chain slightly.

I gasp at the sensation. "Oh, Honey, I already want you to make me cum," I say, pressing into its rhythm.

"I think we'll save this for a little later in the evening," he says, pulling my dress down, standing up and turning me to face him.

"How does it feel, Katarina?"

"Good, but the pressure doesn't go away. It's going to make me feel needy all night isn't it?" I ask, looking into his gleaming eyes.

"Baby, it's going to make you very needy if that's the word you like," he says, taking my lips in his own and kissing me with restrained passion. "We should go before we're late," he says, guiding me out of the bedroom with a hand at the small of my back.

The limousine is awaiting our landing and we slide into the back-seat of the vast car. Chase pulls me close to his side as the doors are closed.

"We've got our best teams in place in and around the sky-rise, but I want both of you on GPS tonight," Jay says, glancing at us from the rearview mirror.

"You won't get any complaint from me and I promise not to throw it on a park bench and make your men go chasing it around all night," I say, recalling with embarrassment one of my previous attempts to elude security.

"Chase, we're getting confirmation that paparazzi is in full swing tonight. The sky-rise is inundated. Nate is already in place, but there are going to be cameras everywhere. The team is planning to allow you approximately five minutes to smile for the camera and answer any questions you choose, just like we ran through earlier today. If you have any thoughts of deviation we should discuss it now," Jay says.

"No, I'm going to provide them with a few pictures, a brief summary on Prestian Corp's vision and I'll deal with any other questions on the fly. Let's stick to the five minutes and you'll know by my lead if I need more time," Chase says.

"Sounds good," Jay says, pulling up to the entrance of the glass and chrome sky-rise that towers above all the other buildings in the block. The Prestian Corp logo is displayed across the top of the high-rise and the entrance is roped off allowing security to keep the crowds of people with cameras at a safe distance.

The back door of the limo is opened and I am assisted out of the car. Chase places his hand on the small of my back and guides me in between the ropes toward the entrance of the building. He stops in front of Nate Collins, the freelance journalist that writes exclusively for him, and pulls me close as the camera's shutters click around us. One journalist calls out, "Mr. Prestian. We understand you have been cleared of all charges. How does that feel," while another asks, "Mr. Prestian, how does it feel to be married and how was the honeymoon?"

"Ladies and gentlemen. I appreciate your interest and would be delighted if you could assist me in raising awareness of why this property is opening. Prestian Corp and Torzial Consulting both have a shared vision to vastly improve healthcare in the United States and around the globe. You are aware, my wife Katarina is the Torzial consultant responsible for overseeing the strategies which are currently starting to change healthcare as we know it today. While we continue expansions of patient centered healthcare designs we believe it is critical to be part of the communities we serve. Meaning, we pay taxes, we donate, we provide local jobs in those areas that we support.

"On a personal note, it was a monumental relief to be cleared of the wrongful drug trafficking charges last month. Once that was behind us, Katarina and I enjoyed a relaxing honeymoon. We both greatly appreciate you taking the time to come out and help us celebrate the opening of the new Prestian Corp facility," he says as the camera shutters continue clicking around us and Jay and Sheldon lead us up the steps to the entrance in front of us.

The red carpet trails into the magnificent stone floors of the foyer. The twinkling crystal chandeliers hang from the vaulted ceilings and the rich cherry wood of the reception area is polished to a high sheen. Waiters and waitresses are carrying large silver trays, handing out champagne in fluted glasses to the throng of guests. Chase takes two glasses from the waiter who stops in front of us. "To a change in healthcare as we know it today," he says, clinking my glass.

"I didn't expect there to be so many people," I say, taking in the crowd.

"L.A.'s environmental landscape is starting to change and this is a boost the city can use. I've already received more requests for space than we have to offer," he says.

"Chase, your dad's here. Over near the buffet," I say, spotting Don.

"Excellent. I knew he was coming, but wasn't sure what time he would arrive," he says, weaving us through the crowd towards his dad and Emily.

He shakes hands with his dad and gives Emily a hug. Don hugs me and smiles. "You both look so tan and very happy," he says.

"We are, Dad. What time did you get in?" Chase asks.

"Just a few moments ago. Carlos and Karissa were going to fly in with us, but they got held up. They should be here shortly, though," Don says.

"Actually, there's a lot going on and Carlos and Karissa are going to stay in New York tonight," Chase says, stopping a waiter to give Don and Emily a glass. Don gives Chase a furtive look.

Emily takes a sip of her drink. "The champagne is excellent and everything's been organized so perfectly," she says.

"Chase's staff took care of most of it," I say.

"The Torzial expansion in the New York City offices is going very nicely. Jenny is getting a lot of visibility since the Houston clip went live," Don says.

"I know. It's been hard to keep up to the requests. She's had to bring on more people just to answer the phones and triage the requests. It's pretty exciting though," I say, looking through the crowd to see if I can locate her before sending a text.

Message: Chase and I are here. Where are you?

Reply: Still with the tour group. Back to first floor shortly.

"Jenny will be down soon. She's finishing up with the tour groups," I say, explaining to Don and Emily before taking a sip of my drink.

"We have a table reserved for the ceremony, why don't we find our seats before it starts and she can join us when she's finished," Chase says, guiding us through the crowd. We make our way through the throng of people and maze of round tables covered with crisp white linen that have been set up for the event. He holds my seat out for me as we reach the reserved table at the front of the room before sliding into the seat next to me.

Don and Emily take their seats and begin talking with a couple at our table and Chase pulls me close to him. "Feeling needy?" he asks while the others are busy conversing.

"Very, I'm not sure if I can last."

"The night is young, Baby," he says before Jenny finds our table and sits next to me.

She is absolutely glowing in a mint colored gown that accentuates her long brunette hair that has been pulled to one side allowing her long wavy tresses to fall gracefully around her shoulder. "How did the tour go?" I ask.

"Absolutely amazing. The entire building is already leased. There's one more tour that I want to go on after the ceremony. One of the clients renting the entire 26th floor is bringing his wife through. She apparently owns a decorating company and is interested in seeing the space personally."

"I'm so excited for you," I say, before turning my attention back to the master of ceremony who is beginning to speak. The mayor is then announced and shares the vision for the revitalization of the down-town area before Chase is introduced.

"Prestian Corporation is proud and excited to be part of this monumental undertaking. This facility will become the focal point in this area and assist in drawing new business and renewal to the city. I'd like to ask that a representative from each of our new partners help us with the ceremonial cutting of the ribbon," he says, standing to the side as one by one the members who have signed leases begin making their way onto the stage and are handed ceremonial scissors. The cameras from members of the news teams begin flashing around us as applause from the audience erupts.

Chase and Jenny return to the table while the mayor concludes the ceremony. "To a great year," Chase says, leading our table in a toast.

"To a great year!" Don says.

"If you'll excuse me I'm going to head upstairs with the last tour group," Jenny says before making her way to the procession who has gathered outside the large conference area.

"I wish Brian could have made it for the ceremony. He was instrumental in procuring this deal," Chase says to me.

"I thought he was planning to be here," I say.

"Business delay. He should be here momentarily," he says, glancing at his phone.

The other members of the table are absorbed in conversation and Chase leans over and whispers, "Keep your eyes on me and do not cum, Katarina," before a slight movement begins between my legs, slowly tightening around my clit, a slow methodical suctioning of the most private part of my body. I am in a daze, mesmerized by the dark green eyes, capturing mine, holding them like a magnet with his own. The vibration increases slightly and the pulling sensation causes an almost instant desire to cum requiring every ounce of willpower in order to control the urge and remain still in my seat.

A voice across the table begins to speak and I turn toward the sound, and thankfully Chase responds."Yes, the reviews of the Prestian Medical Center work have far exceeded our expectations, but Katarina would be in a better position to tell you about that," Chase says to Dr. Johnson, one of the chief medical officers at an area health organization.

The vibration subsides and I am on autopilot as I recant the various quality goals and outcome measures of the Houston project along with the improvements made in the Chicago facilities.

"Well, we are certainly interested in learning more about it as we begin looking at options for building new facilities in California," he says.

"Excellent, let us know when you're interested in going over the statistics. We're at a pivotal point in changing the face of healthcare," Chase says.

"You can be assured of that," the man says.

"If you'll excuse us, Katarina and I are going to mingle for a while," he says to Dr. Johnson, Don and Emily.

Chase places his hand on the small of my back, guiding me through the room, stopping to introduce me to people from various corporations before heading to the open elevators. He presses a code into the keypad and the doors close and at the same time the vibration between my legs begins. "You have forty floors, Baby. Don't cum or I will punish you far worse," he says, pushing the long ringlets of hair from my face and kissing me gently. "Your face is flushed, your eyes are full of desire and your breathing is shallow. So very captivating," he says.

I audibly moan as he captures my lips, kissing me roughly, pulling me against him so I can feel the hardness of his arousal. "Breathe through your desire, Baby," he says, reaching above the slit in my gown to gently tug on the chain, leaving me to struggle through the overwhelming need to cum.

"Chase," I say, but he quiets me with his mouth, releasing me right before the elevator opens and the vibration, as suddenly as it began, ends.

"Come," he says, guiding me through the elegant reception area into an administrative suite. We pass a few offices before we arrive at one that has his name on the outside. As we enter, I gasp at the lit up panoramic view of the city-scape sprawled out in front of us.

"The view is amazing," I say as he closes the door.

"It is indeed, but right now I'm having a difficult time focusing on anything but how lovely you look," Chase says, taking me in his arms, kissing me deeply as he finds the diamond and silver chain beneath my gown.

"Honey," I moan as he tugs, harder than before, causing an excruciating ache deep within me.

"Shh.. Baby," he says, guiding me backward toward the large cherry desk without taking his lips from mine. He slides my gown above my waist and then lifts me onto the edge of the desk continuing his slow torturous rhythm on my clit. I am cognizant that the vast windows are uncovered, but couldn't care less as he parts my legs, continuing his torture.

"Oh, Baby. That's what I thought I would find. So wet and needy," he says, turning the vibration on low, pushing one finger and then two deep inside of me, holding them still. "Breathe through it, Katarina," he says, sinking them in again, antagonizingly slow this time as he tugs on the chain. "Your breathing is becoming labored, Baby. Inhale deeply and now exhale," he instructs, removing his fingers slowly.

I am aching to have him inside of me. He unzips himself, pulls me closer to the edge, and lifts my legs over his shoulders. With one thrust he is deeply seated and the heat of his cock causes me to raise my hips in an effort to feel all of him. "Slow, feel me, deep inside of you," he says before gaining speed, driving his cock deep, right where I need it. I writhe from side to side, hoping to stem the tidal wave.

The vibration returns, drawing hard on my oversensitive clit as he lifts my legs higher, pushing deep inside of me. "Cum now, Baby" he instructs and I am helpless to the overwhelming climax that overtakes my body, trembling uncontrollably as wave after wave overtakes me until the vibration finally stops. He pulls me up and against him, crushing my mouth with his as he withdraws from me and lets my feet touch the ground, before turning me around.

"Lay face down on the desk," he says, grasping my hips and pulling me against him as he buries himself inside of me from behind.

"You're so deep this way," I pant, pushing my ass back against him.

"Feel me, Baby," he says, driving into me, agonizingly slow, flaming the desire that has started to rekindle. He knows exactly the spot, thrusting against it time and time again causing my oversensitive skin to ache with need. I hear myself audibly moan as he tugs at the chain from behind, and begins taking me faster and faster, over and over.

"Cum for me now," he says, just as I fear I will be unable to control my need, helpless against the tidal wave that erupts as he continues pushing deep inside of me and finds his own release.

He pulls me back against him, his arms wrapped firmly around my waist and kisses my neck from behind. "Katarina, you did so well, you're everything a man could ever want," he says.

"I almost didn't make it," I say breathlessly.

"I know, Baby. I wasn't trying to push you more than you could handle this time," he says.

I turn around to face him. "Would you do that?" I ask.

"Baby, you know I'm not above doing whatever it takes to ensure that I have control."

"Would you make me cum intentionally so that you could punish me some more?" I ask.

"Only if you wanted me to," he says.

"Like I would tell you no when we're in the middle of... well, you know," I say, feeling my face warm.

"You're beginning to enjoy the anticipation, the waiting. I can tell by your flush and change in your breathing," Chase says.

"It makes the pleasure so intense when you finally do let me, you know," I say.

He smirks. "So shy when I'm not inside of you aren't you?"

"Chase, you tease me unmercifully!"

"Tell me you don't like it and I'll stop. Now let's get you cleaned up. If we're not downstairs soon our guests will wonder where we are and Brian needs to discuss something with me," he says.

I look around at the opulence of the granite countered bathroom. On the ledge of the natural stone shower are two loofahs and all my brands of shampoo, conditioner and soap. I close the door behind me and as I look into the mirror see the long white cashmere robe hanging behind me and try to squelch the giddy feeling that washes over me. *One at every home he owns.*

NINE

He's on his phone texting when I come out of the bathroom. "Your turn," I say.

"Great," he says, not looking up.

"Who are you texting?" I ask.

"Brian. I'm not sure what's going on but he wants to talk to me right away. It's not like him at all. I'll get washed up and we can go downstairs and meet with him," he says, heading into the bathroom.

I take the time to look out the window at the city beyond. The view is mesmerizing from this far up with light in varying degrees of height as far as the eye can see. I feel him behind me and turn. He is watching me, those deep penetrating green eyes hold mine like a magnet. "You like it, Baby?"

"The view?"

"No, the life. I know you struggle with it."

"Chase, I don't feel kept or cheap or worry about what people think of us anymore," I say.

"And the control?"

"I love what we've been doing as far as the sex. Are you worried that I don't?"

"I think you still struggle with some aspects, but I know you like it.

It's my responsibility to understand what you like and don't, and understand your body's reactions. It's also my job to make sure that your emotional needs come first and we can only ensure that if we're open and honest with each other as we progress."

I pull his lips down toward mine, capturing them with my own. "I love you so much I can barely breathe sometimes," I say, pulling him close.

"I love you too, Baby," he says, kissing me and then putting his arm around my waist to guide me toward the elevator. "Let's see what Brian wants and then head upstairs," he says.

"Upstairs?"

"Penthouse. The sky-rise is equipped with a five bedroom, six bathroom condo to eliminate travel and what you would consider wasted time driving to and from work," he says, grinning widely at my surprise.

"Why didn't you take me upstairs to bed then?"

"Patience and anticipation, Baby. All in good time," he says as the elevator opens onto the ground floor and he guides me into the crowd with a hand to my lower back. He looks around and pulls me closer. "Brian's talking to Dad at the other side of the room," he says as we make our way through the throng of people mingling and chatting. As we get closer Brian catches site of Chase and nods to him.

"Talk to Dad and Emily for a moment, I'll see what Brian wants," he says, heading toward where Brian has moved off to a table on his own.

I try my best to make small talk with Don and Emily, but Don sees right through it. "Something going on between Chase and Brian?" he asks, watching them across the room.

"I'm not positive, but it would sure seem that way," I say, sneaking a glance in their direction.

"They are definitely deep in conversation. Would either of you like a glass of wine?" Don asks as the waiter heads our way.

"I'd love a glass," Emily says, winking at him as she puts her empty glass on the tray.

"Katarina?" Don asks.

"Yes, please," I say, having a hard time taking my eyes off the scene in the corner of the room. Both men are clearly upset and when they turn to walk towards us it is hard for any of us to disguise our curiosity.

"What's going on son?" Chase's dad asks as the men return to our table.

"Ty was here. He singled Jenny out and Brian intervened," Chase says.

"What happened, Brian?" I say.

"When I first got here, he was in her face by the elevators. I could tell whatever he said shook her up. The security team must have realized something was happening about the same time I did. I intervened before Jay's team moved in and secured him," he says to Chase.

"Oh, my God. I need to be with her. Where did she go?"

"She took off toward one of the bathrooms at first, but then went upstairs to the Torzial suite. It's one floor below ours," Chase says as I send her a text.

Message: Heard what happened. On my way up.

Her response is immediate and my heart goes out to my friend as I read the message.

Reply: I'm fine. I just need to get some rest.

Message: I am not leaving you alone after seeing that A-hole!

Reply: Please don't, I really need some time alone. TTYT.

"From the sound of her message she just wants to be alone," I say to Chase and Brian. "If we're staying upstairs tonight, why don't I have her meet us for breakfast in the morning and then we can fly back to Chicago together so we can spend some time talking?" I suggest.

"Sounds like a plan. I thought she was flying back to New York tonight, but Matt says she texted him to let him know that she was staying in L.A.," Chase says.

"Good. That will give us time together tomorrow. Thank you so much for helping her, Brian. That guy is bad news. Where is he now, anyway?"

"Let's just say Ty has been removed from the situation," Chase says, his eyes the steely green that I have come to know so well.

"Okay," I say, looking from him to Brian, neither giving anything away. "I think we should mingle and then call it a night," I say.

"The crowd has died down and I think Dad and Brian will represent the Prestian interests

well," Chase says, placing his arm around my waist.

"You kids run along. Brian and I have this covered," Don says, good-naturedly.

"Thanks, Dad, good night Emily. We'll see you in the morning for breakfast. Brian, thanks again," Chase says, shaking his hand before guiding me to the double elevators in the hall entering a code into the keypad, and taking me into his arms.

"Baby, I have wanted to rid you of this dress all night long and I can't think of a more perfect place than in the elevator," he says, fingering the dainty straps that are the only things holding the material on my body.

"The elevator?" I ask, feeling myself grow anxious, but moistening at the mere idea.

"Does it excite you knowing that any moment the doors could open?" he asks, caressing the sensitive lobes of my ear with his tongue and down the side of my neck, inserting his finger between my legs.

"Chase..."

"You're still so needy and wet. I want to see all of you, Baby," he says, slowly moving the straps off my shoulders and letting the silk gown fall to the floor. "Exactly as I pictured you all day," he says, caressing the tips of my nipples with his tongue as he travels south, lingering at my navel, teasing me with the wetness and warmth before he kneels before me, using his tongue to caress around my clit as he tugs on the chain. This looks so beautiful on you, Katarina," he says, trailing kisses back up my body before he picks me up just as the elevator doors open.

"Chase!"

"Shh.... No one here but us," he says, at the same time I realize the door opens directly into the penthouse. He carries me through a contemporary white and chrome living space to the master suite beyond, exposed to his smoky gaze while adorned only by the silver and diamond necklace, bracelets, and clit chain.

"So lovely," he says before placing me on the bed. I am riveted as he begins removing his tie and suitcoat before starting on the buttons of the crisp white dress shirt below. I am mesmerized, my breathing hitches as the sinewy muscles of his arms, chest, and washboard abs are exposed to me. My pussy tightens as I continue to watch. He is erect and his cock is magnificent, glistening in the shadows of the city lights streaming in from the windows high above the city.

"Lie back with your arms out and above your head," he says, walking to me. He takes his time, his eyes blazing a heated trail over my nakedness before unclasping the bracelets around my wrist, affixing them to the loops above my head. "And now your legs, Katarina. Open them wide for me," he says, walking to the foot of the bed as I do what he's asked. "So beautiful," he says, tugging lightly at the chain still attached to my clit.

I moan and move my hips in pleasure. "I guess we will be needing the restraints after all," he says, placing each of the bracelets around my ankles and clasping them to the end of the bed. The slow rhythm of the pull on my clit begins drawing, like a mouth, causing me to writhe while he leisurely walks toward me, watching me as he trails his fingers along my thighs and navel and caresses my erect nipples.

"So sensitive and responsive," he says, reaching behind my hair and unclasping the diamond necklace that lies across the curve of my breasts. He flicks one nipple and then the other, rubbing the sensitive buds between his thumb and forefinger and the sensation goes right to the center of my core.

"Still Baby, is this what you want?" he asks, his body a strong masculine silhouette in the shadows of night.

I can only nod. "Watch Katarina and stay still. I want you to absorb all of the pleasure," he says as the vibration between my legs intensifies.

It takes concentration and effort not to grind my hips into the pleasurable pulsation, but my mind is distracted as he caresses my nipple and then places the jewelry on my right breast. The exquisite pain begins to flame the already pulsing desire deep in my core. He caresses my other nipple lightly; it is erect waiting for his touch. He strokes it, teasing the delicate flesh before affixing the other clip of the necklace to the sensitive bud, causing me to moan aloud.

He settles onto the bed between my legs, laying the silver and diamond necklace attached to my nipples over the curve of my breasts and across my abdomen.

"Tell me how this feels, Katarina," he says, leaning over me.

"It's so intense, the necklace and the chain together. It's making me so needy," I moan, as the moisture pools in my core.

"Your thighs are quivering," he says, never taking his eyes off of mine as he trails a finger from their tops to the shaven folds of my pussy.

"Chase," I moan, but am careful not to move my hips.

"You're doing so well," he says as the vibration on my clit comes to a slow halt and he tugs hard on the chain. This time the suction releases and he runs his forefinger over my sensitive nub. "So needy Baby," he says, bending to kiss, leisurely tease, and caress me with his tongue.

"I want to feel you shake Baby," he says, taking my clit into his mouth, suckling me while pushing two fingers deep inside of me.

I gasp, my body already right on the edge, pushing deep at the same time he pulls on the silver and diamond necklace clamped to my nipples which send shivers of pleasure throughout my body, pushing me over the edge as I crumble around him, helpless to do anything but tremble, as wave after wave washes over me.

He releases my legs and with one movement has positioned himself between them, driving deep inside of me, controlled but intense, pacing himself until I begin to build again. My legs naturally wrap around his waist, drawing him closer. I moan aloud as he removes the clamps on my nipples, causing all the blood to recirculate and everything south to clench his cock.

"You are so tight, Katarina. I can feel you trembling around me," he says, driving deeper, over and over as we both let go, losing ourselves in each other, breathless and finally completely sated. He releases my wrists and rubs them as he pulls me close to his chest, kissing the top of my forehead as our breathing returns to normal.

"That was so good," I say in a sexy sleepy haze.

"I'm glad you enjoyed it Mrs. Prestian. Now, let's get a glass of wine and sit in the whirlpool for a bit," he says.

"Hmm... I could really just fall asleep I'm so relaxed," I say.

"I'm glad you're pleased," he says smirking, pulling me with him as he rises out of bed. "Start the whirlpool and I'll bring the wine," he says, heading out of the master suite.

I take the time to text Jenny with plans for tomorrow before I head into the bathroom.

Message: Want to have breakfast and fly back to Chicago with us in the morning?

Reply: Sounds good.

Message: Text us whenever you wake up.

I turn on the light when I enter the bathroom and look around. It is spacious, with a white dual sink and chrome cabinet, and a white marble and chrome tub in the corner of the room. I smile at the loofah and hair products sitting on the ledge as I start the water. "There's an assortment of fragrances and foams in the linen closet behind you," he says as though reading my mind.

I select a chamomile fragrance and let it drizzle into the water, watching it fizzle around me as I sink into its warmth. Chase sets a glass of white wine in front of each of us and steps into the tub sinking into the water across from me. "That was a much better way to spend time than mingling with a bunch of board members," he says, entwining my legs with his own.

"I couldn't agree more," I say, taking a sip of the crisp sweet wine.

"How did you like wearing no panties and the clit chain in public, Katarina?" Chase asks.

My cheeks turn warm and his eyes light up with amusement at my embarrassment. "I'm never going to tire of your blush, Baby. Tell me," he urges, his eyes wide with delight.

"It made me feel so wanton, so needy," I say.

"You are amazingly sexy with or without the chain, but I have to admit that I love you in erotic jewelry, especially when I have the control button," he says smirking.

"Well, I am glad that you had a world of fun, but you seriously almost made me cum in front of a room full of people," I say, pretending to pout.

"Not likely to happen, Baby. Those moments are private. I told you not to cum and I was watching you closely. There was no possibility that I would let that happen."

"It took an effort to focus though. Seriously, that Dr. was talking to me and I don't even remember what I rambled on about," I say.

"I was following the conversation for you. Tell me you didn't like it," he says.

"You know I can't do that. It was amazing," I admit.

"I could tell, just wanted to hear you say it. You were responsive, your breathing changed, the flush on your cheeks deepened, and your eyes grew hazy. You loved it Katarina and it gave me a great amount of pleasure watching you not to mention an extremely stiff cock," he says.

"Well I'm glad it affected you, too."

"You can only imagine. Was there anything that you didn't like, Katarina?"

"The waiting still bothers me, but it's getting better," I say.

"Good, I want to make sure that even though your body loves it, you're not conflicted," he says.

"I love what you do to me, Chase. The only thing I'm still reconciling is my own feelings about what other people think and... well, you know the waiting," I say.

"Does it still feel like I'm taking your gift away, Baby?" he asks, lifting my chin so I have no choice but to look into his eyes.

"No, the anticipation and patience thing is getting a little easier now that I know how good it feels later. What do you like, Chase?" I ask, sliding towards him to kiss his lips gently.

"The same thing that's always going to turn me on. Your unbridled trust, Baby. Watching you in the throes of passion, it doesn't get any better than that," he says.

"I love that you care so much about how I feel and want to take care of my needs," I say.

"Yes, speaking of which," he says, laying me against the tub's pillow and reaching for the jar on the ledge. He rubs the erect tips and caresses them gently, then begins to rub cream onto my breasts, around my nipple, taking his time and massaging them. I close my eyes, enjoying the feel of his hands on one of the most sensitive parts of my body.

IT IS morning when I wake to find myself alone in bed. I glance at my phone. Only seven, not too bad. I lay back on the pillows allowing my thoughts to drift back to the night before. The look of intense pride in Chase's eyes as he made love to me, slowly and passionately. My heart aches with love for the man that has helped me work through all the trust issues from my childhood and has taught me how to appreciate so much. I stretch lazily and don a pair of running pants and t-shirt before pulling on socks and shoes, excited to go for a run in sunny California. I glance at my phone. No word from Jenny who usually sleeps in, so plenty of time. I text a message to Jay to let him know my intentions.

Message: Heading out for a run in about 10 minutes.

Reply: Does Chase know?

Message: I'm sure you'll fill him in for me! Be down in the lobby shortly. I'm going!

I head into the bathroom to brush my teeth, trying not to be too annoyed, but the security some days is just a little much.

Message: Am I always to expect such total disregard for your security?

Reply: Not funny! Jay needs to chill out just a little bit. It's sunny, we are in Cali, I AM going for a run!

I turn around, sensing his presence behind me. He is standing in the bedroom door, leaning against the doorframe in lounge pants and nothing else. I follow the trail of his broad shoulders, taking in his rock hard abs and the path of hair trailing below. His eyes are watching me intently.

"Chase, seriously. Jay can have anyone he wants accompany me. I just want to go for a run while the sun is shining and it's warm. We are in California. Is that really too much to ask?" I say.

"On the contrary, a run along the coast would seem most fitting. However, as you know Jay has policies and procedures to ensure our safety. One of them is that if you are going to venture out into a new area, different from your routine, you give them some advance notice.

They need to plan out a course, put guards along those areas to keep you safe. That is your number one priority, Katarina."

"Are you saying no?" I ask, anticipating an argument.

"Fortunately, we have enough detail to make sure you are well protected. Jay is getting details in place as we speak."

"But you would say no if we didn't have what you and Jay feel are enough security?" I ask.

"Katarina, I think you already know the answer to that question. I would most definitely say no," he says.

"And what if I wanted to go anyway?"

"Baby, I want you to experience anything and everything your heart desires, but I will not allow you to put yourself in danger. We've had this conversation," he says, his eyes holding mine locked in challenge.

I see the raw emotion in his eyes and suddenly feel horrible for the anxiety that I am causing. "I'm sorry, Chase. I should have given Jay some warning," I say, recalling the incident in Aruba when I was assaulted while running and how bad I felt when they had to scramble so I could get to an appointment the day before our wedding.

"It's okay, Baby. Jay is getting a team together for your run," he says.

"I appreciate that. I'm pretty sure you'd like to paddle my ass red right now wouldn't you?

"Yes."

"Tell me what you want to do to me in the way of punishment," I say, relishing in the sharp intake of his breath.

"I think the lady has earned a sound paddling with an implement of her choice, but right now I think you should go for your run. Jay has a team in place and they'll be with you from the lobby," he says, his eyes hooded and controlled.

"Any particular place I need to avoid?" I ask, trying to be amenable.

"Yes, go north as you exit and you'll be fine for a half hour then turn back. Security will only be a few feet from you in any direction," he says and it's hard to discern the passing emotion I see play over his features.

"Chase, I will be fine. Please stop worrying," I say, reaching up to kiss him before I head downstairs.

I recognize members of the security team as I walk through the reception area and can't help but feel bad and chuckle at their hastily pulled together running apparel. I walk onto the sidewalk and look up into the clear blue skies, enjoying the warmth of the sun shining on my skin. The streets are lined with upscale little shops until I get a little farther from the hotel, where they become farther apart and the landscape becomes dotted with palm trees, cactus in a variety of colors, and bright yellow and red blooming bushes that smell wonderfully fragrant. I lose track of time as I take in the scenery until my halfway song comes on and I turn back towards the new Prestian Corp tower.

The beep in my ear alerts me to an incoming call and I hit accept when I see Chase's number. "Listen carefully. A black car will pull up beside you in less than two minutes. Get into it. Alfreita's men are watching you. Keep me on the line until you are safely in the car. Understand?"

"Yes," I say, trying to maintain my composure and squelch the fear rapidly rising up in my throat.

"Katarina, I don't hear you breathing. This will be over in less than a minute and a half. Let me hear your voice, dammit," he demands.

"I can hardly breathe," I say somehow managing to keep my pace.

"We've got you, Baby. Tell me when the car pulls up and breathe now," he says.

I manage to pull in a supply of oxygen. "It's here," I say as a black Cadillac swerves up to the curb.

Sheldon emerges from behind me and pushes me into the back seat of the car, sliding in next to me. "Go, go, go," he yells to the driver as the car peels away from the curb.

"Katarina, you're safe Baby. You're just a few minutes away from the sky-rise," Chase says into my ear-buds.

I find it hard to take in air, trying to keep the panic at bay. "Katarina, take a deep breath now," Chase says on the other end of the line. I gulp in a breath. "Steady, short breaths, breathe in and blow out. Let me hear you," he commands.

I take a deep breath and then blow out audibly into the phone. "Good girl, Baby. Again," he instructs and I inhale and then exhale, finally getting my breathing to sync and putting my anxiety at bay.

The driver pulls up in front of the Prestian Corp building and we are immediately encircled by a multitude of security guards, but Chase cuts a path through the throng that surrounds me as we make our way inside the lobby. He puts his arm protectively around my waist as we walk through the lobby and into the elevator. Jay and Sheldon are by our side and enter the elevator with us. "Jay?" Chase says.

"Alfreita's men are all over the city. If we don't move forward with our plan they will continue to come at us with everything they have," he says.

"Get ahold of Carlos and his team. I want an agreed on proposal by the end of the day. This ends right now," Chase says to Jay.

"I'm all over it," he says.

"This is no ones fault but my own. I should have given everyone more notice. It was just so nice out and it sucks to have to be looking over our shoulders all the time, but I know how dangerous Alfreita is. I'll try to follow the security protocals better in the future. I really am very sorry," I say to Jay and Sheldon. I don't need to look up to feel the intensity in Chase's eyes.

"We'll get it figured out, Kate. In the meantime we just need to take extra precautions," Jay says.

TEN

"What's the arrangement for today?" Chase says, cutting him off abruptly.

"The Augusta will be landing on the rooftop in approximately thirty minutes. It will take you to a private airstrip where the Gulf will be awaiting. You should be in the air and on the way to Chicago within the hour," he says.

"Jenny was going to travel with us back to the city," I say.

"Jay, get ahold of her and let her know our plans. Have Matt move her along a little bit and escort her up to our suites," Chase says.

"Yes, sir," he says, pushing the override button code that allows entrance to our floor. "I'll message you when it's time to move," Jay says, pushing the keypad to return to the lower level.

I quickly set out to send Jenny a note to let her know what is going on and try to still the shaking of my hands.

Message: Hey, we have security issues. We need to return to Chicago right away.

I wait for a reply, and when one doesn't come I hit her contact. "This is Jenny Torzial. I am currently away from my office and sorry I've missed your call. Please leave a brief message and I will return your call as soon as possible."

I hang up. "Chase, Jenny isn't answering her phone or responding," I say with growing apprehension.

"Jay's checking on her. Security has been outside her suite all night and there's been no movement in the reports," he says, glancing down at his phone.

"Fuck!"

"Chase, what's the matter?" I ask.

"Brian just stopped by Jenny's to see how she is. No answer. I'm sending security in," he says, typing a message onto his phone just as the overhead intercom alerts us of a visitor. "It's Brian, I gave him the code," Chase says, answering the question I was going to ask before I can.

"What's the plan, Chase?" Brian says, before the elevator doors have even closed behind him.

"The team's going in. She was escorted to her room last night, wanting privacy. The plan was for us to have breakfast this morning and fly back to Chicago together. No reports of her moving in or out of the suite last night," Chase says.

"Good. I hope to God she's just sleeping it off, but you didn't see the look on her face when she was dealing with that asshole last night," Brian says.

There is a weighty silence from both men before the intercom announces Jay and his team. I take a seat on the couch as Jay and a swarm of our teams get off the elevator and move methodically toward us.

"Jay, where's Jenny?" I ask, instinctively knowing something is wrong, trying to keep the anxiety and panic at bay.

"All we know is that Ty approached her last night as the tour group returned to the lower level. Brian recognized him, and got him out of her face before my team got him. She went into the ladies room, came out a short while later and told Matt she wanted some time by herself and went upstairs to the Torzial suites. Matt has had his team posted outside all night long and she hasn't moved. Brian was worried and called her this morning, and not getting a response decided to come over and see for himself. She didn't answer the door. You know as much as we know right now. Chase, they just went in. No sign of Jenny anywhere," Jay says, immediately texting a message into his phone.

"Fuck," Brian says, running his hands through his hair.

"There are three possibilities at this point. She either left of her own accord, meaning she pulled one of your tricks and disguised herself on the way out of the bathroom last night and we followed the wrong person upstairs, or she went out the alternative safe escape during the night, which I don't believe is possible. We've had a guard stationed outside of that area all night long," Jay says.

"What's the third alternative?" I ask.

Jay glances at Chase and then at Brian. "Jay, she means the world to me. Tell me, please," I say.

"The third answer is that Alfreita is involved," he says.

"Chase, we have to find her," I say, burying my body into his chest. His arms lock tightly around me.

"We've got everyone on our security team on it, but unfortunately we just learned she took her GPS off. Jay and his team will do everything in their power to find her," he says, kissing the top of my head.

Jay is already on the phone. "No, I want all members of the family on lockdown. Work with Larussio security to make sure Carlos and Karissa are secure. Don and Emily are in L.A. with us. I want everyone in the air in the next half an hour. The Augusta is on stand-by. Bring it in and make sure we've got aerial backup and security in place when we transfer." He pauses a moment. "No, we're using a private strip. In the meantime, I want two more ground teams in L.A. as quickly as you can get them here." He listens to the person on the other line. "Very good, thanks," Jay says.

"We can't just leave Jenny here," I say, feeling sick as he gets off the phone.

"Katarina, rest assured the city is being scoured as we speak. If she's out there, we will find her. In the meantime, we are going back to the estate," Chase says.

"If you'll excuse me, I need to take care of a few things before the chopper arrives," Jay says, walking to the elevator.

"Hold up, Jay, I'm coming with you," Brian says, sliding into the elevator just before it closes and Chase answers his phone. "No, Jay's got the Augusta on standby," he says, his eyes watching me. I turn away and walk towards the bedroom for fear he will see all the fear and anxiety rising within me as I desperately try to keep them at bay. I pack the few items we brought and leave them on the bed, returning just as Don and Emily are announced and get off the elevator into our suite.

"Chase, what's going on son?" Don asks, holding Emily around the waist.

Chase recants the day's events and Don shakes his head. "Son, there's only one way to resolve this," he says.

"I know, Dad. I just got off the phone with Carlos," he says, avoiding my eyes as I glance up at the mention of my father. "The teams are in place and the Augusta will be landing in about five minutes," Chase says, before Jay and the team walk through the door.

"We need to get you moving," Jay says.

"You're not coming?" I ask.

"I'll be back once our teams from Vegas arrive and we've got them deployed to finding Jenny. You'll be in safe hands," he says, patting Matt and Sheldon on the back. "Besides, someone needs to be a buffer between Brian and the security team," he says, shaking his head.

"Brian's staying in L.A.?" I ask, looking to Chase to see if he was aware. He raises his eyebrows and it's clear that he was not.

"He said he wasn't leaving until he met the team coming in and approved of the plan to find her," Jay says, shaking his head as we get into the elevator and Chase enters the code for the rooftop.

"Brian owns one of the most prestigious sky-rises in the Los Angeles area and has a condo overlooking the pacific coast. He may have other work to finalize here with his transition to CEO of the Carrington empire," Chase says.

"Let's keep the door closed until the chopper sets down and we've got the all clear," Jay says, hitting a key on the pad. It is a matter of moments before he glances down at his phone. "Alright, let's move. Security will be around you from the elevator to the Augusta," he says as he pushes the button allowing the elevator door to open. We are encircled by guards carrying long rifles and I cringe at the necessity as we make our way on-board the sleek grey machine.

The four of us are positioned into the interior of the cabin and as we take off are provided with headphones, in addition to helmets.

"Put them on until we reach the strip," Sheldon says over the whirling of the blades. He and Chase appear to be talking to each other and I surmise with annoyance that my headphones are muted, effectively keeping me from hearing the conversation.

The faces on the men are serious and watchful. I can't keep my eyes from wandering to the guns positioned at the floor, no doubt loaded with ammunition, ready to protect at a moments notice. The events of the morning flood back into my memory, the screeching of tires, getting pushed into the car. I barely feel his arm tighten around me. "Breathe, Katarina," he mouths to me.

I glance up at him, finally inhaling, not realizing I had been holding my breath. I try to avoid the penetrating stare, but I am held captive by the intensity. "Exhale," he mouths, rubbing the back of my neck with his thumb until we touch down on the private air strip where two identical gleaming white jets each emblazoned with the Prestion Corp logo await us.

"Chase and Kate, Matt and I will go with you to the right. Don and Emily, we'll have Mark and John on point for your flight home to New York. Let's move, everyone," Sheldon says as we are transitioned aboard the jets.

As soon as we are onboard security closes the door between the living space of the Gulfstream, the security cabin and the cockpit. The room is spacious and inviting, especially pleasing to me because it is devoid of guns and security. I kick off my shoes and curl up on the soft leather couch, buckling into the custom seatbelts and watching out the window as the pilot makes his way down the runway. The strip appears odd, seemingly in the middle of nowhere. The landscape is dotted with cactus and flowering bushes growing wild in the desert. As soon as we lift off I brace myself for the conversation to come.

"Katarina, look at me," Chase says, tilting my face towards him.

The intensity of his gaze is what I knew it would be. The questions, his uncertainty about my feelings, my fear about our future. It feels like hours instead of mere moments and in that time a million scenarios flash through my mind.

"Katarina, talk to me. Tell me what you're feeling," he says softly.

"I know I told you that I didn't need to know what the plan is, that I didn't care, but..."

"Now you do," he says, finishing my sentence.

I nod, moved by the depth of emotion swirling in the deep green eyes before me. "Not for the reason you might believe," I say, finally.

"And that reason would be what?" he asks, the twitch of his jaw belying his agitation.

I can barely whisper the word, the one that has come between us in the past, the one word that has the ability to drive us apart. "Trust," I say, finally.

He begins to speak and I hold up my hand to stop him. "Chase, please hear me out. The reason for wanting to know what the plan is has nothing to do with trusting you. I just need to know what to expect, what to anticipate. I would never have pushed to go for a run this morning if I knew Alfreita's teams were actually in the city, but I had no idea. I feel horrible that I've put our teams at risk. I trust you and love you with all my heart," I say, leaning over to kiss his lips, relieved when after what is only a brief moment of pause, but seems like an eternity, he nods.

"I will tell you everything once we're at home. Right now, however, I want to be deep inside of you," he says, lifting me and carrying me to the master suite.

The captain announces our impending descent hours later and we barely redress and make it to our seats before Sheldon and Matt come into the living room, as we buckle in by the window. I suppress a smile as Chase adjusts his tie which has served as an effective blind fold for the majority of the trip.

"Gentlemen, any updates?" Chase says.

"Actually, yes. We're going to land at O'Hare. The airport has been cleared and there are no signs of Alfreita or his people at this point. There has been some air traffic over the estate though, so we want to avoid giving away the location of the private landing strip," he says.

"Good. Any word on Jenny?" Chase asks Matt.

"Nothing, not a peep out of Alfreita. As soon as we have you safely home, I'm heading back to L.A. and will take part in the search. Jay and the team are out searching today and just finished briefing the Vegas men. They haven't turned anything up at any of the transportation routes, but it's still early," he says, glancing in my direction as the large jet lands onto the runway.

We are whisked to the helicopter and I grimace as security gets into the helicopter cabin with us, taking up vigilance next to the windows instead of riding in the cabin that Chase had designed for them. "We've got the all clear," Sheldon says into his mic, presumably to the pilot.

Chase takes my hand, rubbing his thumb across my palm as we begin to lift off. Sheldon is on the radio constantly and every once in a while texts a message into his phone. "Send in aerial support and let me know when we're clear," he says into his microphone.

I glance at Chase and he's watching Sheldon, too. "Take us around the lake until we get clearance, Mack," Sheldon instructs the pilot.

"Alfreita's got birds in the sky above your dad's estate, too. Air support is handling it now," Matt says to Chase.

"They're sending a message."

"We've got a clear path Mack, take us home," Sheldon says into his microphone.

"They had helicopters flying around the Larussio estate, too, but stayed on the periphery," Chase says, reading a text on his phone.

"Yeah, probably knew Carlos Larussio would drop them right out of the sky," Matt says. I glance up just in time to see Sheldon's fleeting look of disapproval as we set down on the helipad.

"Come on, let's get you inside," Chase says, lifting me by the waist from the helicopter. We are immediately encircled by a blanket of security guards who walk with us the short distance to the front entrance. The house looks magnificent with its broad pillars and archways set against a backdrop of towering spruce trees, whose branches are now heavily laden from the fresh snowfall.

Chase thanks the men inside the door and shakes hands with Matt who is anxious to return to the airstrip and get back to L.A. "We'll do everything we can to find her, Kate," Matt says to me.

"I know you will, Matt. Thank you," I say before Chase closes the door and we walk into the kitchen.

"I thought I heard a lot of commotion out there," Gaby says, wiping her hands on her apron before pulling the two of us into a hug.

"What smells so good? We're starving," Chase says.

"I just made a fresh batch of clam chowder and sourdough bread. Take a seat," she says.

"That sounds excellent, Gaby. You sure you don't need any help?" I ask.

"Sit, sit, sit. It will give me something to do," she says, bustling over to the stove where a chrome pot of soup is simmering. She lifts the lid and the aroma wafts through the air permeating the kitchen.

Chase looks down at his phone, scowling before he texts a message. "Jay just left L.A. Apparently he and Brian went to question Ty and Jay had to literally pull Brian off of him," Chase says, the tension in his jaw revealing his agitation.

"What's going on with him?" I ask, blowing on a spoon full of the thick creamy soup that Gaby has placed in front of us.

"I don't know. Brian keeps his personal relationships to himself, but something's clearly got him uptight," he says.

"Did they learn anything from Ty?"

"Nothing. He even invited them in to take a look around," he says.

"Smug asshole," I say.

"Any word about Jenny?" I ask, nodding to the phone in his hand.

"Not yet, Baby," he says.

"Who were you on the phone with?"

"Your dad. I wanted to make sure he knew I was planning to fill you in on the details of the plan for Alfreita," he says, his gaze measured.

"And, what pray tell did he say to that?"

"You know how he feels about this, Katarina," Chase says.

"Yeah, he wants to keep me blissfully ignorant," I say.

"Katarina, he cares about you and how you view him. He would do whatever it takes not to ever feel the pain of Karissa or you walking out of his life," he says as we finish our meal.

"I won't think less of him or you. I just want to know," I say, watching the fleeting emotion pass over his handsomely chiseled features.

"Thanks for the nice lunch," Chase says, guiding me upstairs with his hand on the small of my back and closing the door behind us when we reach our bedroom.

"Your father's family is in an outright war with Alfreita. He crossed the line when he kidnapped Karissa and the Larussio family snapped back with a vengeance. They severed all supply chain relationships and made it almost impossible for Alfreita to move product which he desperately needs if he is to fulfill commitments."

"I don't understand how that's helping us."

"Baby, Carlos used that as a means to draw him out. He wants to completely put Alfreita out of business. If you recall the men in Miami, they were being blackmailed by Alfreita. They've been working for your father since that time and the intel they provided allowed him to take out Alfreita's largest manufacturing sites."

"God, Chase. I thought he was done with that life," I say, changing out of my travel clothes and into my robe, climbing into bed and sliding my back against the headboard. "He promised my mom that he wasn't running drugs. She believed him, Chase. I believed him," I say.

"Listen to me, Katarina. He distanced himself from all of those business transactions years ago, but you knew the family was still heavily involved. Your grandfather left this legacy to your family making your father executor of his will. Carlos has done nothing but try to balance his father's wishes and his family's legacy with the anguish over losing Karissa as a young man. He did not lie to your mother. He delegated all responsibility for that side of the business to the older brothers, and began focusing on the legitimate side of ventures years ago."

"Then why is he involved in it now?"

His eyes are hooded and controlled. "Tony is gone and with that your father needed to step back in, at least short term in order to protect the empire your grandfather built. Secondly, it's the only way to draw Alfreita out and cause him to show his hand. He didn't go back in without a lot of thought and deliberation around this, Katarina."

"So that was the plan that you and Jay were talking about?" I ask, feeling the anxiety in my throat rise.

"It was, and you said you didn't want to know, that it wouldn't make you think any less of him," he says.

"I know, but God Chase. I didn't expect this," I whisper, trying desperately to get a handle on my emotions.

"Breathe, Katarina," he says, grasping me by the waist and placing me atop him, my legs on either side of him. "Look at me," he instructs.

He tilts my chin up and it is impossible to look away. "You are mine, and there is nothing that I won't do to protect what is mine. This was the only way, do you understand?"

I nod. "Yes, I'm just trying to comprehend it all, Chase."

"Good, because I won't apologize. We needed to do this. Alfreita has leaders at the highest levels of Interpol in his back pocket and now we have communications intel connecting them to the effort to support Alfreita in taking over the drug trafficking industry."

"What the hell!"

"Carlos and I need to bring Vicenti up to speed, now that we know for certain Alfreita's intent was to wipe out not only the Larussio territory, but that of Vicenti's, as well."

"When I went to see him, he was concerned about Interpol's involvement and the relationship they seemed to have with Alfreita, but no one knew the extent of his involvement with Interpol at that time," I say.

"With the help of your uncle he has been systematically trying to discredit both the Larussio family and Vicenti making them appear to be monsters capable of killing people with poisonous product. We originally thought he knew how close our fathers were and took the opportunity presented when I was aboard his yacht, but it would seem that there was that and other motives at play," he says.

"Chase," I say, urging him to continue but afraid of the intensity in his stare.

He kisses my lips gently, pulling me close to him. "Baby, we always knew it had to be about something more than the money. His family is incredibly wealthy," he says, pausing, his deep green eyes appraising mine, searching.

"Tell me," I urge.

"We know Alfreita's original desire was to overtake the Larussio and Vicenti territories. He and Tony had a plan to put your father and Vicenti out of business and control the drug movement across the borders, but once the supply chain was shut down we thought it would slow them down considerably, but they've got other manufacturing sites that we're still trying to find. We believe he's drawing heavily on his family's monetary resources and Interpol connections to move the product."

"How does this connect with Jenny's disappearance?" I ask.

"I wish to God that I had a better answer for you, Katarina, but we just don't know if it does or not. We've laid a net out over the entire city, scoured every means of transportation that could have been used to get out of the city the night before we realized she was gone. Nothing— It's like she's just disappeared into thin air."

"And no word from Alfreita? He was pretty quick to contact you when they had my mom," I say, recalling the dreaded phone conversation.

"No, Jay's had intel monitoring all the communications lines and there's been no inkling about her, but we certainly can't rule it out. We'll know more later once your father and Vicenti meet."

"Does my mom know about any of this?" I ask.

"That's why I needed to talk with him before I discussed it with you. She doesn't and he wants to keep it that way. He intends to do what he has to in order to ensure the family money is secure, reinvested, and that Alfreita is no longer a concern before he removes himself," Chase says.

"These men have a lot of power, don't they?" I ask.

"Indeed. The aerial show around all of our homes was Alfreita sending your dad and me a pretty significant message. This is all-out war, I'm afraid." Chase says.

"I'm surprised he let you tell me, in all honesty," I say.

"Katarina, I didn't exactly ask his permission, but I did want to give him the courtesy of letting him know that I was sharing the information with his daughter," he says.

"I didn't realize, Chase. I hope it didn't put you in a bad position with my father," I say.

"Nothing to worry about in that respect," he says, and I know he is not intimidated in the slightest by the power my father possesses.

His phone vibrates and he glances at the incoming message, shaking his head before pushing a button to dial out.

ELEVEN

"What's going on," Chase says, pausing and scowling at the other end, putting it on speaker as he listens.

"Shit Chase, no disrespect, but the guys know how to do their job and don't need Brian breathing down their necks every minute. They thought he would eventually tire and go home, but he's apparently pulled in security of his own and plans to stay with the guys all night."

"I'll talk to him Jay. I don't know why he's so interested in this, but I'll find out," Chase says.

"Well you might want to do that sooner than later. I overheard him talking to his security team and he's planning to go back to Ty's house. He seriously needs to be reigned in," Jay says.

"I'll find out and get back to you," Chase repeats before disconnecting.

"What the heck is going on?" I say.

"I don't know what the hell has gotten into Brian. Jay had the intel team set up in one of the suites adjacent to the one Jenny stayed in and Brian hasn't left all day, bossing people around and pulling in teams of his own to search for Jenny. I need to call him," he says, getting off the bed where he's been sitting.

"I feel so useless, I can't just sit here and wait while she's out there somewhere," I say.

"Actually, the team has thoroughly investigated any possibility of travel to her mom's. You're free to call her and let her know what's going on. The police plan to do this later today, but it may be better coming from you," Chase says, kissing my lips before leaving the bedroom.

I sit up, still nude and reach for the cami strewn on the back of the armchair. I slip it over my head contemplating what to say. How in the world do you tell someone that their daughter is missing, and that no one has a clue why? I scroll through my contacts and look into the numbers I have listed for Jenny and with trepidation push the button that will connect me with her mom.

"Hello, this is Mira," a soft-spoken voice says on the other end of the phone.

"Hi, is this Ms. Torzial, Jenny Torzial's mother?" I ask.

"Yes, that's right. May I ask who this is?" she says politely.

"Yes, absolutely. How rude of me not to introduce myself right away, Ms. Torzial. I'm Kate Meilers, a very close friend of Jenny's," I say.

"Of course. Jenny talks about you often," she says, and the sudden apprehension in her voice is apparent. "Is she okay, Kate?"

Oh, God, how to tell her. "Ms. Torzial," I begin, but she interrupts me.

"Mira, please," she insists.

"Mira, I am so sorry to have to break this to you, but Jenny was with us at the grand opening last night and hasn't been seen since then."

"What do you mean, she just disappeared?" she says, pronouncing each word slowly and methodically.

"She was at the ribbon-cutting ceremony and then went to tour the facility with a couple of prospective tenants. She ran into Ty, her, umm boyfriend..." I say.

"Her ex-boyfriend. Jenny told me about him. Apparently he was offered a job in California and they went their separate ways," she says.

She obviously didn't tell her about the rape and I decide to keep it to myself, but am puzzled. "Mira, my husband is doing everything in his power to find her. He has a security team that has been searching the city, interviewing anyone she talked to last night, trying to identify any methods of transportation that could have been used to leave the city. I was hoping she may have come to your house," I say.

"My God. She couldn't have simply vanished," she says, her voice a mere whisper, hard to understand from her emotion.

"The police are going to be contacting you, but I wanted you to hear it from me first. You can be assured that my husband has the best teams money can buy working on finding her," I say.

"Thank you. That's so kind and I appreciate everything you are doing and that you took the time to call me yourself," she says, sniffing.

"I wish that I were in person and could give you a hug," I say, wiping the tears beginning to pool in the corner of my eyes.

"Please find my baby," she says before disconnecting.

I let the tears fall, helpless against the fear and anxiety I feel for my dearest friend, my heart in pain for her mother who must feel completely powerless and bereft and will no doubt need to endure the long interview process with police at some point in the day.

I pull on a pair of yoga pants and head into the bathroom to freshen up before heading downstairs to find Chase. His study door is closed and I hear muffled voices coming from the other side and decide to go in. He is sitting behind his desk and the phone is on speaker. "I'll wring the life right out of him if I ever see the fucker again," the voice coming from the speaker says.

"Who is that?" I mouth, closing the door and taking a seat across from him.

He places the call on mute. "It's Brian," he says, before pushing the button to speak.

"Brian, our teams are doing everything they can. Jay's team has a lead," he says and I immediately look up. "A taxicab driver picked a young woman up with long dark hair but it was in a ponytail and she was wearing an adidas zip up jacket. That's all he could remember from the rearview mirror, but he thought it was odd since everyone else he picked up in front of the entrance was dressed up for the grand opening."

"Shit, Chase. Why didn't we know this yesterday?" Brian says.

"He worked the night shift and just got back on duty an hour or so ago. Jay's men are doing everything they can."

"I'd like to know how the hell she got around security then, but we'll save that for another day. Where did he drop her?" Brian asks.

"Here's where it gets a little strange. He said she asked him to drive her around and show her the city. He gets requests like that all the time so didn't think too much of it, but she wasn't paying any attention to him as he pointed out different areas and attractions in the city. She just had this blank look on her face and when he asked her where she wanted to go she asked him to take her back to Prestian Corp," he says.

"What the hell," Brian says.

"I just sent a message to Matt to have him search all the open suites in the building and every vacant room within the block. They were focused on all exit routes out of the city and preventing her from getting too far out of reach when it first happened," Chase says, but Brian is no longer on the phone.

"Fuck," Chase says, disconnecting and pushing a button to connect with Jay. "I think Brian's heading Matt's way to help with the search. As soon as I told him she returned to the building last night and there was a search underway he hung up on me," Chase says.

"I'll let Matt know and about the other thing. The security guard took a break to go to the bathroom and didn't call for backup. Matt's recommending that we fire him and I'm dealing with it, but wanted you to know," Jay says.

"Keep me informed," Chase says to Jay before disconnecting.

"Chase?"

"I don't think Alfreita had anything to do with this. Whatever Ty did or said to her may have triggered a flight response. She probably wasn't in any condition to know where to go last night, so she may be somewhere close," he says.

"She texted me that she just needed to be alone, otherwise I would have been with her. We have to find her Honey, she's my dearest friend and all alone," I say.

"I know, Baby. Let's see if they find her and then we'll decide what we need to do. We don't know for sure that it was her, but I'm hopeful," he says, coming around the desk, taking me by the hand and leading me to the couch by the window. "Sit by me, Baby," he says, pulling me into his lap and cradling my head against his shoulder, rubbing the back of my neck with his thumb, calming me and holding me for what seems like an eternity as we wait.

The vibration of his phone less than twenty minutes later, but what seems a lifetime, pulls me from my reverie. He answers it still caressing the back of my neck with his thumb. My body is wired and I perk my ears up to hear the conversation although it is not on speakerphone.

"Excellent," he says and then scowls as he listens to the person on the other end of the phone. "Jesus, put Brian on the line," he says.

"Matt says you're bringing Jenny home yourself," he says, pausing to listen. "Slow up, Brian. There's no issue with that. I don't claim to know what's going on between you two, but given the situation, Katarina and I would be greatly appreciative if you would escort her back to Chicago," Chase says.

He listens for a moment and nods. "Yes, Jay will take care of all the logistics. He'll have a helicopter take you to LAX and then home from O'Hare. Let me know when you find out where she wants to stay and feel free to offer her our home. We're going to be working from here for a little while with the Alfreita mess and Katarina would love to have her nearby. Thanks again, Brian," he says, pulling me close before he disconnects.

"They found her in an empty suite. She was still in the clothes the driver described from last night and it doesn't appear as though she's slept. She was just sitting on the bed staring into space when they opened the door. Baby, she's going to need help to get through this. Obviously seeing Ty had a drastic impact on her," he says.

I am seething inside at the injustice done to my friend, but so thankful that she is alive and has not fallen prey to Alfreita. The stories my mom told me of how her captors intended to do terrible things to her and then transfer her into human trafficking come flooding back to me and I shiver at the thought of Jenny in their hands, too.

"I need to call Mira," I say to Chase, scurrying off the couch to grab my phone from the desk. "I called her before I came downstairs and she must be worried sick. It was odd, though. I mentioned Ty's name to her and she said Jenny told her he got a job in California and they decided to go their own separate ways. She was so anxious to tell her mom during the holidays, but Mira clearly wasn't aware. At least it didn't seem that way to me, unless of course she didn't know if Jenny had confided in me.

"I am no expert in matters like this, but my guess is she's kept it all to herself," Chase says.

He glances at his phone and texts a quick message out. "Brian and Matt are with Jenny. They just got on the helicopter and are heading to the airport," he says.

"What do you make of Brian lately?" I ask.

"I've never seen him like this, but like I told you he's always kept his personal life to himself, but it would certainly seem that something is going on between those two," he says.

"I seriously don't think so. I would be the first to know something like that," I say, although I recall being surprised at how quick her relationship with Ty had taken off as I think back.

"I was curious to see if they knew each other previously through any of his family's ventures or personally, but everything that Jay's team came up with would lead you to believe that the first time they met in person was on our wedding night," Chase says.

"What, did you have someone research this?" I ask, raising my eyebrows at him.

"Yes, this is not like Brian. I've known him for years," he says.

"Serious control freak," I say under my breath.

"I heard that. Why don't you call her mother? I need to return a few messages and make a few calls, but will join you later for dinner downstairs. Then we can find some delicious punishment for your insolence," he says, leaving me to lust after his protruding frame before he closes the door behind him.

I dial her number with apprehension, but elated that I can at least let her know that her daughter is alive. The phone rings quite a few times and I anticipate voicemail coming on when she finally answers. "Hello Mira, this is Kate, Jenny's friend," I say.

"Kate." One word is all she says and the fear and anxiety on the other end of the phone in just that one word is heart-wrenching.

"Mira, she's alive. We found her. She is on her way back to Chicago," I say and my eyes tear up once again when I hear the sobs of anguished relief coming through the phone.

"I don't know how to thank you. What happened, was she hurt?" she says.

"Mira, no thanks are necessary. She's physically okay, but what you should know is that your daughter may need a little help emotionally. She has been through a rather traumatic experience, but I want her to be the one to tell you about it when she is ready," I say.

"Okay, I can have someone drive me to Chicago so that I can be with her," she says.

"Mira, I think she will end up staying with me for at least a little while and I know you're helping to take care of all of your grandchildren. Why don't I see how she's doing when she gets here and then let you know? She may need a little time to deal with this before she can talk about it, but hopefully that time is very soon. Once she's in a little better place we can have my husband's private plane pick you up and you are welcome to stay in our home as our guest," I say.

"That's so very kind of you, Kate. I didn't realize Jenny had told you so much about our situation, but yes, I am the caretaker for the grandkids. Would you do me a favor and have her call me when you can? I've tried her cell multiple times since I got your call just wanting to hear her voice at the end of the line and every time, the same message, over and over, she doesn't pick up," she says.

"She's in a rather tough place emotionally right now, but it's clear to anyone how much her family loves her and together we'll get her through this," I say.

"Thank you, Kate. Now I know why she cares about you so much," she says before I disconnect.

I spend the rest of the afternoon reviewing the Vegas and L.A. tower plans and send an updated summary related to the quality scores that have just come in from our work on the Prestian Corp medical center in Chicago. I glance at the time and go in search of Chase. I finally find him in the kitchen delving into a two-layer chocolate cake that looks absolutely sinful.

"You'll spoil your dinner for certain," Gaby clucks, shaking her head in mock disapproval as she pulls a pan out of the oven. The aroma of fresh Lake Michigan salmon smells like a mixture of honey and other seasonings.

"Here, have a taste," Chase says, pulling me into his lap and placing a smattering of chocolate fudge icing on his fingers before he slowly slides it into my mouth. "Suck," he whispers into my ear so only I can hear, but I blush as Gaby turns around, pretending to go about her business as if she had not just witnessed this private moment.

"I made a new relish, a honey glaze, avocado and citrus salsa," she says, placing a generous serving of the relish on our salmon before dishing the asparagus and garlic roasted baby gold yukon potatoes onto our plates.

"I'll put the dishes on the table," I say freeing myself of Chase's hold, still slightly embarrassed at being caught in such a compromising position. "It looks and smells amazing," I say, bringing the dishes to the table.

"I hope you both enjoy it," she says before leaving us to our meal.

"I haven't quite yet decided what punishment suits calling one's new husband a serious control freak," Chase says smirking, his lips upturned.

"You know there was a time when I did think you were just a controlling asshole?" I say, looking around to make sure Gaby is still in the other room.

"When you first met me?" he asks.

"Oh, way before that, Honey. You were texting me telling me that I had worked enough and that if I didn't stop working you would renegotiate my contract. Yep, serious control freak," I say.

"Do you still feel that way, Katarina?" he says.

"That you're a control freak? Honey, you are the biggest control freak I have ever encountered," I say, conflicted at the look on his face.

"Katarina, your answers are confusing. Does it still bother you?" he asks.

"Chase, at some point my views have changed. I no longer think of it as a bad thing. When I first met you it seriously pissed me off, but I absolutely love the way you take control in the bedroom, introducing me to knew things, the way you take care of me and our family and our friends, so many things," I say.

"Baby, I'm always going to want to control certain things, but I don't ever want to squash your individuality, your ambition, or the drive that makes you who you are."

"Damn," he says under his breath, taking my hand just as Jay walks into the kitchen with a swarm of men behind him. "Safe room, downstairs everyone! The team already has Gaby. Alfreita's men are everywhere!" Jay says.

This time as we make our way into the elevator and Chase enters the code to the ground floor I know what to expect. The cameras in the lower level begin processing recognition and he is asked for the verbal code before the doors open.

I will myself not to look up, afraid that he will see my fear, the anxiety, and all the doubts of the past.

Chase has a tight hold on my hand and keeps me moving as we walk through a short hall before he opens a door that leads us into an exact replica of the first floor level of the home above. Gaby is already in the kitchen, seemingly unfazed by the disruption to everyday life and I wonder how many times she has gone through this scenario and how many more are in my future.

As the doors close behind us Jay begins giving Chase an update on the situation. "Your father and Emily are already in the safe room. They had one installed in Emily's son's home for them and the grandkids after the last time this happened. Carlos and Karissa are safely in their lower level, but Jenny, Brian and Matt are just getting ready to land. Alfreita is moments away. We've got teams spread out all over the airport, but it's too far to get her here and they know where her house is. We've got ground teams in place. As soon as they land we're putting them on the Augusta and sending them to Brian's. I've already been in contact with him and he has a safe room," Jay explains.

"Brian just landed," Chase says, reading his message aloud.

"Alfreita's men are in the air and moving this way. Jenny finally fell asleep. Her place is not safe. Taking her to mine."

"What is he thinking? She's going to be in a strange place with no one with her when she wakes up," I say.

"Baby, Brian's right. He's mitigating risks. He has a heavy set of security of his own and a safe room in his condo. She's been with Brian for the last few hours and knows Matt and his team. Right now they need to get to his place," Chase says.

"Okay," I say, instinctively knowing that he has things under control.

"Jay, you have an update?" Chase says.

"The aerial teams are holding them at bay, but they need a diversion to reroute without being followed," Jay says.

"What's the plan?" Chase says, his lower jaw clenching.

"We spread word to the Paparazzi that a Saudi Prince just landed. News reporters are all over Alfreita's men, they have the car surrounded with cameras flashing and we've already got the Augusta up in the air," Jay says.

"Excellent work, men. Let's make sure they get home," Chase says to the group.

"We've got teams on the rooftop and aerial support is holding the copters at a distance from the city, but let's keep our eyes open," Jay says into his phone before disconnecting.

"Chase, Brian will be on the rooftop momentarily and the team will get them in safely. The helicopters pushed Alfreita's men out of the city and our way. They have a team scoping the perimeter of the Prestian estate. Snipers are in place, but this may end up being more than we anticipated. You want the authorities called in as a backup?" Jay says.

"No, just get them to the safe room and let me and Carlos deal with this," Chase says.

"Chase, Brian just landed. The teams have them covered and they're making their way to the rooftop elevator. The entire building has been searched and we've got men at all positions," Jay says, relaying a step-by-step account.

"Good work. Just keep Brian informed of what the team's doing," Chase says.

"Chase, right now Brian's calling all the shots. He's been like a bear to my team and pulled in his own security crew to secure the perimeter," Jay says.

Chase lifts his eyebrows. "As long as you are comfortable with the plan don't intercede and text me as soon as they are tucked into the safe suite," he says.

"Chase, we've got trouble at Emily's son's," Jay says, glancing at his phone.

"What's happening?" Chase says, but Jay holds up his finger motioning one moment as he takes a call.

"Do it, make sure they get a clear message of their own!" Jay says. "They surrounded Emily's son's house and tried to break in. Our teams were there with the Larussio group and have it under control," he says.

"Baby, join me in the study," Chase says, leaving me no choice but to follow in his wake. The room is an exact replica of his study upstairs with a Mac sitting atop a large wooden desk. The only difference is there are no windows allowing expansive views to the coast of Lake Michigan or orchards, in fact, no windows at all, only four walls and the door he closes behind us.

He takes a seat in the large black leather chair behind the desk and motions me to the seat across from him. "I need to connect with your father and I want you to hear the conversation," he says.

"Why would you ask me to do that? He didn't want you to tell me, he's not going to be comfortable with me being on the line and at the end of the day, I really don't know if I have the stomach for it," I say.

"You need to know the details, need to be aware of the dangers and of what could happen if your father had not taken this position. Only then can you make informed decisions about how you feel," he says, pushing the button for my father.

"Carlos here," my dad says, his voice deep and much lower then I somehow remembered.

"Chase here, Carlos. I have Katarina with me. Jay just gave me an update on Jenny and Brian. They've landed and should be secure shortly. Alfreita's men were at the airport. It would appear every attempt is being made to apprehend someone close to us. We've got heavy aerial traffic here at the compound," Chase says.

"Here, too, but they had your dad and Emily's son's place

surrounded, too. Thank God the last time it happened Don insisted they install a safe room."

"Dad's been in touch. Everyone's fine," Chase says.

"Chase, it ends now. Katarina, you'll need to decide for yourself if you want to stay for the conversation, but what you hear needs to remain in the strictest of confidence."

"I'm not leaving and completely understand," I say.

"Carlos, Katarina, Jay just let me know that Brian and Jenny are secure," Chase says, and I can feel my heart beat with the anxiety that I feel.

"Good to hear, Chase. As you know I contacted Vicenti this evening. We'll be meeting at his estate in Brazil tomorrow evening. We've cut off all the suppliers that we can and Vicenti is in the process of pulling in some favors and eliminating others as we speak. The information you've gathered with your intel team has been invaluable in identifying them. I don't know how they do it, but God bless them. I appreciate you allowing their support," he says.

"Not a problem, Carlos. I have a vested interest," he says, his green depths holding my own riveted.

"As we all do. He's shown nothing but relentless determination to put our family out of business and now he's trying to abduct someone close to our family in an attempt to gain control of the Larussio invest-ments in the drug industry. It's time to finish this. I'll meet with Vicenti and put plans in place to move forward."

"I don't understand why Vicenti is involved. I thought he was a competitor?" I say.

"Katarina, Vicenti and the Larussio family have been in different territories for many years. Our fathers knew each other years ago and had a great respect for each other. Over the years we have come together to ensure that our interests were sustained as new and different products and suppliers tried to gain footholds into the market," he says.

Chase regards me warily. Gangsters, mafia, doing what they needed to do to protect their piece of the drug industry. My mother's husband, my father. I will myself not to look into his eyes for fear of what he will see. I am unable to listen to any more of their conversation and get up, feeling the burning of his eyes upon me, and walk to the door, closing it behind me.

I head for the safe room bedroom feeling emotionally drained. I peel out of my clothes and slip into the silky down comforter and text Jenny. Still no answer so I decide to text Brian who is usually online and working twenty-four seven.

Message: They said you are settled in for the night. How is Jenny?

His response is almost immediate.

Message: She woke up for a few moments as we arrived, but then fell back to sleep. She's exhausted.

Reply: I'm sorry I can't be there or that you couldn't bring her here.

Message: No need, she'll need your support tomorrow.

Reply: Of course. Thanks for taking care of her Brian. TTYT

TWELVE

I stir, stretch, and glance at my phone. The time on the face registers nine a.m. I couldn't have slept that long, but another look assures me that I have. I glance over at Chase's side of the bed and am reminded of a previous time when he left me alone to contemplate my doubts about him, believing that I did not trust him. A slight tear rolls from my eye as I remember that it caused him to leave me. I wipe it away, but it is replaced by another and then another.

He has been completely honest with me. I wanted to know what was happening, what he and my father were involved with. Against my father's own wishes he made sure that I was not kept in the dark. I should have stayed, maybe asked more questions, learned more about my father's intent with Vicenti. I get up and throw on some clothes, brush my hair and my teeth and go in search of Chase.

I find him where I left him and although he is wearing different clothes it is hard to tell if he has slept at all. "I'm sorry, Chase. I should have stayed and listened to what was planned. You trusted me enough to let me be part of the conversation," I say, pouring myself a cup of coffee from the carafe on the cabinetry.

"I came in to check on you but you were fast asleep. I didn't want to disturb you," he says.

"I couldn't keep my eyes open. I sent Brian a text to see how Jenny was doing and he said she had woken up, but was already back to sleep," I say.

"That's what Brian said last night," he says.

"Did he say how she's doing or anything? He didn't give much a way, but we were just texting briefly," I say.

"Just what I think we already knew. She needs to see her counselor, routinely. It's the only way she's going to be able to deal with this.

"I thought she was going."

"I'm no expert, but if the night before last is any indication she probably needs to go more often or talk more," he says.

"So did you ask him how he ended up being so, well, involved with finding her and stuff?" I ask.

"I did not. They'll share it with us if they want us to know. I was just appreciative he was able to be there for her when we were halfway across the country," he says.

"You're right. It really doesn't matter and I feel the same way. I was glad that he was with her last night in case something happened," I say.

"We've been given the all clear so we can return upstairs. I didn't want to wake you though," he says, walking toward me, taking the coffee cup out of my hand and placing it on the ledge. "Come with me," he says, leading me through the suite, into the hallway and up the elevator to our bedroom upstairs.

He closes the door behind him and pulls me into his arms. "I don't know what to think when you just walk out of the room like that after I was honest with you and included you in the conversations," he says, the magnetism of his deep green eyes capturing my own.

"I know, I'm so sorry, Chase. The emotions of the day and then hearing my dad, it was just a little more than I could take, but I shouldn't have walked out."

"I wish you had stayed, heard him out, then we could have talked about your feelings afterward," he says.

"I know, but you need to know this has nothing to do with my trust in you," I say, pulling him close, relishing in the fresh soap scent of his skin, pressing him closer, feeling his hardness press against me.

"I'm trying to believe that," he says.

"I'm sure there's some just punishment for this," I say, looking up and into his eyes, watching the myriad of emotions play out.

"You need only ask once, Baby. Stay here," he says, walking to the dresser and opening the longer drawer on the bottom. He pulls out a long rectangular black case and places it on the bed. "I think you wanted the pleasure of selecting the implement when it's time. Well, it's time," he says to me.

My nipples tighten at his words and I moisten as he opens the box displaying a row of paddles laying single file, held by black loops across the top of the case. "Chase..."

"Undress for me, Katarina. I want you naked and vulnerable. Do it now," he says.

I do as he asks, slowly lifting my top and pulling it over my head. I reach for the small gold nugget clasp and unlock it, pulling it aside to expose my bare breasts to him.

"Baby, you are so beautiful. Discard the rest," he says and I slide my pants, along with the silky white panties I have on over my hips, stepping out of them to stand before him, completely nude except for my bracelet and necklace. He runs his finger along the line of my jaw, down my neck and across the tips of both nipples causing goose bumps to form all over my body.

"I love that you wear these without me asking you to," he says, fingering the silver and diamond necklace and bangles.

"You can have me like this any time," I say, panting.

"Tell me which turns you on, pick one out, Baby," he says, standing behind me fully dressed while I eye the different paddles with awe. There are black rubber-looking paddles of different shapes and sizes, what appear to be riding crops with silver handles, small black rubber paddles and wooden ones of various shapes, sizes and lengths. I've seen one before. It is the one he used the first time, long and rectangular. He is still fully dressed and presses his hardness into me from behind.

"Pick one and then I will select the rest of the toys," he says and my eyes travel to the bottom of the case where dildos, butt plugs, nipple clamps, and a multitude of other toys lay.

I swallow as I feel the increased moistness between my legs. "What do you want, Baby? Would you like to feel the smarting sting of a slim paddle against your bare ass, or would you like to feel the crack of a wooden paddle, or maybe, you'd like to feel the flick of this crop as I paddle your pussy," he says, running his finger along the silver rod with the little black rubber material attached.

My entire lower region tightens at the prospect. "You like this, Baby?" he whispers, nipping gently at my sensitive ear lobe.

"This is supposed to be your decision Baby, tell me," he urges.

"I like that one," I say, barely whispering.

"Excellent choice, this will make an extremely good punishment," he says, taking the silver mast that holds a small, square, rubber-tipped paddle at its end, setting the case aside on the dresser, pulling the covers down and placing me face up on the king size bed.

"Hands over your head, Katarina," he says, unlatching my bracelets, using them to secure both wrists above me and connecting them to the headboard.

"Spread your legs for me, Baby," he says, taking my right foot and securing it with the bracelet to the right side of the bed before spreading my legs wider, taking the left foot and doing the same.

"Beautiful, Baby. While I might normally blindfold you, I want you to see what this paddle looks like in my hand and on your body," he says, extending the rubber tip across my erect nipples. Let's see, I think we need to decide exactly what you should expect for such impetuous behavior," he says, running the square rubber black tip down my abdomen.

I can't help the moan of excitement that escapes as it trails down my sensitive skin and he runs the tip over my mound.

"Patience and anticipation, Baby," he says, trailing it slowly over my folds. "Have you ever thought about getting spanked here, Katarina?" Chase asks.

"Never, until I saw the paddle and you asked me," I say.

"I like being the only one that has ever made you think of such things," he says, running the tip over my sensitized clit.

"Honey," I moan.

"So close, yet so far," he says, teasing me with its end, running it over my clit along my folds and then back to my mound.

I pull against my restraints needing to feel more of the friction, but he stills me with a hand on my midriff.

"While I would love to continue pleasuring you, I believe punishment is due for such discourteous behavior earlier. You trust me physically, willing to let me spread your legs, letting me restrain you, allowing me to spank the most intimate parts of your body, but then you walk out not willing to hear the entire story leading me to believe that you don't fully trust me," he says.

"Chase, I do, and I'm so turned on," I say, my hips pushing up on their own accord.

"Patience Baby, I want to go slowly with you, but your choice of punishment is making it difficult. It's an amazing turn on, watching as you wait to see how this scene will play out," he says, continuing to run the rubber tip across my clit and slowly through my folds.

I moan as the tip scrapes my sensitive clit and my hips rise of their own accord, but he stills me with his voice. "Still Baby, I want you to absorb this, the intensity, the pain and then the pleasure that follows."

"Pick a safe word," he says, as he walks toward the head of the bed, kissing my lips gently and squeezing my nipples.

"Can't I just say stop?" I ask.

"Pick one," he urges, kissing me again before removing my silver and diamond necklace, unclasping it so the clamps are visible and the long chain hangs down in front of my eyes. He runs the diamonds over my nipples, eliciting a whimper at the coarseness against my sensitive skin.

"Do you want these on, Katarina?" he asks, holding up my diamond clamps.

I can only nod my head in affirmation. "What's your safeword, Baby?" he asks again.

"Trust," I say finally.

His eyes are heavy with emotion. "You need to tell me right now if we are broaching something you're uncomfortable with," he says.

"We're not, just the opposite. I picked it because I trust you with my body and my heart. You asked for my unbridled trust. You have it Honey, but if I use that safeword you'll know how much it means," I say.

He kisses my lips and trails down to suckle on my nipples, allowing them to become erect before removing the warmth of his mouth, leaving them to the cool air of the room before taking one in his fingertips and placing the clamp on the sensitive nipple.

"Honey," I moan, breathing deeply to absorb the initial pain before feeling the resounding pleasure in my core. He places the other one and I have barely gotten used to the feel, slowly getting acclimated before he tugs gently at the silver and diamond chain setting my nipples on fire and flaming the heat between my legs. He trails the paddle over each of them, taunting and teasing, trailing where his mouth has just been, causing the clamps to move, creating a heated desire before traveling lower, across my navel and circling my mound.

"How many strikes, Katarina?" he asks, allowing the rubber tip to run through my folds.

"Fifteen," I say, picking a random number.

His eyes widen. "Let's start with eight," he says, lifting the paddle and allowing it to strike my pussy.

The intensity is a shock and I feel my hips rise of their own accord to experience the second smack even fuller. "Honey," I moan as it connects with my aroused clit.

"Baby, your pussy is glistening. It likes getting paddled doesn't it?" he asks, administering three more strikes in succinct fashion as I writhe against my constraints, desperately trying to absorb the exquisite pain and pleasure he is creating.

"God yes, Chase. I can't take anymore. I want you deep inside of me," I pant, still straining against the bangles that hold me securely in position.

"Three more, Baby, and these will be intense. I want you right on the edge when I get done so I can sink my cock deep inside of you and feel you convulse around me," he says, striking the tip of my extended clit and then doing it again, twice more as I moan and push my hips up to meet the paddle.

He releases my legs and pushes them above his shoulders, driving into that special spot that causes me to moan audibly. "Chase, I can't wait," I say, panting.

"Cum with me, Baby, let me feel you tremble," he instructs and I am helpless, shattering around him as he releases deep inside of me. He eases my legs down from around his neck and releases my wrists, drawing me aside him and curling me into his chest. He pulls me close and I can feel the beat of his heart through his chest, and I snuggle in closer, secure in his arms as our breathing returns to normal.

"Do you have any idea how much I love you," I say, turning to him, rubbing my thumb against his lower lip.

He kisses the tip of my nose and then my mouth, kissing my lips until I open to him, allowing him to explore. He finally pulls away, looking down at me. "Baby, I want to know how you felt about what we just did," he says.

"See, this is why my heart will never be in danger with you around. You take care of my every need."

"I intend to, but I need you to tell me how you felt," he says, pushing a loose strand of hair out of my eyes.

"It was amazing, so hot. I was so turned on and I didn't even mind waiting for the climax," I say, kissing his lip lightly.

"Baby, now tell me something I don't already know. I was the one watching your breathing, seeing your body glisten with desire and feeling you quiver around me. I want to know how what we did made you feel or is going to make you feel tomorrow. Emotionally, how are you processing it?"

I look away and he places his finger under my chin, forcing me to look into his eyes. "Tell me, Katarina," he says.

"I loved what you did to me and it's hard to explain what's changed for me. Things I used to think were important like what people view as normal and what I should feel about certain acts, I just don't care anymore. It's simply no longer important and I don't understand why it really ever was," I say.

"Baby, you've given me your unbridled trust and you couldn't have made me happier," he says, kissing my lips passionately.

"One thing," I say, coming up for air, repositioning myself so I can look into his eyes.

"Anything Baby," Chase says, looking at me with an odd intensity.

"Next time, please don't renegotiate my punishment."

I hear him audibly gasp. "Katarina, fifteen strikes would have been too much, way too soon. I needed to make sure you liked it and were ready emotionally," he says.

"Oh, I liked it," I say, as his lips overtake mine and he makes love to me, gently this time, kissing and suckling my entire body, taking extra care to lick and caress the area he has just paddled before we are both fully sated and spend the next half an hour curled into each others arms.

I am the first to move, stretching my legs and arms above my head. Muscles I didn't even know I had are sore. "Who needs yoga," I say, grinning up at him.

"Anytime I can be of service, Mrs. Prestian," he says, bemused.

"I should give Jenny a call and get some work done on the Vegas project. I need to get the improvements to the standard Prestian Corp design detailed out before the group finalizes the plans," I say.

"I saw your suggestions and they look great. I'll be working in the study today if you'd like to join me, otherwise, I'll meet you downstairs for dinner," he says, brushing my lips with a kiss before getting out of bed. I watch his body as he walks nude toward the bathroom and until he is out of sight before I select Jenny's phone number.

I am almost convinced the call will go to voicemail when she answers the line. "Hi," she says, with none of the exuberance I have come to know.

"I've been trying to get ahold of you. I was so worried," I say.

"I know, I'm sorry Kate. I don't know how to explain it right now," she says.

"Jenny, you don't owe me anything. I'm just thankful that we found you before Alfreita's men did."

"I don't know too much about what happened except that we need to stay here until Chase and your father figure out a plan for him."

"Yeah, we were going to have you flown here where we could take care of you, but his men were swarming the airport and everyone thought it best to have you go to Brian's since it was secure and close by."

"That's what Brian said," she says.

"Jenny, I don't want to push, but you mean the world to me and I'm worried about you. Should we contact your counselor? I'm happy to give her a call and arrange a visit. We'll just have to figure out how to do it safely," I say.

"Umm, actually, Brian arranged for her to come to his condo this afternoon," she says.

"Really, that was incredibly nice of him," I say, trying not to appear nosy, but dying to know what's going on between the two of them.

"It was. Now I just need to figure out what to say. I just don't know what to tell her, how to explain," she says so low that I have to strain to make out her words.

"Jenny, that's her job. She will help you through that part of it, but it's important that you're honest with her and keep seeing her. Would you like me to be with you?" I ask, knowing Chase will hit the roof if I ask to fly into the city right now, but ...

"No, I think it's something I need to work through with her on my own, but I appreciate the offer," she says.

"Okay then I'll call you a little later this evening and maybe by then we'll know more about how long we'll need to stay on lockdown," I say before disconnecting and firing up my mac.

I pull up the blueprints for the Las Vegas Prestian Corp facility. The outside will be an exact replica of the Chicago and New York sky-rises, but in the new facility we have the opportunity to create better adjacencies for departments, allowing workers to collaborate easier and more effectively. I am still reviewing the opportunity list identified by the survey provided to the current occupants of the Prestian Corp facilities when the swooshing sound from my phone alerts me to an incoming message.

Message: Where are you? You've been working all day.

Reply: Not exactly all day... I'm almost done, half an hour?

Message: Fair enough. Half an hour and if you are late I will pick the implement of my choosing.

Reply: I'm getting wet...

Message: I'll need to confirm this personally when I see you. Wear a dress.

I smile at his last message and hurriedly skim the rest of the document to ensure I didn't miss anything before heading to the shower. I finger the silver and diamond bracelets around my left wrist and clasp the diamond necklace Chase gave me after toweling off and slipping into black thigh highs with an adornment of lace, a slim black skirt, and a white button down blouse, allowing the first two buttons to remain open before sliding into the Jimmy Choo heels that buckle daintily around my ankles. I glance at the time again. Still five minutes to go. I take my time, applying a light lip gloss, a little shadow, eyeliner and spritz of the designer perfume we bought on our honeymoon. I glance at the incoming text and smile.

Message: You are now late.

Reply: It would appear that way...

Message: I'm looking forward to your long, slow torturous punishment.

I walk down the stairs and into the dining room and although engrossed in something on his phone, Chase looks up the moment I enter the doorway. He stands and comes to take my hand. "You look absolutely stunning this evening," he says, his gaze skimming over my body, heating my flesh with its intensity. The possessive placement of his hand on the small of my back, guiding me to the table, is such a small touch, but one that sends a shiver of anticipation through me.

"Cold, Baby?" he says, a glint of amusement in his eyes as he takes a seat next to me.

I shake my head, unsure of my voice at this very moment. "No?" he asks, eyebrows raised. "Nervous?"

"Maybe anxious," I whisper, finding my voice, glancing at the garden salad and roasted rack of lamb with a reddish-colored sauce drizzled over the top, baby potatoes and green beans and unsure how I will eat a bite.

"As you should be," he says, pouring us a glass of wine from the bottle on the table.

"Eat, it will help sustain your energy this evening and Gaby has prepared a new raspberry reduction for the lamb," he says.

I pick up my fork and cut into the tender meat, the delicious thickened raspberry sauce a perfect compliment to the delicately mild taste of the lamb. "It's very good," I say.

"I would agree, the dinner is excellent, but you seem a little nervous this evening."

"Maybe a little," I say, swallowing a sip of wine.

"Baby, your lateness was intentional," he says, reaching under my skirt, the side slit making it an easy task, brushing against my wetness.

I glance nervously around, straining to see if I can hear Gaby in the kitchen or elsewhere. "We are alone. Gaby will be spending the evening in her suite upstairs," he says as if reading my mind.

I take a few more bites of the buttery garlic and parmesan roasted potatoes and almond flavored green beans, and then absently push them around my plate. "You should eat, Baby, you need your energy," he says gently.

"I know, I'm not exactly hungry for food right now though," I say.

"Now that I've confirmed your wetness, Katarina, how did earlier make you feel? When you were restrained, completely helpless and your sweet little pussy was spanked?" he asks.

The heat rising up my neck and across my cheeks is uncontrollable and I feel myself moisten even more at his words. "I liked it, a lot," I say through my embarrassment.

"What did you like about it, exactly?" Chase instructs.

"The vulnerability of being restrained, I liked that you were fully dressed and I was nude, you in control, and getting spanked, the feel of the paddle, there," I say, looking up at him.

"Where is that, Baby? Say it again for me," he says.

"My pussy," I say, feeling the heat in my cheeks immediately.

"I like your flush and the glossiness of your eyes when you say that word for me," he says, pushing his finished plate aside and slipping his hand underneath my skirt, brushing against my folds, caressing me lightly.

"Are you finished with your dinner?" he asks, eyeing the few bites of potato and beans on my plate.

"I am, but you haven't had dessert," I say, sipping my wine, trying hard not to grind against him.

"I thought we may need a little sustenance after the evening and I have something else in mind for dessert."

"Hmm... Just what would that be?" I ask.

"Always so anxious and ready, but your restraint is much improved," he says, pushing against the erect nub he has created and causing me to stir against him.

"Oh, Baby, you moved, and you were doing so well," he says, his eyes alight with mischief.

"I want your hand where mine was, rub yourself just like I was doing," he says, taking my hand and placing it on my mound. "Caress yourself, Katarina," he instructs.

My breathing shallows as I do what he's asked, slipping my hands underneath my skirt. The act itself makes me feel wanton and naughty.

His eyes hold my gaze. "Don't stop," he says as I watch him clear the plates, taking them into the kitchen before he comes back for the glasses, making a second trip.

"Stand up now. It's impossible for me to see you rub your little pussy with your skirt in the way," he says, unzipping it and letting it fall to the floor. He holds my hands as I step out of the material, glancing around.

"Does the fact that we are in the middle of our dining room and your pussy is exposed to anyone that could walk in make you wet, Baby?" he asks, taking in my heels and thighs highs, caressing the soft lace around my thighs, before moving upward to my mound.

I can only nod. "Remove your blouse for me, but slowly. I love how your breasts are pushing against the material, nipples are erect, straining to be touched," he says, standing back slightly so he can watch as I do.

I begin to unfasten them, pausing between each button, watching his deep green eyes turn darker hazel. He trails his finger along the open path of exposed skin as I reach the bottom button and slide the material from my shoulders, letting my blouse slide to the floor.

"So pretty, Baby," he says, stroking my nipples. They are erect and more sensitive than usual, straining against the black lacy material of my bra. In one fluid movement he has opened the front clasp, but takes his time exposing my breasts to the air in the room. He kisses the tips of each nipple lightly and then uses his tongue to caress each one in turn. He reaches behind my hair and releases the necklace, sliding it's roughness over the curve of my breasts before pocketing it, walking me backward until my body reaches the edge of the table.

"I've waited for this part of the meal all evening, Baby," he says, picking me up and placing me deftly on the table. He pushes my legs apart so that he can stand in between them and kisses me gently, a soft provocative kiss, slow and stimulating.

He takes the necklace from out of his pocket, letting it dangle in one hand as he continues rubbing my nipples. I feel it deep in my core, my breath shallow knowing what he intends. "So beautiful and erect," he says, placing one of the clamps on my swollen and sensitive nipple, causing me to moan aloud.

"Shh. . . Baby..." he says, placing the other one, letting the weight of the silver and diamond chain pull at the sensitive buds, allowing me to acclimate to the pressure and the desire it builds.

"Lay back, feel the coolness of the table against your naked body," he says, assisting me, sliding me forward until my knees are comfortably at the end of the table supporting my weight. "Now, I do believe I have waited long enough for dessert," he says, spreading my legs widely, raking his eyes over my body as he runs his thumb gently across my clit, caressing me.

My body has a mind of its own and I am powerless as my hips rise up to meet his touch. "Still Baby, I plan to enjoy my dessert very slow, savoring its sweetness and if you cum or move I will add another swat to the intense spanking I plan to give you tonight," he says, causing my core to clench with anticipation as he caresses me lightly with his tongue. I moan softly, calming myself enough to remain still.

He is slow, deliberately hitting that delicious spot each and every time, building my desire, stroke after stroke, while the sweet pain of the clamps continues fueling my need, sending waves of pleasure throughout my core. I try not to move, but I am struggling, at the brink of climax. "Chase," I moan audibly, my legs shaking.

"Let me hear you, Baby," he says, as I move from side to side, trying to escape the extreme pleasure his tongue is creating. The tug of the necklace pulls the clamps to the edge of my nipples, setting them on fire and igniting my core. "Honey," I moan softly as the exquisite feeling begins to build deep inside of me. "Hush Baby, let your body feel that," he says before taking my clit into his mouth and tugging lightly at the end of the necklace. The pain in my nipples sends an intense desire to my core and I am helpless to the rise in my hips. "Baby, you're so wet and sweet, but you weren't supposed to move," he says, licking me until I am sure I will explode.

"Not yet, Baby," he says, unzipping himself, pulling me to the edge of the table, raising my legs over his shoulders and plunging deep inside of me.

"Chase, you're so deep," I moan, willing myself to remain still, but desperately wanting to raise up to meet him thrust for thrust.

"If you move, I will paddle you harder and won't allow you to cum," he says and his words both excite and frustrate me, causing me to moan as he drives in deeper. "Quiet Baby, take control, don't cum," he instructs, as he continues to sink into me, pulling my body onto his as he explodes inside of me.

He pulls out of me and assists me up, pulling me against him, kissing me passionately. "You showed amazing restraint, Baby. Now let me show you the real pleasures of patience and anticipation," he says, carrying me from the table onto the elevators and into our room.

"Stay here," he says setting me down gently, walking towards the closet and returning with a pillow of sorts.

"What's that?" I ask, eyeing it suspiciously as he pulls the covers to the foot of the bed and positions the cushiony looking thing in the center of the mattress.

"I want you to lay over the top of the pillow. It will ensure you are comfortable and that your ass is on display for me while I spank you. Let's take these off before you turn over though, Baby. Inhale deeply," he instructs.

I do and at the same moment he removes the clamps, it sends a spike of desire right through me. I moan as he takes my nipples between his fingers, squeezing, slowly allowing the blood to flow back into them, watching me, knowing his touch has a straight line to my core before assisting me onto the bed.

"Tonight you are going to learn how intense and erotic delayed gratification can be. Tell me how turned on you are right now?" he asks.

"Very," I moan as he releases my bracelets and extends my arms over my head before securing me to the headboard.

"I think this will do," he says, traveling down my body and securing my ankles as well.

"Honey," I moan.

"Since it was my turn to pick out the paddle and it was clear you were late intentionally, I thought you may be ready for something a little more intense than what we've done in the past," he says, stepping in front of me so that I can look at his implement of choice. It is long, wooden and intimidating. I swallow, my need becoming heated and I will myself to get my breathing in sync.

"Baby, your breathing has become shallow and low, I want you to take a deep breath, inhale now," he instructs and I do, filling my lungs with oxygen.

"Now slowly exhale," he says.

It is challenging to take my eyes off the paddle, my body's desires taking over and making it difficult for me to focus on anything else. The rectangular length of the wooden paddle, similar to the one we've used in the past, but a little longer will cover the expanse of both cheeks with no problem. My ass is lifted in the air, on display to him.

"Katarina, you have the power. Do you still want to play?" he says.

"I do, very much," I whisper without hesitation as he walks behind me.

He swipes a finger underneath me, entering me. "Baby, you're absolutely soaked," he says. "I'm going to spank you and this is going to be more intense than you have ever felt. I want you to tell me if it you want to stop, Katarina," he says and I nod my affirmation.

"Honey, I want this so bad," I say, my voice strained by my own desire.

"Very good, Baby," he says, trailing a finger down the length of my spine, over my ass cheek and my thigh. "We are going to start and I want you to count with me," he says.

I nod my affirmation and the sting of the paddle comes down, square across my ass cheeks. It is harder than at any time before and my core clenches deliciously right before the next one is delivered, and a third and fourth. The smarting on my cheeks causes an overwhelming desire between my legs, deep inside. I push my ass in the air and am rewarded with three more succinct paddles to the ass leaving me needy and desperate for release. I moan audibly. "Baby, I need to hear how you are doing," Chase says.

"I'm so close, Honey," I say, before another three paddles come down, one by one, causing me to squirm and to raise my ass to the extent my restraints allow.

I feel the weight of his body as he positions behind me. "I want you to cum with me this time, " he says, sliding his rigid cock into me, pushing deep inside of me, over and over, holding me on the brink, the tidal wave building, rising and then his command, "Cum for me, Katarina," and I am helpless, trembling around his cock, clutching his girth inside of me as we both find our release, helpless to stop the violent shuddering that overtakes us. He releases my ankles and reaches up to free my wrists, pulling me into his arms, both of us reveling in the aftermath.

"You're still breathing so hard, Baby," he says, whispering into my ear, causing goose bumps to form along my arms.

THIRTEEN

"Mmm... it was so good," I say, pushing against him to snuggle in even closer, enjoying the feel of him inside of me for a few more moments, before he slips out of me and turns me toward him.

"How did that make you feel?" he says, pushing the long curls out my eyes.

"Vulnerable, submissive, wet and wanting to do it again. It's everything I thought it would be except..."

"Except?"

"I have a feeling you still took it pretty easy on me, I mean don't get me wrong it smarted, but, well, you know what I mean," I say, trying to control my blush.

"My goal was to punish you, push you to control your climax for as long as you could, not to hurt you physically," he says, kissing my lips.

"It was perfect, Chase. I am slowly greatly beginning to appreciate delayed gratification and developing some restraint. I realize what a gift it is now," I say, grinning.

"I could tell by your breathing, the way you were trying not to push back but couldn't control your body's desire. It was amazing to watch, Baby," he says.

"I'm still not sure how I would feel if you were actually to deprive me," I say, blushing as I recall one of our previous conversations about punishments.

"Well, then let's make sure that level of punishment does not become necessary," he says, his eyes alight with challenge.

I begin to say something but his phone vibrates. "It's your dad. We should take this," he says, kissing me lightly on the lips before answering the incoming call. "This is Chase," he says, sliding up so that he is sitting against the headboard of our bed before pulling me against him and engaging the speaker.

"Hi Chase. Just wanted you to know everything's set. Jay's team has been working day and night to gather the necessary intel on Alfreita's whereabouts and that of the Interpol operatives his family works with. Greatly appreciate you allowing the team's support," he says.

"Yes, of course. Jay's been keeping me informed on that front. It appears Alfreita may be holding something over each of the three department heads."

"Sounds like Alfreita has documents and photos of them taking money to look the other way on multiple drug shipments, that and a few little romps their wives may not want to see," Carlos says.

I look up, meeting Chase's gaze. The guilt about keeping what's going on from my mother stabs at my heart. "Yeah, his modus operandi. Look what he did to the men in Miami," Chase says.

"I won't allow Karissa to live in fear or my father's legacy to disappear," Carlos says.

"Carlos, you know this is as personal to me as it is to you," Chase says, pulling me closer as he speaks.

"How is Karissa? Do you want me to have someone pick her up and fly her to stay with us?" Chase asks.

"I'd like nothing better actually, but she's working with a couple new clients and was adamant about staying at the estate. I talked to your dad earlier and he'll keep an eye out for her. I think she's a little excited about having some dedicated alone time to get their marketing plans laid out. I've had my team increase the perimeter patrol and overall security everywhere, but I would appreciate it if you keep Jay in constant contact with them."

"Consider it done. Jay gave me the update on the plans from the airport to the estate, the perimeter control and eyes on the inside," Chase says.

"Yeah, the cameras Jay's team used last time are in place and they just had to send a link to reengage them. I'd like to steal that young man away from you," he says.

"Not a chance of that, but I'll have him take care of things," Chase says, his jaw tightening.

"I'll text you before I leave, but once we're out of the compound I'll use the secure lines," he says.

"Sounds good," Chase says, looking down at me and raising his eyebrows.

I shake my head. Carlos clearly would not have wanted me to hear the conversation, was not aware I was on the line, and I wouldn't know what to say to him at this point. My mind is focused on pulling the pieces of conversation together as they wrap up their call. My mother will be alone, Don is aware and will be keeping his eyes on her. I'm not sure what that means as they live at least ten miles away from each other north of New York City. Jay will be heavily involved in the security, but something about the conversation nags at my conscience.

"Are you okay, Katarina?" Chase says, lifting my chin so that my eyes are forced to return his gaze. The depth of emotion I see in his eyes causes me to swallow hard.

"I'm not sure. I can't even describe how I feel about my mother not knowing any of what's going on and my inability to tell her. She doesn't have any idea where he's going, perhaps she thinks he's going off to a fun little business trip," I say, hating the sarcastic tone of my voice.

"Baby, he's trying to keep her sheltered."

"And what if he doesn't come home? What if something happens and she never had the opportunity to say I love you for the last time? What if... " I start, but he silences my protests with a passionate and powerful kiss.

The urgency of his mouth on mine takes me away, helps me refocus, and brings me back to the now. "Chase," I moan, straining against him, clasping my arms around his neck, holding him close to me.

"Baby, do you know how much you mean to me? Your mother means that much to Carlos. You can't imagine the sheer desire that he or I have to keep our families safe and we will do that at any cost. Do you understand, Katarina?" he asks, lifting my chin to his.

I nod, returning his kiss as he captures my lips once again, pulling me into his arms, wrapping me in his embrace. I entwine my legs against him and try to leave the conversation in the recesses of my mind. Something keeps creeping into the surface of my memory. "Baby," he says, kissing my neck, slowly working his way down its side..

I murmur in response, but then sit straight up in bed, taking us both by surprise. "What did he mean by the cameras Jay's team used last time are in place?" I ask, leaning my back against the headboard, pulling the sheet up to cover my nakedness.

He sighs and slides up beside me and puts his arm around me.

"Tell me, Chase." I say, turning to look him in the eyes.

He sighs again. "There were cameras set up before you entered Vicenti's estate, Katarina. You flew halfway across the world to talk to one of the biggest crime lords in the world and expect me not to do anything I could to protect you?" he says, running a hand through his hair.

"It was my fault we didn't have enough security in place to prevent you and my father from getting ambushed. I had to go."

"We've been over this. It was not your fault and I'll be damned if you'll continue to harbor that kind of guilt or I apologize for wanting to protect you. The only way I could make certain that my team could intervene if they needed to was to have the cameras installed before you got there," he says.

"How? You didn't even know where we would be. I mean seriously, you were in a jail cell when I went to meet with him, and Jay was in the hospital. Does your reach have no limits?"

He lifts his eyebrows at the question. "Katarina, I'm never going to allow you to be in harm's way. I've not made that a secret."

"No, but I didn't know you had cameras set up watching me," I say.

"Protecting you," he corrects.

"Fine, but how did you get them into his compound? The place was locked down like Fort Knox. Armed guards everywhere," I say.

"Let's discuss something else. How about the leg trick? I must have rerun that part of the video more than a hundred times."

I swallow, recalling the need to distract Vicenti, keep his penetrating gaze from seeing through my guise.

"He was starting to intimidate me, I needed a moment to clear my head and..."

"Shift the balance of control. In one small movement you completely threw his intent to intimidate you off course, and ensured that you had the upper hand for the conversation," Chase says.

"I'm not sure about that," I say.

"Baby, while I have to admit seeing red when I saw his desire for you pass over his eyes, you were impressive."

"Chase, it was nothing. A spur of the moment thing to distract him," I say.

"Katarina, nothing about the trip or that meeting was not thought out on your part, except perhaps intel and more in-depth security precautions that my team took care of."

"I'm not sure I know what you mean by that," I say, wishing the conversation had not shifted from him and my father to me.

"All of your clothes were hand selected by you. Seductive, hot, my ring on your finger, all intended to portray a certain image at the time they were needed. You anticipated that need and were prepared for it when it arose," Chase says.

"You give me too much credit, Chase. I never put that much thought into it. I seriously didn't have the time," I say.

"It comes instinctively, Baby," he says, gently kissing my lips, capturing my tongue gently with his own, allowing us to savor each other without rush. I experience the familiar tightening of my nipples underneath the cool satin sheets, but we are disrupted by his phone.

"Sorry, Baby, I need to take this," he says, looking at me as if he wants to say something else. Instead, he gets out of bed completely nude, pulling on a pair of lounge pants and nothing else as he listens to the caller and heads downstairs, presumably to his study.

I am left alone with my thoughts about what has transpired over the course of the last couple days, but I push it aside, needing to hear Jenny's voice.

I hit her contact button and she answers within a few rings.

"Hi," I say.

"Hi Kate. I figured it would be you," she says.

"Of course, your daily pain in the ass," I say.

There is a pregnant pause on the phone and I wrestle with the need to fill the void with conversation or just allow the silence. I will my restraint, counting inside of my head, but the mere moments feel like hours. "Ty was at the grand opening," she says, finally.

I audibly let out the breath I had been holding hoping that she did not hear it. "That's what I understand, Jenny. I'm so sorry," I say.

"He threatened me, said a lot of vulgar stuff and well... anyway, I guess it just brought it all to the forefront again," she says.

"Was your counselor able to come over this afternoon?"

"Yeah, Brian had his men disguise her to get her into the building. The entire sky-rise is surrounded with paparazzi after all the pictures last night," she says.

"Just glad she was able to see you. Did you have a good discussion?" I ask.

"Yeah, it was the longest and best session we've ever had. She needs to see me a few more times and run some other tests, but she thinks I may have post traumatic stress syndrome," she says, her voice barely above a whisper.

"Jenny, after what you went through that would make complete sense," I say, recalling her split lip and the harsh marks on her skin, evidence of the way she had fought against the ropes of her captor.

"She says that it can cause you to crawl into a shell of your own, pull away from the people that love you and cause you to become emotionally detached," she says.

"Jenny that all makes complete sense. The sleeplessness and night-mares after it happened," I say.

"Yeah, she said that seeing Ty and hearing his voice may have been a trigger and it could have all come flooding back. My mind may not have been able to cope with it so I just shut it out and well, you know the rest," she says.

"I am so sorry. I contacted your mom when you were missing. She loves you so much and is really worried," I say.

"Yeah, she's been leaving messages. I called her after Dr. Worthing left to let her know that I was okay. She said you told her I was dealing with some stuff and that I may not be able to talk about it for a bit. Thanks for doing that, Kate," she says.

I can hear the shallow breathing and the quiet sobbing that she is trying to cover up and my heart breaks for my best friend. "You know I'm here for you. Anything you need, Jenny," I say.

"Thanks Kate. I hate to ask, but I need a little time away to work through this. I know you have a million things on your plate and are dealing with the Alfreita thing, but…"

"Jenny, anything. Just tell me what you need," I say.

"If I have my emails redirected would you be willing to take care of things?"

"Of course, you copy me on just about everything that goes on. I'm happy to assist. Please don't worry about Torzial. Everything's going well with the medical facilities and the new site for Prestian Corp in Vegas is going on schedule. Redirect the emails and I'll take care of things until you return."

"I don't know how to thank you. There's just no one else that I could ask or trust with the business," she says.

"It's not a problem at all, Jenny. You would do the same if the situation was reversed," I say.

"You're such a good friend," she says.

So, Brian told you what's going on with Alfreita?" I ask, hoping to get her attention on something less troubling for her.

"A little. Brian said we have to stay here because his penthouse has a safe room and no one can guarantee my safety if I were to leave and go home. He told me that Alftreita's after any of the family members or people close to Carlos or Chase that he can get his hands on," she says.

"I'm so sorry that you have to deal with this on top of everything else that you're dealing with, but glad you're with Brian and safe," I say, restraining the multitude of questions I have about their relationship.

"It's okay, I've actually been able to sleep a little lately," she says, and I hear the repressed yawn on the other end of the phone.

"Jenny, why don't you get some rest? I'll call you tomorrow and we can talk more then. In the meantime, if you need anything, anything at all, call or text me," I say.

"I will Kate. Thanks for checking on me," she says before discon-necting.

I pull on a pair of leggings and a sweatshirt and forego the bra recalling Chase's mention that Gaby is spending the night in her room. I slip into multi-colored merino wool socks before heading downstairs to find Chase, anxious to give him an update on Jenny. At the end of the stairs, I stop at his study, checking to see if there is a light or voices coming from beyond the door, but there is not.

I head into the spacious kitchen, ravenous. The light above the stove allows me to find my way over to the counter without turning the large overheads on. The space is adorned with Viking and Subzero appliances and equipped to handle meals for Big Brothers and Sisters, Boy Scouts of America, and whatever other entertainment that Chase wants to do in the lakefront community. I look around at the vastness, feeling small and overwhelmed at the situation swirling around me, the danger, the unknown.

I open the refrigerator. Gaby has labeled a clear glass container with, "Dill Soup.. Heat 2 minutes in the microwave. Next to the bowl is a stoneware pie dish that has been covered with plastic wrap and affixed with a label. "One piece, one and a half minutes in the microwave, one scoop of ice cream," the notes says. Comfort food, it's what we can use tonight.

I pull out the pie dish and am reaching overhead to get dishes out of the cupboard when at the same time he puts his arms around me from behind. "I was just getting you dessert," I say, pulling the stoneware from the cabinet.

"I was just trying to decide what I want, a piece of pie or that luscious little ass of yours," he says, rubbing up against me.

I turn around and look up and into his smiling green eyes, full of mischief. "You've already had that," I say.

"Are you saying no?"

"No, but aren't you hungry?" I ask at the same time my stomach growls.

"Actually yes, and you obviously need to eat something," he says.

"I hate to admit it but I think you're right. I'm absolutely starving,"

I say, turning to place a generous helping of pie on each of our plates as he reaches into the freezer for ice cream.

"The note on the dish said one scoop," I say, laughing at the ginormous servings on our plates.

"Shh... it will be our little secret," he says as we sit down at the small round table in the corner and begin digging into the apple crumble pie. The cinnamon mixed with nutmeg, melded with the slightest hint of lemon juice complement the apple mixture and the crisp brown sugar topping makes it absolutely scrumptious.

I look up and Chase is watching me. "What, it's so good," I say, smiling back at his infectious grin.

"Just glad to see you eating, that's all," he says, taking another bite of his pie.

"I know, I've been so worried about Jenny. She said Ty threatened her at the opening and after that she must have just blocked everything out. Her counselor came today and it was a good session, much longer than normal. It may be post traumatic stress syndrome," I say.

"I know, Baby. Brian's been keeping me posted this afternoon too, and he's taking good care of her," he says.

"Did he say what's going on with that? I couldn't bring myself to ask and she seemed comfortable where she is. Says she's sleeping a little bit," I say.

"No, just that he had it under control. Brian's a good man. Whatever's going on with them, he'll take good care of her until we can get Alfreita out of the picture," he says, placing our dishes in the sink and leading me upstairs to our room for the night.

I WAKE in the morning to my phone alarm, scowling, turning it off and groaning at the seven-thirty a.m. time. I slip out of bed, jumping into the shower quickly washing and towel drying before sliding into my robe while I attempt to at least dry some of my thick hair before heading to the closet. I have Skype calls scheduled and while just on video conference and not in person, I decide to slide into a grey, patterned pair of thigh highs that end with little pearls and lace that outline my thigh, a slim skirt, and sweater. The nylons are a gift from Chase and feel like butter against my skin. I slip on a pair of black lacy panties and matching bra, pulling the sweater on before I reach for my skirt. Gaby is in the kitchen and looks up when I enter. "Hi, Chase is already working. Would you like a bite to eat now or want to wait?" she asks, knowing I'm not a morning person normally.

"Actually, I'm absolutely ravenous," I say, feeling my cheeks warm with the memories of last night.

"Chase asked me to make you a hearty meal," she says kindly, handing me a plate with an English muffin and a healthy topping of mango slices, blackberries and blueberries.

"It looks wonderful," I say, opening the muffin to reveal the layer of Egg Beaters and provolone.

"You made a breakfast sandwich with Egg Beaters. That was so nice of you," I say, touched by her caring.

"You need your proteins with all your running and I know your aversion to eggs," she says, sashaying to the kitchen counter.

"Thank you, Gaby. It's absolutely delicious," I say, taking a bite of the muffin sandwich.

"It's an absolute pleasure. You make an incredible difference in his life. You are good for that young man," Gaby says, winking at me.

"Thank you. I love him so much," I say, taking a few more bites.

"Oh, the feeling is mutual sweet girl. He can't take his eyes or mind off of you," she says.

"I thought he would be down here for breakfast, where is he?"

"Caught up with business in his study," she says, rolling her eyes upward.

"Can you make a plate for him?" I ask.

"Love to," she says before sliding a plate piled high to the center of the breakfast nook.

"Thank you, now to find my husband," I say, heading towards his office with breakfast in tow.

I open the door and he is concentrated on the monitor in front of him and looks up as I walk in. "Morning, come sit by me," he says, letting his eyes roam over my outfit, finally settling back to my eyes.

"Katarina, while you know that I want to keep you sheltered from anything ugly, you have a right to know, to understand what it is we are navigating and what harm may lay in wait for us. No more secrets, it ends here," he says, hitting the button to connect the flashing light and incoming call while still on mute.

"What you are about to hear is to be held in the strictest of confidence, the conversation is untraceable, overseen by the most powerful intel units in the business. I obviously have clearance and they will be unable to tell that you are with me. Saying that, it means you won't be able to comment on the conversation, only listen. Are you okay with that?" he asks, lifting my chin so that my eyes have no escape.

"Yes, I just appreciate you letting me hear it for myself," I say, kissing him soundly on the mouth. A brief connection, meant to convey how much it means to me that he trusts me with this information.

His control dissolves and my lips are captured by his own, his passion soaring into a fever, evidenced by the way his tongue captures my own, imprisoning it, leading them through a well orchestrated dance, tongue on tongue, tongues on lips, lips capturing lips, before ending, finalizing our pact with a playful bite to my lower lip as the speakerphone engages and my father's voice permeates through the room.

I straighten, and look at the speakerphone on the desk, the flashing light alerting us to the fact that they are unable to hear us. "Chase, we've got everyone on the line," my father begins.

"Thanks, Carlos. On this end you know we have intel monitoring the conversation for any disruptions in security. Jay the floor is all yours," Chase says.

"As we discussed yesterday we've learned a great deal about the hold Alfreita currently has over three men, all in senior positions of Interpol. Things progressed nicely last night and we now have interventions in place to counteract the blackmail of said members. I won't go into detail, but suffice it to say that we should have this rectified within the week. In the interim, let's just say they will be cooperative while maintaining appearances of alliance to Alfreita."

I am watching Chase. He is listening, but I know nothing being reported out has not already been reviewed and cleared by him.

"Carlos, Vicenti is not aware of this. While we wanted to make sure you knew the concerns were mitigated, we don't want to share that bit of information just yet," Jay says.

"Great work, Jay. Of course I'll keep that in the strictest of confidence. Any news on the family front?" Carlos asks.

"Yes, but I would feel better if we were farther along. We've picked up communications from your two youngest brothers. They've been in constant contact with your uncle in Italy. It appears he is concerned about family name, the reputation, the Cosa Nostra if you will," Jay says.

I glance up at Chase, recalling the word from the research I did on my father, but his eyes are hooded and controlled giving nothing away. Cosa Nostra, a term used by the Sicilian Mafia. The Italian family members still working together, residing over different villages and territories.

"This should be of no concern to him. The work Vicenti and I will discuss has nothing to do with the Italian family, a few simple shared investments, but easily dissolved. Keep intel on them, but if everything goes as planned we'll reach an agreement with Vicenti," Carlos says.

Chase hits the mute button to engage in the conversation. "Carlos, you and I both know those ties run deep and everything is intertwined. I've asked Jay to expand surveillance and communications ops in that area so you know what you're up against."

My father is not to be deterred. "We're moving forward, with or without a family blessing. Next I'd like to go over the security plans," Carlos says, dismissing the conversation.

"Carlos, we've got the arrangements all set. Your plane will leave shortly and will touch down in Brazil at approximately nine p.m. Brazil time, just shortly after six our time. We'll have the helicopter waiting. It will take you to Vicenti's home on the coast for the meeting at ten tonight. You know the late hour is intended to mitigate potential observers and air traffic. We only have a short window of time where air traffic records can be altered," Jay says.

"Jay, I assume your security team has taken all precautions, communications and visuals are in place, clearances have been completed?" Chase says.

"Yes, everything is in place and working well. They've already completed a sweep of the compound and none of our monitoring systems were picked up," Jay says.

"Very good. Carlos, I don't have any other questions for you or the group. Give me a call once the conference has concluded," Chase says, disconnecting.

"So, what is it that he and Vicenti are planning that my great-uncle doesn't like?" I ask.

"See, you are just too smart for your own good, Baby. These details, they need to come from Carlos. When the timing is right he'll go over everything with you. I owe it to him to let him tell you himself," he says, kissing my lips lightly.

"I have more questions than answers now," I say.

"The answers will come in time, for now just know that everyone is working to keep our family and friends safe and to put Alfreita behind us."

"I don't doubt that for one moment. It's just hard that I can't talk with my mom and I hate that she's in the dark but I do understand. I need to get a little work done. I told Jenny I would help her out with a few things," I say, intentionally leaving out the fact that I will be overseeing Torzial until her return. A conversation best left for another day with everything going on.

"Jay and I have some work to finish. Let's plan to meet for dinner and hopefully by that time your dad will be on his way back to the States," he says.

"Sounds good," I say, relieved that he is clearly distracted with whatever work he and Jay need to get done and I will have a chance to get a handle on Torzial affairs in Jenny's absence. "I think I'll work in the library," I say.

"Good, and remember to eat lunch," he says, kissing my lips gently before turning to leave. "Oh, and Katarina, only the necessary work," he says, his voice low, threatening, and seductive all at once, taking on the characteristics of the dominant man I love in the bedroom and the one that keeps me challenged and impassioned by day.

"I'll let you know how long once I sign on and determine how much time it will take and I'll be sure to let you know which implement you should use if it's going to be much past six p.m.," I say, looking at the clock on the wall.

"Baby, you need only be one minute past that time and I will show you exactly what happens, but the implement will be of my own choosing this time," he says, walking out of the room, leaving me moist, filled with anticipation and a growing desire to disobey him.

FOURTEEN

I head into the library, glad to see the fire is crackling with fresh logs and the blanket is still laying on the overstuffed reading chair. I take the laptop from the desk and enter in the password to get through the security servers and snuggle in to get started.

I quickly skim my emails, responding to some and deleting or saving others, leaving the one requesting me to redline the detailed designs until the end. The changes outlined will generate more space for collaborative areas that will be equipped with video conferencing abilities to align with the way future work will be done globally. I have a few more closing notes after a couple hours and send it back to the designers and copy Chase, Brian, and Jenny.

The swoosh of my phone is almost immediate.

Message: Glad to see you are almost finished. Design notes look great.

Reply: Thx! But, not finished.

Message: You have three simple rules to follow.

Reply: Where's the fun in that?

Message: Seeing your ass redden and pussy moisten will give me great pleasure.

I shake my head slightly, trying to hide the smile that threatens and open the new folder that has been created which now contains all of Jenny's email correspondence. I audibly gasp at the amount of email that is currently marked unread. Almost a hundred emails that have not been opened since the evening before the grand opening.

I slowly begin making my way through them, deleting the ones that I have been copied on. "Damn, that only takes care of a quarter of them," I say aloud, tucking my feet under myself and creating a makeshift laptop table with the blanket in front of me, quickly becoming engrossed in reading emails about aspects of the Torzial corporation. I walk my way through those, ensuring the managers of the different divisions are included in replies. I click on the next message and stop short. It is from Ty, received the day after the Prestian Corp grand opening in Los Angeles.

DEAR JENNY,

You appeared a little ashen at last evening's festivities. Perhaps a little too much to drink or were you thinking about something in particular? Perhaps the special night we shared? I sincerely hope that is the case and if so that you continue to dream about that every night until I can repay you for all the joy you have brought me and we can be together again. Until then your secret about Torzial is safe with me.

Yours always, Ty

I AM COLD, fear and anxiety for my friend grips me and sends goosebumps down my spine. I read it again, slowly this time, absorbing the evil malice of its intent and physically shiver. I send it to myself, unsure at this point what to do with it, uncertain if deleting it from her email account will impact evidence if needed later. I leave it on her email praying that she doesn't see it until I can talk to Chase.

I try to refocus and flip to the next email when Gaby's voice comes over the intercom. "I was waiting for you to come for lunch. Shall I bring you a chicken salad croissant?" she asks.

"I'm so sorry. I was absorbed in work and didn't realize it was so late. I can come out and get my own sandwich," I say.

"Nonsense, I'll bring it in shortly," she says over the speaker.

I am just contemplating this when the sound of my phone alerts me to an incoming message.

Message: Missed lunch, broken rules, so many possibilities.

Reply: Was absorbed in what I was doing. Eating shortly.

My response goes unanswered and for a moment my mind conjures up all kinds of possibilities for the night.

I am getting near to the end of the Torzial emails when I see an email from my dad.

DEAR MS. TORZIAL,

The Vegas properties we discussed last week are in the process of being purchased. Once complete, we would like to move forward with the development of four of the largest and most impressive casinos and hotels Vegas has ever seen. Please contact my assistant at your earliest convenience.

Thanks,

Carlos Larussio

I PULL up Google Maps and hone in on the location of the future Prestian Corp towers in Vegas and that of the Larussio properties named in the attached pending sales agreement. Neighbors, literally adjacent properties in the most sought after block on the strip. I shake my head, letting the information that my father and Chase have literally purchased a block of land in the most prestigious part of the strip sink in, along with the complexity of the agreements and demolition requirements of the existing properties.

I look up as Gaby walks in with a small tray. "Just a light lunch," she tuts as she lays the plate of fruit, chicken salad croissant, and a glass of water on the table.

A couple hours later, almost to the end of the documents my father has sent, I am duly impressed with the proposal laid out for the

Larussio investments in Vegas. I Google Larussio and am in awe of the information that comes up. I read on, fascinated by the family history, which can be traced back hundreds of years in Sicily and now creates a mark of its own in New York, Chicago, Philadelphia, Vegas and Los Angeles. I glance up at the clock on the wall and grab my cell as the swoosh of a text captures my attention.

Message: Almost finished?

Reply: Not quite. The Larussio history has my interest.

Message: You were googling your family?

Reply: Yeah, it's interesting.

I wait for a reply, but there is none, only the dead silence of the phone in front of me until finally a text pops up.

Message: Meet me in my study. Your dad will be connecting shortly.

I hastily close my laptop and lay it on the side table, shimmy out of the blanket that has been covering me most of the afternoon, and take off toward his study.

"She won't be going within a thousand feet of him in this life if I have my say," Chase says, his eyes locked on me as I enter.

"I'm not asking her to be anywhere near Alfreita, only to answer questions if they are asked in the future," my father says.

"What does that mean exactly?" I say, closing the door behind me, sizing up the conversation, my father's voice all of a sudden quiet and Chase ready to do battle if needed.

"Katarina," Chase says, taking my hand, leading me to the loveseat that sits adjacent to the mahogany desk in the office. I look away, out at the view, taking comfort in the heavy snow accumulating in between the branches of the pines, creating a natural privacy fence on this side of the home.

"I need to know what's happening," I say, turning back toward my husband and the speakerphone that has gone silent.

"You do need to know, but I'm going to let your father explain," Chase says, eyeing the telephone in the middle of the conference table.

"Dad?" I say, walking towards it, "tell me."

"Is it not enough that I am on my way home and will take care of this once I arrive in the States?" he says.

"Take care of what? Tell me, Dad!"

"Chase, I trust that you will take care of my daughter and anything else that needs attention," Carlos says.

"Dammit Carlos. You know I will, but tell us what the fuck is going on. You cut all ..." Chase says.

"Enough!" Carlos bellows through the phone. "I'm trusting you and Don to take care of things. In the interim, I'm taking the next flight out, and for the record Vicenti is more than interested in buying the business out, but not until we get the family under control."

"Carlos, we can discuss it when you get home," Chase says, at the same time Jay walks into the room, motioning Chase and pushing the mute button. "Keep him talking, we need three more minutes," Jay says, releasing the mute button.

"Carlos, there's one thing that's been on my mind that I need to tell you about," Chase says.

"Chase, I need to get on the fucking plane," my father says impatiently.

"Carlos, I need to give you a heads up about the Vegas properties," Chase says.

"Nothing can go wrong with those, Chase. You know that's the Larussio family's future," he says.

"Carlos, we'll work everything out, but you need to know that we're getting some serious push back on the properties. Someone is attempting to block state approvals," Chase says.

"Dammit! Thanks for letting me know Chase. We'll talk when I get home, but right now I need to get in the air," he says, as Jay gives Chase the thumbs up and Carlos disconnects.

"Jay, what the fuck is going on?" Chase says.

"You were right about Carlos. As soon as he got to Vicenti's he cut all eyes and ears from the devices we had fitted on him. Fortunately, he didn't know about the plants we had on the property. The teams are pulling the feeds together as we speak and I'll have something to share with you shortly," Jay says.

I look at Chase and then Jay. "So the same recording methods you used when I went to see Vicenti?" I ask.

Jay looks to Chase uneasily. "Jay, it's fine. She knows we had surveillance in place when she was in Brazil."

"Sorry, Kate. We couldn't let you go in there without protection," Jay says.

"It's fine. I really appreciate the fact that you were there for me even when you were still in ICU. I need to know what's going on with my father. My mother is at home completely oblivious. My heart is hurting for her right now," I say.

"Just a moment," Jays says, holding his hand up, signaling that he's listening into a call on his headset.

"Send in air support, do it now!" he says, walking toward the panoramic window that at this time overlooks nothing but late afternoon duskiness settling around the property. "Chase, we've got the Augusta circling, trying to keep a clear path for Carlos to the airport."

"Whatever it takes," Chase says.

"Shit, Chase, we just received a shots fired message- they're taking on fire. Shots out team," he yells into the mic hanging low from his headset.

"Update," Chase says almost immediately.

"Chase, safe room! Let us take care of this. Stay on the burner," Jay says.

"Dammit," Chase explodes, taking my hand and leading me toward the kitchen where Gaby is bent over reading a cookbook.

"We're heading downstairs. Tell us what you need," Chase says to her.

"Let's move. You know I'm prepared for anything. You think that refrigerator downstairs isn't stocked just in case you give the say so?" she says.

He smiles and kisses the top of her hair. "Excellent, let's move," he says, leading the two of us down the main elevators. We enter the safe room, which is an exact duplicate of the floor above. "If you'll excuse me, I'll be in the kitchen," Gaby says, sashaying out of the spacious living room.

"Chase, tell me what's happening," I say, sitting on the soft taupe leather sectional that is an exact replica of the one upstairs.

"Katarina, you know as much as I do right now. Something turned sideways, I need to talk to your dad, but you heard Jay. He's under fire, Jay's doing everything that he can to get him out of there.

"Chase, Jenny's texting me. She said Brian's making her go into the safe room with him."

"It's for their own protection. My father and Emily's family have been moved, too. Jenny's family will also be rounded up and protected," he says, pushing a strand of hair out of my eyes.

"Why is it that you know this but Jay didn't mention it?" I ask.

"Baby, it's standard protocol. Our family and friends are on the list that I review with Jay routinely," Chase says.

"Everything planned out in advance just in case shit happens. I am so thankful that you are the biggest fucking control freak in the universe," I say, shaking my head.

"Baby, nothing is left to chance where you or our loved ones are concerned. I've told you that and I'm never going to apologize if that's what you're looking for," he says, tilting my chin so my eyes meet his own.

"Chase, I'm not looking for an apology. I trust you with my life and that of my family," I murmur, caught up in the tenseness of the moment.

He nods, but picks up the ringing phone and listens for a few moments to the person on the other end. "Dammit, make sure there's a plan to infiltrate communications so we know what's going on and get him home safe!" he says, before placing the phone into his pocket.

"What happened?"

"The helicopter crew turned back. Fortunately Jay anticipated that Alfreita may have a watch on your dad's movements and had enough fire power in the air to disrupt their plan. Unfortunately, your family in Italy is involved. Your father will need to fill you in on all the details, but what you need to know from me is that if it comes down to Jay giving the order to take anyone out that harms Carlos and your family in Italy, he has my order to take care of Carlos. Jay's certain he cut all communications to ensure his uncle's family wouldn't learn about his plan for Vegas."

"Thank you," I say, wrapping myself in the warmth of my own arms to ward off the bone chilling fear that has overtaken me and trying desperately to ward off the onset of tears that threaten.

He stands and picks me up. My arms instinctively wrap around his neck and I bury my face in the comfort of his shoulder, the clean scent of his skin calming me as my tears begin to flow. He presses the button on the keypad to the elevator that will lead us to our room and only places me down when we are in the bathroom. He begins to run the whirlpool.

"Undress, I want to see all of you, Katarina. Do it now," he instructs. The commanding sound of his voice brings me out of my contemplation. I look up and the emotion is raw and concerned and I begin to shed my clothes, allowing them to drop to the floor around me.

"Good girl, now join me," he says, taking my hand to support me as I step into the deep square whirlpool tub.

I sink into its depths and allow the jetting bubbles to begin relaxing me. "Katarina, I need to know what's wrong," he says, sliding in across from me taking my hands in his own underneath the water.

"I'm scared."

"Tell me why," he says, his eyes searching, reminding me of all we've been through around trust.

"Of everything happening, the timing, but mostly how I feel," I say, finally, hating the questioning look reflected in his eyes.

"About Alfreita?"

"About Alfreita, my great uncle and the threats Ty is making to Jenny," I say. The tears that I thought were under control begin to fall again.

"We need Alfreita out of our lives. The plan is coming together, Baby. Just hang in there with me a little bit longer," he says, wiping a tear from my eye.

I trust you completely Chase, and know you will take care of us. I just wish it was over and I'm sorry I ever doubted the way you handled things in Miami. I've come to understand that everything you've done has been in the best interest of your family and that of the people involved and I couldn't be more in love with you," I say.

"Baby, please don't give me credit where it's not deserved," he says, rubbing his thumb against my lower lip.

"Chase, freeing those men in Miami, after what they did, was pretty incredible. I know your heart better now. You always try to do the right thing whenever possible," I say, swirling my hands in the warmth of the water.

"If it wasn't for you, I may not have been such a good man this time," he says, rubbing his thumb over my lips before gently grasping the nape of my neck before pulling me in for a kiss. His lips cover mine, his tongue exploring, enticing me and capturing my lips. "Katarina, I am not going to let anyone harm you or our children," he says, lifting my chin. His eyes are deep green pools of emotion, gauging mine.

"You want children?" I say, sobbing, wishing I could stop the flood of tears but the dam has been opened and I can only attempt to wipe them as they fall.

He nods. "Baby, I want you and to have a family with you," Chase says, rubbing his thumb across my lower lip.

"I know you will get us through this Chase, I'm just scared," I say, wishing I could remove every bit of worry etched along the strong jawline and ease the tension I see on his handsome features.

"What did you mean by the threats that Ty is making. Did Jenny tell you something about what he said to her?" he asks.

"No, actually I forgot to mention it with everything that's been going on. I came across an email that he sent to her after he cornered her at the grand opening. It sounds as though he's still trying to hold something over her head," I say.

"I need the email, Katarina," Chase says.

I nod. "I wasn't sure what to do with it so I sent it to myself from her email but I didn't want to delete it in case it was needed in her inbox for evidence or something," I say.

"We'll figure it out in the morning," he says, applying body wash to the loofah that sits on the stone ledge, first warming it with the lukewarm water of our bath before reaching for me. "Put your hair up," he says, handing me a clip that I often use in the shower.

I sweep my long hair up, twisting it into a messy bun and slide the clip into place. "Lean back, against the pillow, put your hands behind your head and close your eyes. Don't move or open them until I tell you to," he says.

I slide down, laying against the pillow and the automated warming and massage features begin to slowly knead the muscles in my neck as he begins to rub the soft side of the loofah across my body, starting with my arms, shoulders, across the nape of my neck, and then gradually trailing a path across my breasts, my navel and then back up again to start all over. "That feels so good, Chase," I say.

"Spread your legs for me. I want to see you," he says huskily.

I open to him, unable and not wanting to deny my desire. The soapiness of the loofah is already south, rubbing against me. "Open wider," he instructs, his masculine thighs helping me with the task as he rubs the soft side of the loofah over my mound again, circling, creating a slow burn deep inside of me. He moves the loofah lower and the rough side of the loofah grazes my clit.

"Gah," I say, raising up, but the palm of his hand on my midsection calms me.

"Still Baby, close your eyes, pretend you can't move. You are completely restrained, unable to see and all you can do is feel," he says, his voice calming me, centering me.

The soft side of the loofah circles again, the warmed body wash allowing it to flow sensually over my mound, causing my hips to raise in need, wanting it to dip lower.

"All in good time, Baby," he says, continuing his slow torture. The finger of his other hand traces the curve of my breast, one then the other, squeezing my pert and erect nipples, never missing the slow sensual rhythm he has created.

"God, Chase," I moan as he rubs the other side of the loofah against my sensitive and erect clit, swollen with the desire he has created.

"Stay still, absorb the pleasure Baby, cry out if you need to, but don't move and do not cum," he instructs, rubbing the rough material against my clit again.

My hands are over my head and I need desperately to let them claw into something. I instinctively want to move away from the intensity, but once I can't, it turns to pleasure, causing me to rise up and meet it head on, stroke for stroke. My clit is on fire and I feel the waves of a climax that I fear I will be unable to control.

"Chase, I'm so close..."

He enters me, hot and rigid, finding the spot that he knows will send me over the edge. "Cum for me now, Katarina," he says and I am lost to the sensations crumbling around me, taking me higher and higher, a climax that leaves me shaking and trembling. He does not allow me to come down, grasping my ass, positioning my hips so that every time his cock drives into me it pushes against that hypersensitive special spot. My hips rise of their own accord, clenching around him, pulling him deeper and deeper until we find our release in each other and the waves slowly begin to subside.

My hands are still above my head. I can't help the smile that crosses my lips as he captures the smooth silkiness of my nape between his lips, suckling, keeping my nipples aroused and on point. "Honey," I moan, as he continues his onslaught capturing my earlobe, penetrating the sensitive canal with his warm wet tongue, causing goose bumps to float over the length of my arms.

"Tell me you're worry free," he says, whispering in my ear.

"I can't think of anything but you right now," I say.

"You've taken all my energy and I need to replenish. Let's see what Gaby has for dinner and get an update from Jay," Chase says, kissing me on the lips before assisting me out of the tub to towel off. He unclasps the clip that has held the long strands of auburn hair off my neck and it tumbles around me falling over my breasts. "So beautiful, Baby," Get dressed before I take you back to bed," he says, kissing me gently.

"That's not a very good incentive," I say, smiling into his eyes.

"Probably not. Go, I need to eat," he says, spinning me around and swatting me playfully on the ass.

I rummage through the selection hanging in the closet before settling on a green sweater dress and boots for dinner.

Jay is already at the table when we arrive and Gaby has made lasagna, garlic bread and a tossed salad. "You made my favorite," he says, grinning at her as he snags a piece of bread from the platter.

"Chase told me you would be joining them for dinner," she says, her eyes twinkling.

Chase holds out my chair for me as I'm seated before taking his own beside me. "So where are we at?" he says to Jay, as he passes me the salad bowl.

"Much better position. No sign of anything suspicious in the air right now and they're making good time. Our men will be on the waves all night," he says, serving himself a large piece of lasagna before passing the dish to Chase.

Chase places a piece onto my plate before taking some for himself and setting the pan back in the middle of the table. "Gaby has outdone herself," he says after taking a bite.

"That lady can cook, that's for damn sure," Jay says.

"Do we know who was shooting at him?" I finally ask after finishing my dinner and listening to them talk for awhile.

He glances at Chase and I see his head nod slightly and I scowl at their exchange. "We think it was Alfreita, but we don't know yet if uncle was part of it or not," he says.

I am just about to ask him something else when my mother's ringtone comes through. "Excuse me, it's my mom," I say, just as Gaby brings in a round chocolate cake for dessert.

"I'll have some later," I mouth to Gaby before answering my cell on the way to the library.

"Hi Mom," I say.

"Hi Sweetie. Just thought I would call and see how you're doing. It's been a little lonely here today. Your dad had a business trip and won't be back until well into the night," she says.

I listen as she tells me about her day, trying to contain my guilt, knowing that anything could have happened on this trip and thankful that he is safe and on his way back to her. "We're on lockdown here with everything going on, but I have plenty of work to do from home and am using the time to try and get ahead a bit," I say.

"Yeah, Carlos doubled the security here, too. He wanted me to stay with you and Chase while he was gone, but I had so much work to do. He worries so much," she says.

"They're just being careful, Mom," I say.

"I know, but we shouldn't have to be prisoners in our own home. It's ridiculous," she says. Don called to check in with me earlier and told me that he and Emily and her family are all on lockdown, too. They think it may last another week or so," she says, clearly upset with the situation.

"That's not so long, Mom," I say.

"It is like being in prison, only it's in our house. Ridiculous!" she says.

I try to take her mind off of the situation and give her an update on Jenny and we talk a little bit more before disconnecting. I glance at the clock and it's early yet, just after seven, so I quickly hit Jenny's number to check in with her.

She answers on the first ring. "Hi there," she says, almost breathlessly.

"Hi yourself. You just get off the treadmill?"

"Umm, no, but I did have an amazing workout."

"Oh, what kind of workout would that be?" I ask, grinning.

"The best kind if you ask me," she says and I can almost feel her smile through the phone.

"Aren't you supposed to be resting, young lady?" I ask.

"That's all I've been doing, sleeping, reading, talking. I think this is exactly what I needed."

"Well I'm very happy for you. Chase thinks the world of Brian. I'm assuming it's him you're talking about," I say.

"It is, but I need to go. He should be done with the calls he needed to make," she says.

"You sound so much better today. Give me a call tomorrow. If you don't I'll track you down," I say before disconnecting and turning on the overhead television monitor, surfing through a gazillion channels before coming upon a movie that I haven't seen in a long time. I curl into the chair pulling the blanket around me, stifling a yawn as I watch.

The door opens a short time later and Chase walks into the room, his shadow outlined by the light of the television monitor. He closes the door behind him and stalks toward me. I smile when I see the dish with a piece of cake on it that he places on the table before he scoops me up and slips into the chair and pulls me into his lap. I thought I might find you in here," he says, kissing my neck before reaching for the cake and putting a bite to my lips.

"Mmm, sinfully good," I say, nuzzling into the strength of his arms around me as we watch the movie. It is hours later when I rouse, barely aware as he picks me up and carries me to our bed, laying me down, sliding in behind me and pulling me close into his body. "Sleep Baby," he says.

FIFTEEN

When I wake up, Chase is already up and gone. I glance at my phone for the time and decide to get a quick run in before I find him. I am just heading upstairs to shower when the swish of my phone alerts me to an incoming message.

Message: Where are you?

Reply: Just got done with a workout. Heading upstairs to shower.

Message: Meet me for an early lunch?

Reply: Yes! I'm starving!!

I feel refreshed after a quick shower, and blow dry my hair just enough to take the moisture out of it, leaving the rest to air dry. I shimmy into leggings and a long crème- colored sweater before pulling on a pair of boots and heading downstairs.

Chase is reading a news article on the computer and puts it aside when I walk in, opening his arms for me as I get to the table. I slip into his lap and he pushes my hair out of my face, bringing my lips to his. "Your dad arrived home last night," he says.

"That's great news. I was talking with Mom last night and felt horrible the entire time she was talking about his business trip. I know it was technically business, but it was hard knowing that he could be in danger and that he may not get to come home to her," I say.

"I know, Baby. They let me know when he landed late last night, but you were sleeping so soundly by that time I didn't want to disturb you," he says.

"So are you going to tell me about the trip?" I ask, slipping into the seat beside him.

"No, I meant what I said last night, I think your father should explain the details. He'll call you a little later," he says as Gaby walks into the kitchen preventing me from voicing the retort on the end of my tongue. Instead, I pretend to scowl at him behind Gaby's back as she walks to the coffee pot and he winks at me in return.

We have barely finished our lunch when Chase's phone vibrates. He glances at his messages and looks up at me. "Your father is hoping to call us shortly," he says.

"Lunch was delicious," Chase says to Gaby who is busy at the counter rolling crust before taking my hand and leading me to his office and closing the door behind us.

"Should I be nervous?" I ask wondering what it is that is so important that my father wants to tell me himself.

The phone on the desk rings and I look up surprised he didn't call Chase's cell. "Safe line," Chase explains, hitting the speakerphone button.

"Hi Carlos," he says to my father.

"Afternoon Chase. Is Katarina with you?" he asks.

"Hi Dad, I'm here in the office with Chase. I have to admit I'm a little nervous about whatever it is that you're going to tell me. He said that you wanted to tell me yourself."

"I'm sorry if it's made you apprehensive, but I'm glad Chase allowed me a chance to share this with you myself. You know the history of our family wealth from conversations with your mom, so I won't spend too much time on that. Over the years, I have slowly been diversifying into many legitimate and I might add very lucrative business ventures."

"I believe Chase may have mentioned that when I told him that you were my father," I say.

"You also know that I went to see Vicenti, but not why," my father says.

"I'm listening."

"Katarina, while I do not actively manage the business of moving illegal product, the money it brings in does go through my companies, distributed throughout the enterprises we own and then dispersed to the family. I have wanted to get out of the business for quite some time and there's never been a better reason than when you and your mother came into my life. I want to change the legacy that is passed on to you and my future family," Carlos says.

"Dad, that's admirable, but I don't understand how it involves Vicenti," I say, looking to Chase but while his eyes hold mine, they give nothing away.

"As Chase told you, my father's brother is the head of the Italian family and we learned that while my two younger brothers were not in any way associated with Tony and Alfreita, they have strong reservations about discontinuing the trade. Unfortunately, my uncle and his family can be very persuasive. My father left me in charge of the entire Larussio legacy, wanting me to ensure his family's future generations always had a good start in life, didn't have to come up the way he and Don's father did," he says.

"I knew you and Don were great friends. I didn't realize that your father's knew each other or that you had grown up together," I say.

"Katarina, I would like nothing better than to share some of these family stories with you, but they aren't all good. The history of our family is not something I was ever ashamed of until your mom walked out on me twenty-six years ago. That was the day I knew there had to be another way, a better way. It's taken me time to diversify, cautiously planning investments without unsettling the current infrastructure, putting my part of the proceeds into legitimate start up businesses. Today, I can proudly say that my portfolio is minimally financed by the proceeds of that business, but to my family it is their way of life, the legacy they know," he says, pausing for a moment.

"Dad, are you okay?" I ask.

"Katarina, I'm more than okay, but I'd be lying if I said I wasn't a little apprehensive. The time has come to completely diversify which brings me to Vicenti. He is willing to buy us out, completely. Take over the entire works."

"Really, that's great, right?" I ask.

"Yes and no. It's a wonderful opportunity, the price is excellent, but somehow my uncle became aware of it before I could share my plans with the family. You see it's not as easy as just selling off that part of the empire and splitting it among the remaining siblings. My father's wishes were for me to ensure his legacy continued, which means that in order to honor his dying wish, I must continue to ensure they can always remain financially independent and according to my father's will, the money must stay in my control. It is how the families have been raised for generations," he says.

"I actually think it's pretty honorable that you want to uphold your father's wish to safeguard the families' futures," I say.

"Katarina, some people won't think very much of the business I've invested most of our capital into. I can only hope that you're good with it," he says.

"It has to be better, tell me," I urge.

"The money will be invested in two large casinos on the Las Vegas strip this year and with two more anticipated the following. We were able to find prime property and will soon be in the process of building what will be known as Larussio Lane."

"Wow! So, maybe I should share a little bit of information with both of you at the same time," I say, watching Chase who raises his eyebrows in question.

"You know Jenny hasn't been well lately and that her business means the world to her. It was started with money that her father left her and it will be the legacy to her future family. Dad, it means as much to her as your legacy does to you. She financially takes care of her parents, siblings and their children much of the time. Unfortunately, she's not well, and I've been overseeing her accounts and plan to continue to do so until she's better," I say, averting my eyes from Chase's gaze.

"You're aware of the consulting work for the demolition of the other properties and design of The Larussio that I've requested of Torzial?" my father asks.

"Not only aware, but will be in charge of all of the accounts until she returns," I say, feeling proud of Jenny's trust in me.

"I'm not sure what to say. The firm came highly recommended, obviously Chase can't say enough about your work, and the Houston outcomes have caught the country's attention. Torzial is making a name for itself in consulting circles outside of design, as well, so I hired them. I hope you realize I wasn't aware you would be personally responsible," he says.

"No, I realize that. I just needed to get this out there, make sure you don't have any issues with conflict of interest or anything else," I say.

"I don't have any issues except that you already have more than a full time job. How are you going to manage both?" my father asks.

"In all honesty, I'm hoping that I don't have this charge for very long. I'd like nothing better than for Jenny to get well and be able to take back the reins very soon, but until she can I need to do this. She's my best friend and I'm going to be there for her, until she can," I say.

"Chase, you've been pretty quiet. Any conflicts or issues we need to discuss related to Katarina's involvement with Torzial and our buildings?" Carlos asks.

"Outside of the hours that Katarina will need to work? Carlos, it sounds as though she's given this a great deal of thought and is committed to ensuring Jenny's legacy remains in tact while she's ill. I can't think of anything that she doesn't have the capability to manage and would be delighted for her to handle both The Larussio and Prestian Towers accounts," Chase says.

"So a couple questions that I have. Have you shared this with Mom and how are you intending to work through your uncle and brothers' reluctance in selling?" I ask.

"Katarina, I'm going to be honest with you. I didn't anticipate any aversion from my uncle. The families have always been close, but kept the various businesses separate. I need to pull a family meeting together and let them know the intent is to ensure they have the income they are accustomed to, but far richer and legitimate. I've worked years toward that goal. Don's father took that path many, many decades ago and while I appreciate the life that my father left for us, I want part of the legacy for my future family to be legitimacy," he says.

"Dad, I think it's wonderful and I'll help in any way that I can with the designs and you've got Torzial Consulting backing you. You haven't shared any of this with Mom though, have you?" I ask.

I can hear the heavy sigh. "No, I haven't yet. I was hoping to have it all sealed up before I told her but we need to get through the family's aversion first," he says.

"So for the record, Mom and I have never kept secrets and this is going to be a strain for me. Do whatever you need to do to fix this and tell her. I can't even imagine how ecstatic she will be to learn what you've shared with me today. I don't understand why you're leaving her out of helping," I say.

"Katarina, she left, walked right out, disappeared from the face of the earth carrying my child because of my lifestyle. There's no part of me that wants to bring her remotely close to this until I can look her in the eye and tell her that we live legitimately. I just need a little time," he says.

"I understand, Dad and I'm glad that you cared enough to share it with me. Do what you have to do and let me know how I can help. In the meantime, I saw your email and have been researching the property for The Larussio. I have several lean consultants that will be assigned to the job and will begin identifying key stakeholders. They will identify the ultimate customer experience, and then we'll lay plans for design around that," I say.

"You don't know how happy it makes me to have you working on this project," Carlos says.

"Last thing Dad, why sell to Vicenti instead of your uncle?" I ask.

"Katarina, if I sell to your uncle my younger brothers will align and they will continue the cycle of criminal activity. Our families can have greater prosperity through casinos and the legal businesses associated with them. If I sell to Vicenti, it's done. I want to take all of the money and reinvest in the casinos to ensure our future," he says.

"One last question. Does Alfreita have anything to do with your plans, Dad? I mean he and Uncle Tony wanted to take over the entire market. He's still out there," I say.

"Katarina, Chase may be in a better position to answer your questions," he says.

I look at Chase and his eyes are hooded and controlled, not giving anything away. "Chase, tell me," I say, squeezing his hand.

"Thanks, Carlos. I appreciate you allowing me to share the story, but there are pieces that you may need to fill in," he says, watching me, his eyes never wavering.

"You sure you want to do this now?" Carlos asks.

"Yes, I want Katarina to know everything, no secrets, right or wrong, good or bad. She needs to know. Jay and I had a long conference call this morning.

"It would seem the indictment last year was just another contrived way to bring shame to the Prestians. The night on Alfreita's yacht last year was not what it appeared. Jay has reason to believe that my presence was a preplanned and a well-laid-out attempt to indict me for the largest drug seizure in the area. Tony and Alfreita thought it would serve both of their purposes. I would be in prison and my father would be devastated, and Tony would discredit Vicenti's product in an effort to take over the market," Chase says.

I look at Chase. His eyes are hooded and controlled, giving nothing away. My heart aches for the man that I love. "This is not going to end until we end it. Your father will pull together a meeting with the family in Italy, and Jay has everything in place to draw Alfreita out," he says.

I nod. "Whatever it takes."

"I promise you, this will be over soon, Katarina," he says, turning away from me and towards the speakerphone. "Carlos, I'll be in touch and let you know when Jay has plans in place for us to travel," he says, disconnecting the line.

"I told you that I didn't need to know, but tell me that whatever the plan is you aren't putting yourself at risk like the last time. It's all I've been thinking about. I don't care what happens as long as that man is out of our lives for good and he can never reach out and hurt you or our family, but I'm petrified that you're going to do something that places you in harm's way. I couldn't take it if anything happened to you," I say, trying unsuccessfully to keep my tears at bay.

"Come here," he says, pulling me into his arms. "This is going to be over shortly and there is nothing for you to be concerned about, but it does mean that I need to be away from you for a short time," he says, holding me close.

"You're going to be involved, aren't you?" I say, looking up at him, his eyes hooded and controlled but filled with emotion.

"Baby, it's the only way. I need to be there."

"You're breaking my heart, Chase. I don't want you anywhere near the man that wants to hurt you, but you're going anyway and there's nothing I can do about it," I say, wiping the tears that are falling faster than I can wipe.

He pulls me close, kissing the top of my head while I cry into his chest and then lifts me into his arms carrying me to the couch, and settles me into his lap. "Katarina, I won't be gone long and Jay will be with me. We'll be okay. I'm coming home to you and our family, understand?" he says, lifting my chin so that I am forced to look into his eyes.

I nod, still unable to stifle my sobbing. "When are you leaving?" I ask.

"Tomorrow afternoon," he says, pushing the hair out of my dampened eyes.

"How long are you going to be gone?" I ask, attempting to push my fear down.

"Hopefully only two days," he replies.

"Where will you be?" I ask, wondering if it will be in Aruba or somewhere else.

"Baby, I think story time has come to an end for now. But, we should talk about your work with Torzial. You didn't mention it?" he says.

"She just asked me a few days ago and I really haven't done too much except field a couple contract questions and review the documents that Carlos sent over for the Larussio land. It appears as though the Prestian building and the Larussio properties will be neighbors. Did you know that when you started the build?"

"I knew your father's plan, but I wasn't certain if all would go as well as it did with Vicenti, but I think it's my turn to ask questions," he says.

"Just what questions would that be, Mr. Prestian?" I ask, smiling at the amusement in his eyes.

"Oh, I'm pretty sure taking on the Torzial work for Jenny will cause you to break a few rules, or did you forget?" he asks.

"Forget what?" I ask breathlessly, watching his eyes intently.

"Forget that when you work too many hours I will be forced to come and remind you of the time. If you're in the library working I may come in quietly, close and lock the door behind me. You'll be at your desk and glance up. You'll know by the look on my face that your time is up and that you'll be punished. As soon as you realize this, your body will begin to respond. Your breathing will change, it will become shallow and your body temperature will rise. I'll be watching you and when I see your little intake of breath, I'll know that you can feel yourself moistening for me, just like now," he says, pushing a strand of hair out of my face.

"Then what will you do?" I ask, feeling myself becoming moister and moister as he talks to me.

"Sorry, Baby, I need to take it," he says, pulling his vibrating cell phone from his pant pocket.

"Damn it, I'll be ready," he says, disconnecting.

"Katarina, there's no easy way to say this. Things are escalating and I need to leave shortly. Jay's having the helicopter take me to the private field and will have the jet waiting from there. I don't have much time," he says.

"Nothing I say will stop you," I say, trying desperately to put on a brave face and suppress my feelings about the plan I know nothing about and failing miserably. The tears begin and I am helpless to stop the flood that pours down my cheeks.

"Katarina, I'm sorry. It's the only way, Baby," he says.

"I know, just go, Chase," I say, as he pulls me tight against his chest and kisses me on the forehead.

"I'll text you whenever I can, but if you don't hear from me, it's because the signals aren't clear. I'll contact you when it's safe and will be thinking about you every minute," he says.

"Chase, your bag is packed and your ride is here," Gaby says over the intercom system.

He looks like he wants to say something and I put up my hand, too emotionally drained. "Go, Chase. I will be fine," I say, knowing it's a lie.

"I love you," he says, kissing me on the cheek before he opens the door and closes it behind him. I do not have the energy to go upstairs and curl up on the couch by the window, pulling the afghan that lays on it around me. I am unable to control my tears, fearing the unknown, where he'll be, what will happen.

I wake to a gentle prodding of my shoulder. "Kate, it's way past dinner time. Are you hungry?" Gaby asks kindly.

"What time is it?" I ask, searching quickly for my cell.

"It's seven, you've been sleeping for hours. I just wanted to make sure that you're okay," she says.

I nod. "Thank you. I'm fine, but I really am very hungry," I say.

"What do you feel like?" she says.

"Any chance I could get a bowl of your tomato basil soup and a grilled cheese?" I ask.

"I keep a few servings in the freezer for just such occasions. Why don't you relax and wake up a little while I put it together," she says, sashaying out of the study and closing the door behind her.

I skim through the missed messages on my cell and put it down. All I know is that he made it to his private airstrip and was preparing to take off. No clue where he is going or when he'll return. I pull myself together and go upstairs to freshen up before heading into the kitchen to find Gaby.

"Smells fantastic," I say, as the basil and smell of bubbling cheddar wafts through the air.

"Take a seat, it will be done soon," she says as Sheldon walks in.

"Hi there," I say, eyeing him ruefully.

"Hi there yourself. Gaby said you were sleeping most of the afternoon. Wanted to make sure you hadn't put someone on the couch in your place and given me the slip again," he says, grinning widely.

"Sheldon!" Are you ever going to let me live that down?" I ask, recalling with a smile how I gave him the slip by going into a public bathroom in one outfit and leaving in another and a beret to cover my hair.

"Probably not, but on a serious note I did want to check in and make sure you were okay.

"I appreciate that, but I would be much better if I at least knew where Chase was right now. Do you know?" I ask.

"I can honestly say that I don't. I'll be staying in the guest quarters while Chase is away. Just wanted to let you know so you'd feel safe for the night," he says.

"I do, Sheldon. I know you'll take care of anything that arises," I say as my phone rings. The telephone number is unfamiliar, but I recall Chase saying he may call on a secure line. "Excuse me, I just want to catch this in case it's Chase," I say.

"Hello, this is officer Patrick," a deep male voice says.

"You've reached Kate Prestian. How can I help you?" I say, hitting the speakerphone button so that Sheldon can listen to the call, trying to get a handle on my climbing heart rate, fearing the worst for Chase.

"I'm looking for Mrs. Katarina Prestian," he says.

It is moments before I find my voice, my breath catching in my chest. "This is she, I go by Kate," I say as my body begins to tremble with unexplained fear for Chase.

"Mrs. Prestian, I'm sorry to have to give you this news, but your mother has you listed as the emergency contact in her cell phone. She and your father have been in a grave accident and were rushed to the New York Trauma Center."

"My parents?" I say, trying to comprehend what the officer is saying.

"I'm afraid so, Mrs. Prestian. I'm not a medical professional, but the car accident was one of the worst I've seen in a long time. If they were my parents and I wanted to see them one last time, I'd be on the next flight home," he says.

"Of course, thank you for calling me," I say, tears welling in my eyes.

"You're welcome and I'm sorry to have to give you such bad news. If there's anything I can assist you with please feel free to contact me back at the number on your cell," he says before disconnecting.

"Sheldon, can you arrange the helicopter and the Gulfstream? Let's use the private runway. I don't want to waste time traveling to the airport," I say.

"I'm already on it, Kate. I need to confirm the legitimacy of the call first though. It's going to be a few minutes before we get arrangements in place."

"Do what you have to do," I say, trying desperately to hold myself together as I head upstairs to pack. I am just about finished when I receive Sheldon's message.

Message: Kate, helicopter is ten minutes out and the jet will be on the runway waiting. We need to move.

Reply: On my way.

I sift through the messages one more time frustrated that I can't let Chase know where we're going in case he is in an area that can be picked up. Instead I hit the contact for Chase's dad.

"Hello."

"Don, this is Kate. I'm sorry to disturb you this evening," I say.

"It's no bother. Is everything all right?" he says.

"No, not at all. The New York police just called to tell me my parents were in a car accident and were transported to New York City Trauma Center. Chase is gone for the next few days, and I know how close you are to Carlos, so I wanted you to know. Sheldon has arranged to take me to the hospital and we'll be leaving shortly."

"Kate, while this could certainly be an accident, we need to make sure it's not a ploy to draw you out of the complex while Chase is gone. Do you mind if I speak with Sheldon?" he asks gently.

"No, of course not," I say, walking into the kitchen with my bag and handing my cell to Sheldon.

"Chase's dad wants to make sure the accident is legitimate and that they are at the hospital," I mouth quietly to Sheldon.

He nods and takes the phone. "Mr. Prestian. Nice to speak with you sir," he says, pausing briefly to listen to Don.

"I contacted the New York City police department and confirmed the accident and connected with the trauma center. I also spoke with the head of Carlos's security team and he confirmed that they are both there, and our team was able to corroborate this with a little search," he says, looking at my raised brows and pausing to listen to Don.

"The helicopter just arrived and we should be at the airstrip in twenty minutes, up in the air no later than thirty. I sent a secure message to Jay, but it's been silent to this point, sir. A team is securing the perimeter of the hospital as we speak and will maintain security during the night. Yes, sir. We'll meet you at the hospital," he says.

"Everything okay?" I say.

"Yep, we're good to go. Have everything you need?" he says.

"Here, take this for later," Gaby says, tucking a little plastic bag into my handbag.

"Thank you, Gaby," I say, hugging her close to me.

"Okay, ready as I'll ever be," I say, following Sheldon out the door to the awaiting helicopter.

SIXTEEN

The trip to the airstrip is uneventful and the pilot and crew are awaiting our arrival as the helicopter puts down. There are two cars with security guards already on the ground and Sheldon and Dereck escort me to the plane and up the ramp, introducing me to the pilot and crew. Once we are settled in I reach for my phone and call Jenny.

"Kate, how are you? I was wondering when I would receive my next call," she says, jokingly.

"I'm sorry I didn't call earlier. Chase is gone and I just learned that Mom and Dad were in a bad car accident. Jenny it doesn't sound good. They rushed them to the trauma center," I say, unable to stop the tears and thankful the guys are busy talking with the crew and I have a little privacy.

"Kate, Brian is with me and I'm putting you on speakerphone. Are you going to see them?" Jenny asks.

"I'm on my way right now. We just boarded the jet and will be taking off in a few moments," I say, trying my best to sound stronger than I feel.

"Kate, this is Brian. I'm sorry to hear about your parents. Sheldon is your security point, correct?" he asks.

"Yes, he's been great. He contacted the hospital and the police department to confirm the accident and has security blanketing the perimeter of the hospital. We should take off in a few minutes," I say, trying to sound calm although my emotions are at the point of screaming.

"Kate, I know you aren't able to contact Chase right now and I want to make sure you're okay while he's gone. Don't trust anyone, and don't go anywhere on your own. I know it's hard to think about safety while your concern is for your parents, but you need to understand that Alfreita's team may know that you're out of the complex," he says.

"I understand, Brian. I called Chase's dad and he pretty much told me the same thing and talked to Sheldon, too. I really appreciate you both looking out for me," I say.

"Call or text when you arrive. I'll connect with Sheldon and sincerely hope all is well with your parents when you arrive," he says before disconnecting and I buckle in for takeoff.

"Everything okay?" Sheldon asks, peeking into the cabin just as I wipe the tears that have escaped from my eyes.

"Yeah, I'm good. When can I get onto the internet?" I ask, needing so badly to throw myself into work.

"As soon as we take off you should be good to go. Chase has it set up so he can work the entire trip," he says.

"Perfect, I have a lot to do," I say, slipping off my shoes and curling my feet underneath me on the soft leather recliner, hitting the remote to reduce the lighting and igniting the floor-to-ceiling fireplace that lets off an ambiance of blue sparkling warmth in the otherwise dimmed room.

The takeoff is perfect and once we're in the air I set about signing on to my email to take care of all the Prestian Medical facility needs. The Chicago designs have been approved by the state and the detailed designs inside the approved footprint are starting to shape up nicely. I send a few notes on the proposed workflows to the lean advisors and sign onto Jenny's email.

I peruse the emails and respond to some, but catch my breath as I see the one from Carlos Larussio which was sent earlier in the day.

. . .

KATARINA,

I can't tell you enough how pleased I was to hear that you will be temporarily overseeing the purchase of land for the future site of The Larussio in Las Vegas, the demolition of existing properties, and design of the casinos. I have attached the vision for the venues, which should assist your design teams. Please let me know if questions exist or further assistance can be provided. I am most excited and privileged to be working with you.

Carlos Larussio (otherwise referred to as Dad).

I BEGIN REVIEWING the documents he has attached and can't suppress the emotion and tears that overtake me as I read through his vision for the organization going forward. The luxury of the hotel rooms includes whirlpools and private balconies which overlook the city or mountains depending on desire, the spa is set up to pamper and cater to the sensual desires of those that stay in the hotel, and the in-room amenities include tuck down service, couples massage, room service and basically anything you would want for a couples weekend or longer in Vegas. I recall the conversations with my mom about his family's history, what I've read and come to learn about my father's earlier years, and can't help but feel proud of what he's trying to achieve for his family going forward. The tears slide down my face again realizing the very real possibility that he may never be able to recognize his dream.

The captain announces the impending descent and I take the next couple of minutes to finish responding to email before heading into the master bedroom to compose myself. I wipe my red rimmed eyes with a cool cloth and apply a light dusting of powder to my face along with a little lip gloss and hope that it doesn't look as bad as what I see in the mirror before heading back to my seat to prepare for landing.

As we touch down Sheldon comes into the cabin to lead me to the awaiting limousine. "Let's go," Sheldon says to the driver once he and Dereck are seated. We ease into the New York City traffic with a black caddy in front of and behind us, armed with guards and I feel nothing but appreciation for their presence. The driver pulls up to the entrance and Sheldon and Dereck escort me into the hospital. My mind reverts back to the time Dad's brother shot him in the chest and he was barely alive. I can only pray that he will be so lucky this time.

Sheldon speaks with the receptionist and we are soon on our way up a bank of elevators, arriving into a large waiting room with an expansive window looking out into bright lights of the New York skyline. Don is leaning against the glass, gazing out over the city, but turns as we walk toward him. "Kate, I wish you weren't here under these circumstances," he says hoarsely, pulling me into a hug.

"How bad is it?" I ask, hoping against hope that the emotion in his eyes is not an indicator.

"Your mother is listed as critical, but what they're considering stable condition. She has multiple neck and back injuries, contusions and lacerations. They have her heavily medicated and she may need surgery to correct one or two of the disc injuries," he says.

"What about my dad?" I ask, bracing myself as his voice cracks. "Kate, he's not doing as well. There's just no easy way to say this. He's had severe brain trauma caused by the head-on impact. His brain was swelling at a rate they couldn't control, so they had to place him into a coma," he says.

"Can I see them?" I ask, wiping the tears from my eyes as quickly as they appear. The nurses' station is right around the corner. Let's see if they'll let you in," he says, placing his arm around me and guiding me to the desk.

"Miss, this is Katarina Prestian. Her parents, Mr. and Mrs. Larussio are in the trauma section. Any chance she can see them?" he asks.

"Absolutely. Families do best when they have loved ones surrounding them. If you give me one moment I'll take her back unless you are part of the immediate family," she says.

"Yes, Carlos is my brother, I'll let my son know to join us, as well," he says, walking around the corner to where Sheldon is watching with raised eyebrows at the exchange. He joins us and the nurse guides us down a hall and through a double set of doors before we enter a unit that has patient rooms around the perimeter with a large nursing station in the center. There are monitors above each patient's door and the entire unit seems to be beeping and humming with a flurry of activity as nurses and physicians enter and exit patient rooms. She guides us to the desk and speaks with a tall ponytailed blonde lady.

"This is Mr. and Mrs. Larussio's daughter, brother and nephew and this is Alison. She'll take care of you from here," she says warmly before heading back to her station.

"The police officer who arrived with the ambulance let our intake staff know that you had been contacted but were a few hours away. I'm happy to meet you and glad you were able to get here so soon. Before we go in I want to prepare you for what you're going to see," Alison says.

"Your mother has significant facial lacerations, bruising and swelling. This will heal with time and I don't want it to unnecessarily alarm you. The brace around her neck is to ensure she doesn't hurt herself moving in her sleep. She is heavily sedated and while she won't be able to answer you, feel free to talk to her. Research that shows patients respond much better when family members are close by. When we go in by your father, you'll see more of the same. The trauma to his head caused intensive swelling of the brain. The physicians had to place him in a coma in order to slow down the brain activity and are currently working to reduce the swelling with medications," she says as we reach my mother's room.

"Thank you," I say, finally finding my voice as I walk into the room. I gasp audibly and put a hand over my mouth to keep from crying out at the vision in front of me. There are tubes, oxygen masks, IVs and monitors surrounding her. I reach her bedside and the tears begin to fall as I take in the battered and swollen face of my mother. The lacerations are numerous, having sliced through her face diagonally. I take her hand squeezing it gently, avoiding the needles that have been taped down to the outer side of her wrists.

The nurse puts her hand on my shoulder. "I can only imagine how it looks to you right now, but please know the lacerations are superficial. None required suturing, it's her back and neck that we're most concerned about. She's doing great and they will heal over time," she says gently.

"Thank you for your kindness. Would it be possible to see my dad and then come back and sit with her for awhile?" I ask.

"Absolutely. He's in the next room. We currently need separate care teams and room equipment so they have different rooms, but we may at some point in the future be able to put them in a larger room together," she says.

I nod. "I'd like that very much when possible," I say, as she leads us to the next room and to the bedside of my father. His face is battered and bruised and he has a bandage across his left temple.

"Unlike your mother," he had a pretty bad gash that required suturing," she says, as if reading my mind.

"What happened to his arm?" I ask, taking in the plastic sling-like device that has my father's arm outstretched.

"The impact of the truck fractured the humerus, scapula and clavicle. The bone in the top of his arm, shoulder and collar bone have all been broken in multiple places. Again, with time these will heal. We're most concerned with the pressure in your father's head, which is why we had to place him in the coma," she says.

"They were hit by a truck? I don't even know what happened, just that they were in a bad automobile accident," I say, attempting to wipe the tears falling from my eyes away.

"I'm sorry, unfortunately that's all I know, but the police officer who contacted you knew you wouldn't arrive for a few hours, so planned to come back," she explains.

"Thank you so much for your kindness," I say, taking a tissue from the bedside to wipe my runny nose. I glance up as Don joins me at my father's bedside and the minute I look at him and see the pain in his eyes the tears begin to flow even faster. He squeezes my hand.

"Carlos is a fighter. He's been through hell and back and this will not stand in the way of his dreams, Katarina," Don says.

"I hope you're right," I say, wiping my nose and trying to contain the tears that continue to fall.

"Sheldon, would you escort Katarina to her mom's room? I'd like to spend a little time with Carlos and then I'm going to hang out in the waiting room tonight if that's okay with you," Don says to me.

"Nonsense, you're family. You mean the world to him, you know that. If you're going to remain at the hospital, just stay in his room with him. It would make me feel so much better to know he's not alone and I can't be in two places at once," I say, patting his shoulder before allowing Sheldon to escort me back to my mother.

"I hate to ask you logistical questions right now, but what are you planning for the night? If you want to stay here we've got the entire perimeter and interior covered, if you want to go to a hotel to rest, we can make that happen, I just need a little time to secure the facility," Sheldon says.

"No problem, Sheldon. You can plan on us being here for a while. I brought a few pairs of comfy clothes and a toothbrush. I'm good," I say, settling into the recliner by my mother.

"Very good," he says, pulling the sliding sofa out and removing the cushions that expose a makeshift bed. He opens the closet and pulls down a pillow and blanket, laying them on the bed for me.

"Thanks, Sheldon. You didn't need to do that," I say, glancing up at the knock on the door and the two police officers entering the room.

They glance somewhat nervously at my mom's feeble body. "Mrs. Prestian, we hate to interrupt time with your mother. However, we were wondering if we could have a few moments with you, preferably somewhere private? The nurses suggested that we use one of the family conference rooms just down the hall," the tall one says.

"Of course. This is Sheldon, and he'll be accompanying us," I say, following them along the hallway to a small room that contains a sleek black oval table and eight chairs. I glance around and although there are no windows, the hospital staff have made it cheery with white-boards, scenic pictures of nature, and a coffee bar. The shorter, dark-haired police officer pours coffee into one of the Styrofoam cups. "Would anyone else like one?" he asks.

"I'd welcome some caffeine," Sheldon says, taking the cup the officer hands him before situating himself at the end of the table facing the door.

"We apologize it's so late. We wanted to allow Mrs. Prestian time to travel and spend a bit with her parents before we intruded, but also need to share what we know with you. While you may have heard it on the news, there's a lot to the accident that doesn't make sense. Your parents were hit head on by a semi driver, Mrs. Prestian. He pauses at my gasp. "I'm sorry if this is hard for you to hear, but it's important for us to find out if your parents may have had any enemies, anyone that may have wanted to do them harm. We're well aware of your father's, um, position, and unfortunately this appears to be an orchestrated hit," he says.

"You mean someone intentionally drove a semi truck into their car," I say, slowly trying to digest this information.

"While we can't be certain, there are enough details that lead us to believe that it was not an accident. Unfortunately, we can't release those specifics just yet, but we need to learn if you know of anyone that would want to harm your parents, Mrs. Prestian?" he prods.

I do not look up, recalling the multiple times that Chase has not prevented the police from doing their job, but kept them out of the way so that his own men could do it faster.

"Gentlemen," I say, finally leveling my gaze at them. "As you referenced, my father is well-known in this city and across the country for that matter. He has many business investments and at any time someone could take issue with a deal that didn't go the way they intended it to, an investment that went sour, or any number of things. I wish I could provide you with something helpful. If someone deliberately tried to murder my parents, I would like nothing more than to have them brought to justice," I say, meeting their watchful eyes head on, hoping my eyes are as hooded and controlled as possible.

"If you think of anything, anything at all, we would welcome a phone call," the tall guy says, standing up and pushing his chair in. He offers me his card. "I'm glad you could be here for your parents and my thoughts are with you and your family," he says before they leave.

The door closes and I feel a sense of relief, finally able to let down my guard. "Kate, you did a great job answering their questions. Excellent job and such a poker face. Chase will be so proud," Sheldon says.

"Do you know anything more than what they've told us?" I ask, knowing he does but not sure if he'll divulge it.

"Chase pays me to know more than them, but I didn't know before they called you. I should have though. The security team Carlos has in place should have gotten hold of me right away since Jay is off the grid. We're looking into why that didn't happen and they'll need to answer to Carlos and Chase, but I can tell you what we've learned since if you want to hear it," he says.

"Tell me, Sheldon."

"It was completely orchestrated. The police are right, but they know so little. Your parents were supposed to be on lockdown. Your mother wasn't happy about the situation. Apparently it was some sort of special anniversary date and he doubled security, booked an entire restaurant so that he and your mother could have a nice dinner out. The semi was stolen approximately seven hours before your parents set out on the highway to the restaurant. I've engaged our intel teams to tap into Carlos's security and see if they can find a plant. They had to have one in order to know his exact plans if they knew they were driving into the city instead of taking the helicopter. They also had eyes in the sky since the truck driver knew exactly when to accelerate, bear down, and cross the center line. Your father didn't have a chance of correcting, Kate," he says gently.

Inside my body is raging with emotion, screaming at the injustice, an inferno that will not be put out easily. Outside I appear calm, evenly overly collected.

"Thank you, Sheldon. Please keep me apprised as you learn more. I assume you have people screening my father's help? This is the second time that an inside job has occurred. His head of security should be fired. If you'll excuse me, I'm going to check on my parents and then get a little rest before the physicians start their morning rounds," I say, standing and walking toward the door.

"We'll have someone stationed right outside your mother and father's door all night. If you need to leave the room for any reason, they are going to follow you."

I begin to protest, but he interrupts. "Kate, this is not up for debate. Security will be accompanying you everywhere, at least until we get to the bottom of this since I'm the one that's in charge of keeping you safe, not to mention that I need to answer to your husband when he returns," he says.

"I'll do my best to behave then," I say, smiling to myself as I walk back to my father's room

Although it's the late at night, the nurses' station is alight with activity. Physicians moving in and out, signing ledgers, talking on phones, and discussing patient progress with nurses. I nod to Dereck who is on duty outside my father's door before I go in. Don is sitting in the recliner next to him and glances up from his phone when I walk in. My father does not appear to have moved or be in any different state than when I left him.

"Just letting Emily know I won't be home tonight," Don says, pocketing his phone and coming to stand next to me at my father's bedside.

"Any change?" I ask, watching my father's lifeless appearance.

"No, the physicians were in a short while ago, and they said that time will tell if the medicine will take affect. The swelling appears to be the same, and they'll know more in the morning," he says gently.

I say a silent prayer that we'll have better news by morning before telling him goodnight and returning to my mom's room. I slip off my shoes and get comfortable in the makeshift bed, watching my mom's chest rise and fall, and the waves of the monitors that surround her. I glance down at a message eager to see one from Chase, but it is Jenny checking in to make sure I'm okay. It's hard to keep the tears and rage at the injustice at bay, watching my mom, knowing that while she may make it, my father may not. I glance at my cell to see it's one thirty in the morning. While Chase has only been gone twelve hours it seems like an eternity. I open my purse, pull out my MacBook, and rummage through the bag that Gaby sent with me, smiling at her thoughtfulness. Cheese, grapes, and my favorite oatmeal cranberry cookies. I take a couple bites as I begin googling the accident, but my appetite quickly turns to nausea as I view the scene of the accident and the wreckage. While I don't learn any more than Sheldon has shared I can't get the visual of the massive semi bearing down on my parents and the collapsed car out of my mind. I finally shut down my computer and after another hour of tossing and turning, trying to get comfortable, I finally fall into an exhausted and fitful sleep.

I dream that I hear Chase's voice, the deep timbre piercing through my sleep, giving me comfort. I pull my pillow closer, but then hear it again. "Do what you need to keep him alive."

"We need to have this conversation with your wife. She's the next of kin," someone says, as I slowly rouse to take in my surroundings.

"Chase?" I say, finally able to open and focus my eyes on the two men standing next to my mom's bedside. He turns at my voice and comes to sit next to me, pulling me into his arms.

"Baby, I'm so sorry. Your father developed a blood clot from the cranial bleed. They need to make a decision to relieve the pressure. I'll let Dr. Moore explain it to you, but they need to act fast," he says.

SEVENTEEN

"**Mrs. Prestian, I'm sorry** we have to meet under such dire circumstances. I'm the surgeon on call and your father's medication, while managing to keep the swelling from increasing, has not been able to bring it down as quickly as we had hoped. Additionally, a clot has formed that we need to remove. I'd like to remove it and try to release a little of the pressure while I'm in," he says.

"What do you mean, while you're in?" I ask.

"Mrs. Prestian, the procedure I'm recommending is a small hole inserted into the cranium. The official term is a craniotomy. It will allow me to find the blood clot, remove it, and at the same time relieve a little of the pressure that's built up. The statistics and results of this procedure are good, but time is of the essence."

"I'm familiar with the procedure. I worked on a process improvement for the procedure a few years ago. Do what you need to do to keep my father alive and protect his mental capacity. I would far rather this procedure than a craniectomy," I say.

"You can be assured, Mrs. Prestian, I will do everything in my power to do just that, and we will reserve the procedure you reference as a last resort," he says, shaking our hands before leaving the room.

"Does your dad know? He stayed the night with him. We should tell him what's happening," I say to Chase.

"He's aware. We were talking when the physician came in for his rounds this morning. Sheldon said you didn't get to sleep until late. I didn't want to wake you," he says, pulling me close.

"You've talked to Sheldon, so you know what happened? You know someone intentionally did this to my family? Somehow they found out that my dad was taking my mom out for dinner and they put a plan in place to run them off the road with a fucking semi truck, Chase. A semi truck! Have you seen the pictures? The Lincoln didn't have a chance in hell. I want you to tell me if the same person that keeps coming after us is responsible for what happened to my family. I need to know, Chase," I say.

"The communication leak was confirmed a couple hours ago. It's Alfreita's men, but unfortunately it's not as simple as that. After your father's uncle learned about your father's intent to sell parts of his business portfolio to Vicenti it appears he began working with Alfreita for the same reasons your uncle Tony did. They want to take over your father's market and at the same time put Vicenti out of business. Your father didn't want to sell to your uncle, didn't trust that he had not started selling the cuts that are poisoning people at a growing rate. Katarina, it was Alfreita that put the hit out on your father, but we're not sure how involved your uncle was in the actual planning of it.

"I want Alfreita gone! Out of our lives forever. I want that monster dead, I won't be happy until I am at his funeral and see his hateful body buried. My mother is still having nightmares, still dealing with the emotions of being kidnapped, and just think about what he would have had them do to her if you hadn't stepped in? Now both of my parents are fighting for their lives because of him. Do you know what a craniectomy is? They are going to drill fucking holes into my father's skull, and if that doesn't work they are going to saw off the top of his skull so they can relieve the pressure to his brain!"

"Katarina..."

"I realize I've gone both ways on this and I was naive. I didn't realize they wouldn't stop. I just want him out of our lives," I say, finally letting my mask slip and the tears to fall uncontrollably.

"Baby, we'll get through this. I promise you," he says, pulling me into his arms, rocking me back and forth as I cry into his chest.

"I hate to interrupt, but they're prepping your father," Chase's dad says, coming into my mom's room.

"It's okay Don. I need to tell my mom what's going on. I know she's on a ton of morphine and probably won't be able to hear me or understand what I'm saying, but the research says people can and do hear these types of things," I say.

Chase holds me to him and brushes the hair out of my eyes. "Dad and I are going to step out for a bit. Take all the time that you need," he says, brushing my lips gently with his own.

I walk to the edge of the bed and take my mom's hand, holding it tightly. "Mom, it's me, Kate. You and Dad were in a horrible automobile accident. We've been with you all night and your vitals are getting stronger. You're going to make it. Dad's still alive, but he's fighting, Mom. He has a lot of pressure and a blood clot on his brain and they have to take him into surgery. This could go either way, good or bad," I say, wiping the tears that fall uncontrollably down my cheeks.

The hand in mine squeezes me. I look down at her small frail hands thinking maybe I dreamed it, but it happens again. She squeezes my hand tighter and I return the gesture.

"Mom, I love you," I say, not even attempting to wipe the tears that are streaming down my cheeks.

"Love you, Sweetie," she says very low, almost a whisper.

"Mom, do you need anything?" I say, bending so that she can hear me better.

"Your dad," she says, tightening the grip on my hand.

"Tell me what you want," I say.

"Talk to him," she says, her head moving side to side trying to come out of the medication-induced sleep.

"Hang on, Mom. Just hang on," I say, kissing her forehead before I run out of her room to my father's next door. "Wait, my mom wants to talk to my dad before you take him to surgery," I say to the men starting to move the gurney.

"Ma'am, we've already started the prep. We need to move the patient to surgery rather quickly."

"Let me be just a little more clear. I wasn't asking if it was possible, I want to know how we make this happen. The best thing for my father before he undergoes surgery is to hear the woman he loves, the reason he has for being on this earth, talk to him. How do we make this happen? I ask.

"Gentleman, is there a problem?" Chase says, walking into the room.

"No sir, we're happy to move him, it's just the timing. We need to be quick," he says, beginning to push the bed my father is on past us. "We'll pull him right up beside her, but then they'll only have a few moments before we need to have him on his way to surgery," the guy says.

"Thank you," I say, running ahead of them to reach my mom before they enter her room. "Mom, Dad's prepared for surgery, but he's coming to see you first. You can talk to him," I say, just as they wheel him next to me.

"Mom, are you awake?" I ask.

"Hmm. Your dad?" she says.

"He's here, Mom. You can say anything, here touch his hand, hold it," I say, placing his hand next to hers, startled when she grasps it and squeezes.

"Come back to me. I love you," she says, and I see the squeeze of her hand again.

"Dad, Mom is going to make it. She's going to be okay. She loves you and wants you to get better. Do you feel her squeezing your hand? You need to be strong to get through this and come back to her and me. We love you, Dad. Please get through this," I say, squeezing both of their hands before I release them and let the transporters take him to surgery. My mom's eyelids shutter and she falls back asleep before Chase guides me to the couch and pulls me into his arms as I watch my mom's chest rise and fall with sleep.

"Lay down, Baby," he says, settling my head in his lap while I stretch out on the couch and he places the blanket over me. He pushes my hair to its side and begins slowly rubbing my neck, massaging it, tracing patterns around it and down my back. I follow the patterns of his hands on my skin and slowly begin to relax.

I wake to voices and people scrambling about the room. I raise my head and my mom is sitting up and has nurses around her checking her blood pressure, adjusting her pillows and giving her sips of water. My heart catches, just seeing her upright, her eyes open and taking in liquid. I wait until the nurses finish and leave before rising from the couch. Chase is sleeping sitting up, and I kiss his lips gently and place the blanket over his body. I walk to my mom's bedside and take her hand. The battering of her face, purple and green eyes, and bright red lacerations make my heart ache. I kiss her forehead gently, careful not to move her neck which is still in the white brace.

"Dad should be out of surgery shortly," I say, glancing at my phone. "It's been over an hour and a half since they took him downstairs," I say just as a nurse walks into the room.

"Mrs. Larussio, your husband is out of surgery and is in recovery. He'll be back in ICU within half an hour. The surgeon will be down to speak with you shortly," she says.

"Thank you for letting us know," I say, squeezing my mom's hand and reaching over to wipe the tears that fall from her lovely blue eyes that are filled with shadows of pain and fear.

"He's going to be okay, Mom. He's a fighter," I say, feeling her tighten the hold on my hand.

"Mrs. Larussio, wonderful to see you awake," a man in blue scrubs says, removing his mask as he enters the room. Chase wakes to the sound of his voice and comes to stand next to me.

"How is he?" Chase asks, shaking hands with the surgeon.

"The procedure went well, we were able to relieve some of the pressure and remove the blood clot. We are already starting to see reductions in the swelling which is a great sign. We'll continue monitoring and keep you apprised of his condition. Do you have any questions for me?" he asks.

"No, we're excited to hear the surgery was such a great success and appreciate everything you've done for my father," I say, shaking his hand.

"You're more than welcome, Mrs. Prestian. If you need anything please ensure the nursing staff are alerted. Mrs. Larussio, your husband should be returned to the room next to you shortly," he says before walking out the door.

My heart tugs painfully at the tears slowly rolling from my mom's eyes. "Mom, he's getting better." I wipe her eyes and kiss her forehead, giving her a little taste of the ice chip water. I reach into my purse and pull Chapstick out and gently run it over her dry and cracked lips. "Feel better?" I ask.

"Um-hum. So tired though," she says.

"Get some sleep," I say, squeezing her hand and realizing that she has already fallen back into a deep sleep.

"They just wheeled your father into his room. Let's go see him and then I'm taking you to Dad's condo. It's not far from here," Chase says, pushing the hair back from my eyes.

I nod, knowing they need rest and that they are in good hands, and I need rest. "I'm going to take a call while you visit," he says, connecting his incoming call as I walk out of the room and am escorted to my father's room by Sheldon.

I knew what to expect, the marks and helmet-looking equipment atop my dad's head all indicators of the earlier procedure. I grimace and take his hand. "Dad, you're going to get through this. You have so many dreams to fulfill," I say, holding his hand. I don't know how long I am there, until I feel a slight touch to my shoulder. "Let him rest, Katarina. He's in good hands. We'll come back later in the day," Chase says, taking my hand and leading me down the hall, nodding at Sheldon and Dereck as we pass. His cell vibrates. "I have to catch this, Baby. It could be about your dad," he says, answering while keeping his hand on the small of my back.

He listens for a moment and nods. "Excellent news, Jay. When will you have definitive confirmation?" he asks, listening for Jay's response. "Keep me apprised. No, he's still critical, but the swelling is starting to recede which is a good sign. Sheldon and his team have everything under control. Katarina and I are just leaving the hospital," Chase says, placing the phone in his pocket.

"Jay?" I ask.

"Yes, there's been a development," he says, taking my hand.

"It sounded like a good one from what I heard," I say.

"Better than we can imagine. Alfreita is dead. It's over. Interpol received evidence that Alfreita was supplying deadly product. He and his men opened fire and they had no choice but to take him out," he says, squeezing my hand.

My heartbeat picks up a little. "That's the best news we could have hoped for. The world is a much better place," I say.

"Do you want to know the details?" he asks, pushing the hair that has fallen over my eyes behind my ear.

I shake my head. "No, I'm just happy that he's gone and that we won't have to deal with any of this mess in the future," I say.

As we exit the hospital we are swept into an awaiting black limo. The paparazzi are held at bay as the doors close behind us and I sink into the strength that is Chase.

EIGHTEEN

Chase's arms tighten around me, pulling me close as we navigate through the congested morning city traffic and pull up in front of one of the few sky-rises in the area, dwarfing the other buildings in comparison. The door is opened for us and Chase guides me into the elegant facility, over the marble floors and towards the elevator. He runs his key fob over the security panel and only then does it begin to move upward, seemingly forever until we reach the top floor. The doors open into an elegant living area, but the draw is the entire wall-to-wall windows overlooking central park.

"Chase, it's magnificent," I say, walking through the spacious living room, classically designed with high ceilings and decorated with a soft leather sectional, fireplace, and large overhead screen television mounted on the wall.

"Dad used to spend a lot of time here after Mom died, but not so much now that he and Emily are together. It's empty almost year round so if you or Jenny are in the city working the condo is usually available," he says.

I laugh outright. "Chase, since we met, how many days have we been apart? Oh, wait, I take that back... How many hours have we been apart, because it wouldn't be hard to calculate," I say.

He raises his eyebrows at me. "Katarina, are you complaining? Would you like more space, more time alone?" he asks, pulling me close, pushing my outerwear off of my shoulder, throwing it over the couch before taking my hand and leading me down the hall, through the master bedroom and into a bathroom with a large whirlpool in the corner. I can't keep the smile from my face glancing at my shampoo and conditioner and a sole loofah hanging on the faucet. "Chase, how did all this stuff get here? You had no idea I would be in New York."

"Does it bother you?" he asks, helping me out of my sweater.

"Chase, it makes me feel like it doesn't matter where I am, what situation that I am in, that you are taking care of things and I don't need to worry about it. It's like..."

"Total control?" he says softly, rubbing his thumb along the bottom of my lip. I look up at him and his eyes are glistening as he frees me from the confines of my bra, and then helps me to step out of my pants.

"No panties?" he says.

"I was just hanging out at home waiting for you when I got the word," I say, blushing and not wanting him to know that I cried myself to sleep and stayed there until I learned about my parents' accident.

"Well, I'm pretty sure that I am going to immensely enjoy the punishment that comes with you not wearing underwear in front of our staff," he says.

It's my turn to raise my eyebrows as he steps out of his pants, walking toward me as my eyes take in his chiseled frame and erect manhood before he slides into the water across from me.

"You like the control, don't you, Honey," I ask, looking at the loofah, my bathroom products, knowing now that as soon as he knew what was happening he already had a plan to console me and put me at ease.

"Baby, I do, and that's not likely to change. But more than that, I like that you like when I control the situations," he says.

"I do like it Honey, it makes me feel absolutely treasured," I say.

"You are treasured, Baby and I do want control over just about everything. I want to keep you panting and on the edge underneath me and the power to ensure your safety, but there's one thing that I no longer want control over," he says.

"What's that?" I ask.

"Your work hours," he says.

"Really? That seemed like the one thing you didn't want to relinquish control over," I say hesitantly.

"You're right, it wasn't. In fact, it was the one thing that I wanted control over more than anything, well, except sexually."

"What changed, Chase?" I ask.

"I've come to realize that your strength, the passion and desire to help people regardless of your own needs is what drew me to you in the first place. My initial instincts were selfish. I thought protecting you from working long hours was just that, protecting you, but I've come to realize and appreciate how much the work you do changes peoples lives and how much that means to you. Katarina I am in awe of the work you do," he says.

"So you don't want to punish me for working too many hours?" I ask, not sure how I feel about this. How is it that in a matter of months I have gone from an independent, hardworking female that couldn't trust any man to one that wants and needs this man desperately, trusts him completely with not only my life but my heart and craves to be punished for whatever reason is at hand?

"Oh, Baby, no one said anything about not punishing you when you work too many hours, but I understand why you push yourself, where before I would have wanted to simply forbid it," he says.

"So, you still want total control, sex and otherwise, but because you understand why it's important you're good with me working when I need to?"

"I'm still going to challenge you to work less with the same outcomes. I'm pretty sure that's the lean methodology, continuous improvement Baby," Chase says, smirking with amusement at me before glancing at his cell.

I take a moment to absorb what he's said. It's what I wanted initially, for him to stay out of my business related to my hours of work, but that was before I knew him, before we made our pact and he broke down the walls I had created around my heart.

"Chase, I'm not sure if I understand, Honey. I'm trying but what exactly are you telling me?"

"Basically, I no longer want to control the hours you work. The compassion and dedication you put into improving the lives of those around us is inspiring. Until now with your parents both in the hospital I don't think I've ever quite realized how much getting the patient experience right means to you. I knew how important it was to me, but I didn't want you working odd hours of the day and night for me or for what I wished could have been different in healthcare for my mom. I thought I was protecting you from working too many hours, while in fact I was smothering your ability to accomplish this critical work. It would be selfish to ask you to give your aspirations up by limiting your work," he says, tilting my head to him.

I move into the warm bubbling water, walking towards him on my knees. I take his face in my mine and kiss his lips, relishing in how much he has come to mean to me.

"Chase, while I love you for wanting to take care of me emotionally, as well as physically, these terms are completely unsatisfactory. You see when limits are set, I find myself exceptionally moist and pleased with the knowledge that if I push the boundaries, you will test the limits of my pleasure later. It's the anticipation of what's to come that makes me delirious with desire, moist as I contemplate disobeying you. So while I appreciate your offer, I am unable to accept and would like to renegotiate terms," I say, watching the swirling emotion in his deep green eyes.

"You want to renegotiate our contract?" he says smirking, eyes alight with amusement.

"Oh, I do indeed, Mr. Prestian."

"And what terms would you propose, Mrs. Prestian?" he asks.

I look into the deep green eyes of the man I love, at peace with my acceptance of total control and the power of absolute trust and devotion. "We agree that you have total control over my safety, my working hours and most definitely my orgasms. I will sincerely do the best I can not to deviate from any safety practices, but try as I might, will often times need to be punished for my total disregard and disobedient ways when it comes to my work schedule," I say.

"I see you have become an expert negotiator," he says, pulling me astride his thighs and kissing me with a fevered passion that takes my breath away.

DOWNLOAD a free copy of my exclusive story, "A Promise" to receive updates, sneak peeks and fun and games through my newsletter.

READ THE EXPLOSIVE NEW, enemies to lovers novel, Rule next. Katarina's Italian cousin, Giovanni Larussio falls hard for Serena who wants nothing to do with him or his crime family. As a bonus, follow Chase and Katarina as they stand up to the ruthless side of the family.

WANNA FIND out what happens to Jenny when she meets a hot, cocky billionaire with mafia connections? Read Shattered where the passion is fiery, and the stakes are high.

THANK YOU

Thank you for reading Degrees of Power. Reviews help other readers connect to books they may love. Would you be willing to help your fellow readers learn what you love about Chase and Katarina? If so, please leave a review

ACKNOWLEDGMENTS

Wayne, my husband, thank you for always believing in me, supporting my passions, and helping me make my impossible dream come true.

My parents and family have been a steady reminder that you can achieve your goals with determination, hard work, and commitment. Thank you!

Karla, my dear friend, who read the first book first and encouraged me to keep going, and who recommended getting other beta readers, because "You can only read a book for the first time once." Thank you for your unconditional support through all the insanity!

A special thank you to all the people who diligently bring all the aspects of these novels together. It takes an army, and I may be a bit biased, but this team is fantastic!

Debbie, my amazing street team, and all the groups, bloggers, and book lovers who spread the word about these stories, thank you!

Via's House of Vixens, is a "private" Facebook group for readers and fans to connect. If you would like to be part of this group, request to join for loads of fun!

I hope you continue reading Rule to find out what happens next!

ABOUT VIA MARI

Contemporary romantic suspense author Via Mari likes to keep her readers on the edge, fanning themselves as the action unfolds and the heat rises. Her books, featuring the most handsome, intense males, exemplify extreme romance, with powerful men who will stop at nothing to protect the women they love.

Via was raised in both the United States and United Kingdom. Since childhood, she has enjoyed reading books that carry you away. In fact, you can still find her in the early hours of the morning, curled up in an overstuffed chair by a crackling wood fire, reading a page-turning novel, especially during the harsh winters of the Midwestern United States.

When not writing, Via spends her days with her husband. She enjoys gardening, shopping at the local farmers market, and walking in town or around a big city. And she loves traveling to research her next novel.

She also loves interacting with her readers, so feel free to connect with her on the following social media sites! If you want to stay updated on the latest releases and claim a copy of an exclusive story, **sign up for her newsletter.**

www.ingramcontent.com/pod-product-compliance
Lightning Source LLC
Chambersburg PA
CBHW050025040726
47599CB00015B/1548